It's Always You

by Autumn L. Belle

Copyright © 2025 by Autumn L. Belle
All right reserved.

Cover design: CoverDesignAI

This book is a work of fiction. Names, characters, places and incidents are products of the author's imagination, or are used fictitiously.

References to real people, events, organizations, establishments, or locations are intended to provide a sense of authenticity and are used fictitiously. Any resemblance to actual events, locations, organizations, or persons living or dead, is entirely coincidental.

All song titles, songs, and lyrics mentioned in the novel are property of the respective songwriters and copyright holders.

No part of this book may be reproduced in any form or by any electronic or mechanical means, including information storage and retrieval systems, without written permission from the author, except for the use of brief quotations in a book review.

CONTENTS:

CHAPTER 1	1
CHAPTER 2	16
CHAPTER 3	30
CHAPTER 4	45
CHAPTER 5	52
CHAPTER 6	66
CHAPTER 7	77
CHAPTER 8	96
CHAPTER 9	119
CHAPTER 10	142
CHAPTER 11	152
CHAPTER 12	167
CHAPTER 13	188
CHAPTER 14	202
CHAPTER 15	215

CHAPTER 16	228
CHAPTER 17	236
CHAPTER 18	246
CHAPTER 19	255
CHAPTER 20	271
CHAPTER 21	283
CHAPTER 22	293
CHAPTER 23	314
CHAPTER 24	336
CHAPTER 25	341
CHAPTER 26	349
CHAPTER 27	361
CHAPTER 28	367
CHAPTER 29	377
CHAPTER 30	384
EPILOGUE	397

EPILOGUE II 407

EPILOGUE III 411

Playlist

Custer – Slipknot

Circus Psycho - Diggy Graves

Insanely Illegal Cage Fight - Dal Av & Jackson Rose

liMOusIne - Bring Me The Horizon feat. AURORA

Sugar – Sleep Token

Whore - In This Moment

Farewell II Flesh - Ice Nine Kills

Popular Monster - Falling In Reverse

Psychosocial - Slipknot

I'm Not A Vampire (Revamped) - Falling In Reverse

Decode – Paramore

Stay – Ghost ft. Patrick Wilson

Ivy (Doomsday) – The Amity Affliction

Paranoia – A Day To Remember

R U Mine? – Arctic Monkeys

Psycho Killer – Talking Heads

Jaws – Sleep Token

Hypa Hypa – Electric Callboy

Daisy – Ashnikko

Death Note – PI3RCE

BEG! – Vana

Dead Memories – Slipknot

do you think of me? – hazel

Satanized – Ghost

Blurb

This is a standalone in the It's Always You series. The books can be read in any order, however it is recommended to start with It's Always You.

Veronica

I've been obsessed with everything morbid ever since my parents were brutally murdered when I was a kid. That led me to my chosen career as a Forensic Autopsy Technician. And starting work with the Medical Examiner's Office is what changed everything for me.

My job is where I met Felix Drakos. He's witty, charming, and his soul is just as dark as mine. But here's where the complication comes in, my masked stalker, V. It's time for me to find out if Felix and V are the same person, and if they're not, I need to make a decision that will change my life forever.

Felix

Five years ago, my little sister was attacked by a monster, and the law did nothing to help her.

That's when I decided to take matters into my own hands and start my little hobby of vigilante justice. My hobby led me to my dream girl, Veronica Woods. But what will she do when she finds out what I spend my nights doing?

I want her to be my everything, and I'll do anything to make it happen. I'll even hunt down the person who killed her parents. And if I have to, I'll hunt Veronica too.

Trigger Warnings

This book is a dark romance with an unhinged, obsessive, and morally grey MMC who will do anything for his girl. The topics discussed in this book may be triggering for some. Your mental health is important, please read at your own discretion.

For a full list of trigger warnings, please scan the below QR code:

Chapter 1
Felix

"Look man, please. I didn't do it. I don't even recognize her, man." Royce Mills pleads, strapped to the cold metal table.

Royce's tone is whiny and annoying, grating my ears. They always deny, deny, deny. But the evidence doesn't lie.

I hold up the picture of a woman in her early twenties. She smiles, her bright blue eyes crinkling at the corners and her teeth in perfect white rows. Her straight blonde hair falls around her shoulders and frames her face. I bring the picture right up to Royce's face, holding it close enough so it's all he can see.

"Her name was Chloe King. Did you know who she was or did you just see her while trolling and decide that she was the one to satisfy your sick urges?" I doubt he'll fess up so soon. These pieces of shit usually go through all five stages of grief before I end them. Royce is still in the denial stage.

"What the fuck is wrong with you, you freak? I told you I don't know her." Royce combines anger with denial this time. How refreshing.

I sigh. It always goes the same way. Denial, anger, bargaining, depression, and then acceptance. Just once I would like to skip right to the acceptance part. I could finish this and kill Royce now, but it's less satisfying than breaking them apart piece by piece. I wonder if Chloe felt those same stages of grief as Royce brutalized, raped, and murdered her.

I grab the next photo, this one of Chloe's death scene. Her body lays bruised and broken, thrown away like trash on the side of a road. By the time her body was found, rigor mortis had already come and gone. Her once lively eyes had become milky white, open wide in fear but unseeing. The skin that used to have a golden glow was pale and ghostly, her lips tinged blue and her back mottled by the settled blood. The smooth blonde locks that were so perfectly coiffed had become a tangled mess, with chunks torn out, leaving only blood encrusted bald patches.

I shove the new photo in Royce's face, taking his entire field of vision. Royce feigns disgust, curing his lips in a grimace, but the emotion doesn't reach his eyes. His eyes are dead and flat, no light or warmth behind them. I'm almost sure I see a flicker of pride cross his features before he schools his mask back into indifference.

"Fuck man. You're fucking sick." Royce spits, still trying to appear revolted by the photo displaying his work. "I'll fucking kill you for this!"

And now we've moved onto anger.

"You can give up the act, Royce." I chastise. "Your DNA was underneath her fingernails. She had been raped, but you must've used a condom, either that or you couldn't get your tiny dick to work properly. Unluckily for you, a couple of your pubes were left on her."

A whimper escapes Royce's throat. Seems as if he's catching on quick and ready to move onto stage three, bargaining.

"Please. It was consensual man. She begged me to fuck her. Just let me go. I won't tell anyone about this, I swear." Royce's face is covering in a sheen of sweat now. Subconsciously, he realizes how royally fucked he is. That doesn't mean he won't still beg.

"Was the murdering her part consensual, too?" I respond, keeping my voice light, as if I'm talking to an old friend. We both know that nothing that happened between this piece of filth and Chloe was consensual. Her body showed signs of trauma, her entire pubic area was bloody and bruised.

My casual tone does nothing to soothe Royce. Fat tears roll down his cheeks and he sniffles, sucking a glob of snot back into his nose.

"Gross, dude. Get yourself together. What's next? You going to wet your pants?" I tease.

I've had enough of this psychological torture. It's time for something physical. I like to make my guests experience the same things that they put their victims through.

I wheel over the metal tray filled with all sorts of goodies. Scalpels, razors, jigsaws, bone saws, thick needles, knives, hammers, wire, rope. Based on the ligature marks around Chloe's throat, wrists and ankles, and the fibers left behind, the medical examiner determined that nylon rope was used to bind her.

"I've bought a present for you, Roycie-boy." I sing-song, picking up the rope and wrapping it around my fists. "The fibers found on Chloe were from an orange and black nylon rope. Lucky for you, I found a matching one at the hardware store down the road. Now tell me, how'd it all go down? Did you drug her drink at the bar? Sneak up behind her and knock her on the head? Did she go willingly with you at first and then change her mind?"

His eyes widen as he looks at the rope coiled around my hands. Royce's tears roll faster down his chubby face, snot leaking from his nose down the side of his cheeks.

"No…no…no…God, please…no" Royce chants, praying to a god that won't help him now.

"God isn't here. It's only you and me." I lean down, whispering into Royce's ear. "I'm going to go with scenario numero uno. And who are we kidding? We both know you drugged her. The toxicology report clearly stated that Rohypnol was found in her system."

Royce continues his obnoxious chant of no's and pleases, throwing a prayer to God in every once in a while and a 'why me'. He's moved quicker than most through the grief stages, firmly settling in stage four now, depression.

With the rope wrapped around my fist, I swing my arm, sucker punching Royce in the nose. His nose cracks and sprays blood over his face and my hand. Royce coughs and gags as blood leaks into his mouth, splattering me with more of his blood.

"What the fuck, man?!" I mock, conjuring an impression of his earlier tone. "Why me?" I fake a sob, sniffling. My fist connects with his face again, this time hitting the left side of his jaw, causing his head to whip to the side. "How about we ask the real questions? Why did you feel entitled to Chloe's body? Who gave you the authority to take her life?" I strike him again, this time uppercutting him and snapping his jaw upwards, forcing the back of his head to hit the metal table with a rattle.

"Just kill me." Royce sobs.

"And there it is, acceptance." I let out a contented sigh. Now it's time for the real fun.

***

Last night I dumped Royce's carcass in the same spot that Chloe King was found. It's poetic, if you ask me. I started doing all this vigilante shit around five years ago, when I was twenty. A lowlife piece of shit had viciously attacked and raped my little sister, Gwen. Shane Adams, a rich white boy who had 'his whole life ahead of him', got off scot-free because his dad was a senator and had the judge in his pocket. Shane destroyed my sister's life. She's still afraid to leave the house and suffered mild brain damage from the blow to her head Shane used to disable her.

So, Shane was my first kill. It obviously didn't go as smoothly as Royce's elimination did, but I've learned a lot over my years. I've made it my mission in life to take care of the scum that the justice system lets go. Hell, I even started a business doing crime scene clean-up and transport of bodies just to push my way into the system. It also helps that Dr. Terrance Vargas is an old family friend.

Terrance gives me first dibs on picking up the bodies that need to be transported to the Medical Examiner's office. And he often gives me confidential intel on the victims of murders. Dr. Vargas could get his license revoked for giving me information, but he doesn't think I'm going to do anything with it. He's just a family friend talking with his best friend's son.

And like magic, my phone rings. Dr. Terrance Vargas is on the line. Who would've guessed?

"Hey doc, got something for me?" I answer on the third ring.

"Felix! How you doing, son? Yeah, I've got another one for you. Royce Mills, thirty-two. He's off of Highway 74, near exit 39." Terrance's jovial voice greets me.

"Be there in thirty, doc." I reply, already hanging up the phone. Of course, I already know exactly where Royce's corpse is. I was the one who put it there, after all.

I send off a text to Sav, telling him I'll be there in ten minutes to pick him up. I met Sav in high school, and he's been my ride or die ever since. He's the only one I trust to help me pick up the bodies, although he has no idea that I'm the one making the corpses. Sav's parents were real pieces of work. His mom was a druggie and his dad was abusive. Sav's full name is actually Savage. Like I said, his parents were shitty.

But even though Sav had a fucking nightmare of a childhood, he's still chill, kind, and reliable. Sav huffs as he plops down in the passenger's seat, his sandy brown messy, and his hazel eyes tired.

"Lix, dude. I'm happy you gave me a job and all, but it's fucking early. And I've got a hot piece of ass back at my place just waiting for me. Couldn't you have the other team take care of it?" Sav complains when it's just the two of us in the van, his eyes flashing to me.

Sav is serious when it comes to handling crime scenes and bodies, but that doesn't mean he won't complain about it.

"You know I fucking hate it when you call me Lix. And bro, it's fucking nine in the morning.

It's not that early, and also, how do you already have a chick in your bed?" I shake my head.

"She came home with me last night, and she's fucking hot, so I figured I wouldn't mind keeping her until the morning." Sav shrugs.

I sigh. Sav still lives like a frat boy, even though we both graduated from college three years ago. He'll fuck just about anything with a hole. Although I'm surprised that he liked one enough to let her stay the night. Maybe he's growing up. Fuck, who am I kidding? The day Sav stops being a playboy will be the same day that pigs fly.

The cadaver pickup goes smoothly, as usual. Sav's a real professional when it comes to these things, at least in front of everyone but me.

"Do you know who the shithead we just picked up is? Vargas thinks he's related to Chloe King's murder. You know I like to work the jobs involving cum stains like him." I explain. Vargas didn't actually tell me Royce's relation to the Chloe King case, but Sav doesn't need to know that.

"Yeah, fine. But let's hurry. That tail of mine isn't going to wait around forever." Sav grumbles, pushing messy hair off his forehead.

We unload the gurney and wheel it in through the back entrance to the M.E.'s office. Vargas wanted Royce moved directly into the autopsy suite.

"Alright, Terrance. Here he is, the man of the hour." I announce as I push through the double doors into the suite.

I look up and lock eyes with the most gorgeous woman I've ever seen. It's like one of those moments in a movie, where time stops and angelic light surrounds the girl. She's wearing blue scrubs and a rubber apron, with her black and green hair pulled atop her head in a bun. Not a trace of makeup on her face, but she's divine without it. Underneath the PPE, I can tell she's a curvy little thing. Her hazel eyes look me up and down, and when she notices I'm watching her, a pretty pink blush colors her pale cheeks. She has piercings in her nostril and septum. Whoever she is, she's my fucking dream girl, that's for sure.

"Felix, meet my new autopsy technician, Veronica Woods." Terrance breaks the silence.

"Nice to meet you, Veronica. First day?" I try to sound casual, but my heart is racing and my cock is hardening just looking at her.

"Yep, yeah...Yes. Sorry." The pretty pink blush gracing her cheeks turns a shade darker. "And you can call me Ronnie, that's what everyone calls me." Ronnie's voice is sweet and sultry, and I'm definitely making her nervous. Does she think I'm attractive? I fucking hope so.

"Well, Terrance here is a real teddy bear. He'll take good care of you." I reply with a wink. What I don't say out loud is that if Terrance doesn't treat Ronnie well, I'll rip his spine out through his asshole and then feed it to him.

"I'm Sav, by the way. Thanks for the introduction, Lix. Not to interrupt whatever the fuck is happening here, but I have plans, remember? We should probably wrap this up." Sav interrupts.

What a cockblock. Sav is my best friend, but right now I want to throat punch the fucker. I don't care if he wants to go home and fuck a case grapefruit. I want to stay here and get to know Ronnie. But fine, we'll unload Royce and then I'll take Sav back home. And then maybe I'll swing by here towards the end of Ronnie's shift and see if I can take her out, you know, to celebrate her first day and whatnot.

We each grab an end of the body bag, hefting the deadweight from the gurney to the metal autopsy table. I catch Ronnie watching me work out of the corner of my eye. She's definitely checking me out. My cock twitches at her gaze. Fuck.

"Right, well, call me if you get any more bodies to pick up Terrance." I nod at Vargas. Turning to Ronnie, I deepen my voice. "It was nice to meet you, Ronnie."

***

I arrive back at the M.E. around six that evening. Ronnie steps out of the office clad in a tight skirt, tank top, leather jacket, fishnets and combat boots. Goddamn. Her hair falls just past her shoulders in waves, and she's put on some black lipstick. Carrying a helmet, she walks over to a black and gray motorcycle, hops on and fastens the helmet. Could she be any fucking hotter?

Now, this may appear creepy, but I never claimed to be one hundred percent normal. Remember, one of my hobbies is torturing and murdering people. But instead of approaching her, I follow her in my Jaguar. She speeds through the streets, heading to downtown Westmound. Where is my little fox going? It takes her about twenty minutes before she parks and walks into Club Profile. Interesting, I didn't take her for the clubbing type, especially not on a Thursday night.

I wait a few minutes before following her into the club. It's early still, so there's no bouncer. I slip into a booth in the back corner, staying hidden in the shadows and just watching Ronnie.

A blonde girl squeals Ronnie's name and runs up to her, jumping up and down before giving her a hug. The blonde looks like a bartender here. I notice another bartender, this one a male, looking over at the girls and with a dopey smile on his face. Who is this fuck? He better not be eyeing my girl.

I decide to hang back and watch for a while, just to see who the newcomers are and what relationship they have with my little fox. I usually don't kidnap, torture, and kill non-scum, but if this dude keeps looking at Ronnie like that, I might have to.

The girls break apart and Ronnie slides into a seat at the bar, talking animatedly with her friend. The male bartender keeps flicking his gaze at the female bartender with a coy smile. Looks like he's got a thing for the blonde, not my girl. He's lucky, because I was starting to get real murdery feeling.

Chapter 2
Ronnie

I pull off my apron and scrubs, throwing my soiled attire into the laundry bin inside of the women's locker room. It was my first day at the medical examiner's office in Westmound. Since I was a little girl, death has fascinated me. My therapist says it's because of the trauma I endured at a young age, witnessing my mother and father being murdered by an intruder. Who knows if that's really the cause, but either way, I've always been interested in things that little girls shouldn't be. Instead of playing house with dolls, I would play crime scene investigation. Rather than playing doctor, I'd want to play autopsy.

My morbid fascinations made it hard for foster homes to want me. I'd try to hide my proclivities, but eventually they'd sneak their way back into my life and scare off the families who took me in. I never really understood why my interests were so frowned upon. Everyone dies, and someone needs to do death related jobs. Not long after my parents died, I knew I wanted to be a forensic autopsy technician. I wanted to work with the dead and decipher their stories from the inside out.

The only constant in my life has been my best friend and sister (from another mister, and misses), Leah Crawford. We met in fourth grade and she became the light to my darkness. Where she's bright, bubbly, and a blonde-haired, blue-eyed girly girl, I'm the exact opposite. When people see us together, they don't get it. My hair is black with emerald green highlights (my favorite color). My eyes are hazel, my skin is pale, and I'm covered in tattoos and piercings. Leah is a typical popular party girl, always clad in mini-skirts, crop-tops and heels. And although she doesn't share my sense of fashion, I will never give up my platform combat boots, she's never tried to change me or been embarrassed to be around me.

I was passed from home to home, school to school, until Leah convinced her parents to take me in during eighth grade. Leah's parents, Jake and Darcy Crawford, were a lifeline for me from fourth to eighth grade. And then they had me live with them, pulling me out of the foster system. Jake and Darcy might not understand me, or my friendship with their daughter, but they never fought it. I was the weird kid who liked to talk about true crime at ten, and instead of trying to change it, they just embraced and encouraged me. They even helped pay for my college education.

The Crawford's support led me to where I am today, starting my new job with the medical examiner's office. I peel off my panties and bra, and then step into the warm stream of water. I'm so glad that there are showers in the women's locker room here. I need to wash the smell of the dead off my body. Just because I'm interested in their stories doesn't mean I want to smell like I'm one of them.

As far as first days go, today was a doozy. The first body that we worked on was a deceased male, Royce Mills, age thirty-two. His body was brutalized, bloody, and bruised. We had to pull DNA from his corpse in order to get an I.D. And wouldn't you know it, his DNA matched that of an unknown perp linked to the Chloe King case. I hadn't started working here when Chloe's body was brought in, but it had been all over the news. She was beaten, raped, and then strangled to death before her body was left on the side of a road just outside of Westmound.

The examiner was able to pull DNA from underneath Chloe's fingernails, as well as a few loose pubic hairs from her body. At the time, no matches existed in the system. But lo-and-behold, a week later a cadaver shows up matching those samples. The Chief Medical Examiner, Terrance Vargas, noticed the similarities between the two deaths. Although Royce Mills was apparently in far rougher shape than Chloe King.

Royce Mills was a rapist and killer, and if you ask me, the world is better off without him. I know how the world works. I've seen it firsthand. Culprits get off because of the fine print. Even with mountains of evidence stacked against them, the bad ones always seem to escape with a slap on the wrist. Good riddance, Royce Mills. You will not be missed. Someone out there decided to take matters into their own hands before the judicial system could fuck it up, and more power to them. Thank you, vigilante justice.

I step out of the shower, toweling myself dry. Leah's working at Club Profile tonight and I figured I would swing by to see her before heading back to our apartment. She usually works evenings, bartending at the club. We live together, but because of our conflicting schedules, we don't really see each other often.

My black and green hair is naturally wavy, and I rarely have to do too much in order for it to look good. I brush through it before warming some curl cream and leave-in conditioner between my palms and then finger combing it into my hair. I apply my signature black lipstick, rubbing my lips together and popping them. I'm not the type to spend hours on my hair and makeup, unlike Leah, who loves getting dolled up. Lipstick, eyeliner, a bit of mascara and I'm good to go.

I brought a change of clothes to work, knowing that I'd be going to the club afterwards. Tonight's outfit includes a tight leather mini-skirt, a black tank top and a black leather jacket. Oh, and of course my combat boots and some fishnets. Like I said before, Leah and I are polar opposites. I'm the goth vampire and she's the barbie.

Grabbing my purse and motorcycle helmet out of my locker, I leave the office. Leah has hated my choice in transportation since I first got my Kawasaki Ninja 500. She's always on my ass about the danger of riding a motorcycle. Honestly, it's sweet how much she cares for me, but I need the danger in order to really feel alive. Maybe witnessing my parents being slaughtered broke something in me. Thrills and risks excite me in a way nothing else does. We're all going to die someday, anyway. Might as well enjoy life while I still can.

Leah is a complete wuss when it comes to anything remotely dangerous or scary. She won't watch horror movies with me, hates haunted houses, detests my motorcycle, and basically abhors anything I find exciting. But she'll still do those things with me and in return I do things I hate with her. Like clubbing, partying, going shopping, and watching chick flicks. We love each other and would do anything for one another. Our bond is unbreakable.

And that's why I'm going to drag her along tomorrow night to Haunted Hollow, the scariest haunted attraction in the metro. It's October, and that means Leah can't say no to doing all things Halloween related with me.

I zip through downtown until I reach Club Profile, where Leah works. The club is not my scene, but Leah loves it. So much so that she started bartending here. After hanging my helmet on my handlebar, I bend over and shake my head, running my fingers through my hair to regain the volume I lost while wearing the helmet. Safety first and all that.

It's Thursday night, but still pretty early, so the club isn't all that busy. Before I can even reach the bar Leah sees me and excitedly waves.

"Ronnie!!!" Leah squeals, jumping up and down before pulling me into a tight hug.

Leah's favorite color is pink. The club requires her to wear black pants with a black button-up shirt, but she accessorizes it with a pink tie and a pink bow holding her long hair back. She's truly beautiful, and even the atrocious color pink looks good on her.

As I approach the bar, I wave at the other bartender on duty tonight, Micah. He one thousand percent has a crush on Leah, and she's absolutely clueless. He's cute, with a 'boy next door' vibe. Tall with golden brown hair and brown eyes. He looks like he definitely participated in several sports during high school. Not my type, but he and Leah would make a cute couple.

"Sooooo…how was your first day? See any dead bodies?" Leah's voice is bubbly and melodic. She slides me a Moscow mule, my go to drink.

"Oh yeah. But you know I can't talk about it, confidential information and all that." I reply. It was my first day and I really don't want to get fired for talking about information outside of work. "What I can talk about is the sinfully hot guy I met there." I say with a wink.

"Ewwww. Don't tell me he was a corpse." Leah sticks her finger in her mouth and fake gags.

"Ew, what the fuck, no." I groan. "Just because I'm interested in death doesn't mean I'm a necrophiliac, Jesus. No, this guy was definitely alive."

"Thank God. I almost thought I'd need to stage an intervention. Tell me about the hot guy." Leah waggles her eyebrows and flashes a grin.

Micah sidles over, interrupting. "Did someone say hot guy? I hope you aren't talking about me behind my back."

"We always talk about you behind your back, Micah." Leah jokes. "But not this time. Ronnie met a guy at work today."

"Was he dead?" Micah asks, his eyes wide.

"Fuck, no!" I exclaim, exasperated. "Why did both of you come to that conclusion? That's fucking concerning. As I was about to say before you so rudely interrupted Micah, he was the transport for the first autopsy we had today. His name is Felix, and he's built like a fucking god. About six foot two, muscular, beautiful olive skin, the most intoxicating green eyes." I stare off into space, imagining Felix. "He had this silky looking black hair that was a bit shaggy and wavy. Oh yeah, and tattoos. He was wearing PPE, but I could see some ink peeking up past his collar."

"Damn girl, he sounds exactly like your type. Tall, dark and handsome. So, when are you going to fuck him?" Leah asks earnestly.

I choke on my Moscow mule; the vodka burning my throat. "Woah, slow down. I don't even know if I'll see the guy again. But damn, I bet he'd be a fucking god in bed. He looked like the type that would make me beg…"

"Ummm, Ronnie?" Leah cuts in, breaking me out of my thoughts. "Not to freak you out, but is that Felix?" She points behind me.

I turn my head to look at who she's pointing out, and oh my fucking god, it is Felix and he's walking right towards me.

Felix slides into the seat next to me. I can smell the leather of his jacket, the mint on his breath and the warm musk of his cologne.

"Hey, Ronnie, right?" Felix says smoothly.

"Hi, yeah. What're you doing here?" I ask and then wince, realizing I came off as rude.

Felix laughs. "I come here now and then to get a drink. It was a long day at work, hauling bodies around."

Leah looks between me and Felix before slyly winking at me, grabbing Micah's arm, and walking both of them to the other side of the bar.

"Do you come here often, Ronnie?" Felix asks. The way he says my name sends a shiver down my spine.

"It's not really my scene." I explain. "But my friend Leah, the blonde bartender, loves it here. We live together, but don't get to see each other much because of our work schedules."

"Mmmm. I see." Felix hums. "And what do you love?"

"Huh?" Not my most elegant response, but his question caught me off guard.

"You said Leah loves it here. I want to know where you love to be, if not here. What you love to do." Felix's response sounds almost sexual.

Baby, I'll do anything you want me to if you keep talking to me like that…is what I say in my head but wouldn't dare say out loud. I'm not sure if he lowers his voice and talks in that sensual way on purpose, or if it's just how he naturally is. Felix is charming and mysterious, and I can't help but to lean closer to him as we talk.

"Oh, um…" I'm not super comfortable talking about myself to other people. I've learned over the years that my dark personality and interests are turnoffs for the general population. "Leah is more of a bubbly girly girl, and I am…not. I prefer morbid and scary things." Might as well let the cat out the bag and be honest up front.

"As do I." Felix drawls.

His warm breath caresses my lips. We've moved closer to each other over our conversation, and now we're only a few inches apart. I'm entranced by his dark green eyes, flecked with browns and golds, and framed by dark, long eyelashes.

If he leaned in and kissed me, I wouldn't even fight it. His eyes flick down to my lips, then back up to my eyes before he pulls back, breaking the spell.

I let out the breath I didn't realize I was holding. My heart drums loudly, and I swear he can hear it.

"I'd like to take you on a date." Felix whispers, his fingers brushing my knee. "Tomorrow night."

Yes, daddy.

I gaze down at his fingers, still touching my knee, but barely. The feel of his warm hands sends an electric shock through my skin. I've talked to this man all of ten minutes, and he's made me feel like no one else ever has. I've dated all types, and it always ends the same way. Every time I start to show my darker side, they bolt. Will it be the same with him?

"I can't tomorrow night." I reply. I haven't actually asked Leah to go with me to Haunted Hollow yet, but Fridays are the only nights where we're both off. "Saturday?"

"Saturday." Felix confirms, a sexy smirk on his lips. "7 p.m. at Sage."

Sage is a very upscale Italian restaurant, not far from here. A place I definitely can't afford.

"Oh, umm…" I try interject and explain that it's out of my budget.

Felix cuts me off. "Don't worry, it's my treat." He says with a wink, before standing up and striding to the door.

Once Felix is out of earshot, Leah scrambles back over to me.

"Bitch, he's fucking smoking hot!" She tries to whisper, but her excitement overwhelms her. "Did I hear him ask you on a date?!"

"Yes!" I squeal. Felix is definitely the sexiest person I've ever had a date with. But unfortunately, I've found the hottest ones are usually the shallowest. Most have as much personality as a rock. Hopefully, he proves me wrong.

Chapter 3
Ronnie

"Wouldn't you rather go have a few drinks somewhere?" Leah complains, a shiver running over her body, but not from the cold.

"Come on, Leah." I plead with her. "We always go out drinking. We only come to Haunted Hollow once a year. You know I love this shit." I give her my best impression of a sad puppy.

"Ugh, fine!" Leah stomps her foot and scowls. "You're lucky I love you so much you little bitch."

I pull her in for a hug and press a sloppy kiss to her cheek.

"Watch out for the makeup!" Leah squeals.

We're both clad in costumes. Leah is dressed up like a sexy cheerleader, pigtails and all. Meanwhile I like to be spooky yet sexy, so I came as a demonic nun with black blood running down my eyes and an upside-down cross necklace hanging between my tits.

Haunted Hollow is only open during October each year. It's right outside of the city, sprawling across an open field. There are six different haunted houses, a haunted hayride, carnival foods, alcohol, bands and other entertainers. I'd come here every weekend of October if I could, but it's not as fun coming alone. Leah will only let me drag her ass out here once a year.

We make it through the ticket entrance, and immediately the atmosphere changes from a normal fall night to the best kind of nightmare. Screams echo around us as the fog from the machines descends around us. The air smells like a mix of fallen leaves and mini donuts, making my mouth water.

"I'm gonna need a drink before we do anything else." Leah grumbles.

"I gotchu." I weave my fingers through hers, dragging her along to one of the liquor booths. "Two hard ciders please."

I hand Leah her cool, crisp cider before taking a swig of my own. Neither of us are beer girls, but give me a cider or a Moscow mule and I'm all yours.

"Chug it down, babe." I gesture to Leah's drink. "You know we're going to the Camp Killer haunted house first." Camp Killer is one of my favorites. It's based off of all those cheesy eighties slasher films about a summer camp that is attacked by a serial killer. Sleepaway Camp, Friday the 13th, etcetera. There's something about cheesy slashers that I just love.

Camp Killer is sillier and more fun than it is scary, so it's the perfect attraction to start with for Leah. Although, she still hates it just the same. But Leah will get her revenge, making me go clubbing with her in the near future.

We get in line, waiting our turn to be let into the area sectioned off for Camp Killer. It's a series of small cabins that we walk through, as well as some 'camp grounds', a shower building, and a dining building. This haunt is a staple of Haunted Hollow, one of the only ones that has stayed since the attraction first opened in 2005.

The revving of a chainsaw sounds directly beside Leah, eliciting an ear-splitting scream from her.

"Not cool!" She shrieks at the masked actor, before huddling closer to me and wrapping her arms around my bicep.

I can't help but laugh. While Leah gets truly frightened during these types of events, I get excited. The adrenaline pumps through my veins, making my heart thrum and my clit throb. Is getting turned on by fear normal? My therapist would say it's a kink I developed due to trauma or some shit. Either way, I love the tingling sensation that skitters over my skin when I'm scared.

The masked chainsaw man continues on, working his way through the crowd while making people scream. We're getting close to the front of the line, and the buzz of excitement grows stronger with each step.

"Oh no…not another one." Leah groans, hiding her face in my jacket while pointing off to my right.

I glance over to see a man standing ten feet away. He's clad in all black, with heavy boots on his feet and a hood pulled over his head. He's wearing a blacked-out goat skull mask with two horns curling out of the top. A red upside-down cross is engraved on the forehead, and mesh covers the eye holes. It's a cool fucking mask. I give him a small smile, appreciating the costume. The man just cocks his head to the side while continuing to look directly at me.

Just then I noticed a glint of something in his hand. Trailing my eyes down his body, I realize he's holding a prop knife. The dark and dangerous vibe the man is giving prickles my skin and makes my breath hitch. I should not be getting turned on by this dude's costume, but well, I am.

I turn back towards Leah, breaking the trance the masked man had me in. "It's fine, Leah. He's just an actor."

Leah only whimpers in response.

"Look, he's not even coming over here." I say, turning back to look for the man but realizing he's nowhere in sight. I shrug it off, he probably went to terrorize someone who would actually get scared.

"Why'd you have to pick a place with a waiver?" Leah grumbles.

In order to get through the doors at Haunted Hollow, you have to fill out a waiver that basically has you acknowledge that the actors can and will touch you.

"It's more exciting that way, don't you think?" I explain. The touching adds another layer of fear and danger. "And besides, they aren't actually going to hurt you."

"Welcome to Camp Killer, counselors. Enjoy your slay." The haunt attendant, whose dressed up like a counselor with their throat slit, greets us before waving us through.

Weaving my fingers back through Leah's, I pull her through the entrance behind me.

"Don't worry, I'll protect you." I give her hand a squeeze. "I know you don't like these things, but thank you for coming with me anyway."

"Like I said, you're lucky I love you." Leah sighs, but squeezes my fingers back.

Our first stop in this haunt is cabin number one. Four sets of bunk beds line the walls. The sounds of screaming, stabbing, and blood splattering fill the air. A floor lamp in the corner is knocked over, the flickering bulb the only source of light in the cabin. The flashes of light and then darkness are disorienting. Dismembered limbs litter the floor, along with stage blood. As we near the exit door, a large figure steps out in front of us, wielding an axe.

"Oh fuck!" Leah screams, hiding behind me.

The actor chuckles darkly, darting towards us with his axe raised. Adrenaline takes over and I pull Leah along, sprinting past the ax man and exiting cabin one.

The actor steps back into place, waiting for the next group to enter the cabin. I let out a deep laugh, breathing heavily from the sprint.

Next, we make our way through the pitch-black shower room. Strobe lights flicker behind the shower curtains, illuminating the scenes behind them. In one stall the shower scene from Psycho is recreated, a man holding a knife over a screaming woman. Other stalls are empty, only revealing shadowed blood splatter on the curtains.

The second to last shower stall has a tall, shadowy figure standing inside, only visible each time the strobe flashes. With each step closer to the stall, the figure moves. We approach, knowing we have to walk past the stall to exit the building. The shower curtain is ripped open by the figure as soon as we stand in front of it.

"Fuck this shit!" Leah screams, letting go of my hand and running right out the door.

"You bitch!" I call after her, feeling betrayed at her abandonment.

I look at the figure, noticing that it's the same man from outside of the haunt, the one with the black goat mask and the prop knife.

He looms closer, but my feet are stuck in place. My heart thumps in my chest, and my breaths become pants. Part of me wants to run, but the other part wants to see what will happen next. My traitorous body reacts to the danger of the man, and heat coils in my core.

"I like your mask." I manage to whisper.

"Shouldn't you be running, little fox?" The man whispers in my ear, his voice deep and sinful.

I shudder. "Yes." His voice is a caress, stroking the most depraved parts of my soul.

The man circles me, raising his knife so it flashes in the strobe lights. He rounds me again, stopping at my back. He trails the knife against my cheek, and I realize that it's made of metal as the cool blade gently touches my face. Is it a real knife? I've never known a prop knife to be made of real metal.

He leans in to whisper. "Run."

My feet obey his command, and I take off, exiting the shower building. Leah waits for me right outside, her eyes wide with terror.

"What the fuck took you so long?!" Leah's voice is high pitched and cracks with her fear.

"Come on. Keep moving." I say, not answering her question.

It is wrong that I hope the masked man chases me? I want him to follow me and find me. I want to see what happens if he catches me. His voice was deliciously dark, filled with promise. The way he growled 'little fox' had my knees trembling. I have no idea what the dude even looks like underneath the mask, but right now I don't care. Something about him makes me want to give into my darkest desires.

We make it through the rest of Camp Killer without another encounter with the goat masked man. Disappointment courses through me, but I shake it off. He's just an actor at the haunt, I don't know why I'm reading more into it than I should be.

Next, we hit up the Haunted School, based off of a Japanese horror film. After those two haunts, Leah needs a break. We grab two more ciders as well as some hot cinnamon sugar mini donuts. Finding an empty table, we eat and drink while watching a fire dancing act on one of the stages. The dancers swirl the lit batons around themselves and the stage, the fire hot and crackling with each move.

"So where are you going for your date with Felix tomorrow night?" Leah asks, sing-songing Felix's name.

"He's taking me to Sage." I reply.

"Damn, bitch. That place is like, super fancy." Leah's eyes are wide.

"I know, it's really expensive." My cheeks flush. "I feel weirdly guilty about letting him pay for dinner there, but he suggested it and said it was his treat." I shrug. If he wants to take me out on a date and treat me to somewhere so expensive, I'm not going to argue. "I've never had a date take me somewhere so…lavish."

"He must be rich. You better hook that man, make him your sugar daddy." Leah waggles her eyebrows.

I smack her on the arm, laughing. "It doesn't matter how rich he is if he's boring as fuck. I'm sick of basic vanilla dudes. I'm looking for someone who can blow my mind."

"Well only one way to find out…" Leah flashes me a mischievous grin.

"The only way he's getting into my panties is if he wow's me at dinner." I roll my eyes. "I'm done putting out for dudes who only want to fuck me missionary, pump twice, come and dump."

"That's my girl!" Leah giggles. "You deserved to be fucked hard, not fucked with." She tries to come off sincere, but then breaks into another fit of giggles. Recovering from her giggling fit, Leah raises her bottle of cider, "To men who can find the clit!" She cheers, bumping her bottle against mine.

"Let's fucking hope so!" I laugh, bringing my bottle to my lips.

We finish our ciders and donuts and head to the next haunt. Now that Leah's had a couple of drinks, she less scared of being here. She actually seems to be enjoying herself now, which I knew would happen once she just let go.

The next haunt is The Chapel. It's a small church building, with a creepy as fuck basement with all sorts of demonic nuns and exorcist shit. I modeled my costume this year off of this haunt. Something about demons legitimately terrifies me. It's about one of the only things that actually gets me spooked, and not in a horny way.

The actor dressed as a priest ushers us through the wooden doors into the chapel. From there we head into the basement, where we're met with demonic growls and screeches. Electric candles adorn the space, lighting the space just enough to see right in front of us. Goosebumps prickle my skin as actual fear grips me. I know this is fake, but the idea of demons scares the shit out of me.

"Let's get through this one quick, yeah?" I whisper to Leah.

"Oh, so this one finally scares you, huh?" She replies, a cocky smirk on her lips.

"As if you aren't pissing yourself too." I snap back.

"You're right. Let's go." Leah drops the brave facade, pulling me through the darkened basement.

A nun with completely black eyes, sharp teeth coated in blood, and pale skin jumps out of us hissing and cackling. We both scream, running past the actor.

The next room in the basement is made to recreate an exorcism, with a woman convulsing on the table, neon green vomit streaking from her mouth. An evil priest stands above her, reciting

Latin text from a book that looks similar to the bible.

We hurry through, getting scared again by an actor dressed as a demon jumping out at us. People in the rafters reach down, trying to grab us as we race by. A ramp switchbacks, taking us back up to the main level of the chapel. The next part is the worst, we each have to go into the 'confessional', but it's an individual experience.

"Rock, paper, scissors to see who goes first?" My voice shakes as I try to sound nonchalant.

"Nah, bitch. You brought us here, you get to go first." Leah replies, shoving me forward.

I glare at her, flipping my middle finger at her, before striding forward and stepping into the confessional. The doors click shut, and I hear the distinct sound of a lock sliding into place from the exit door. I've been through this haunt a few times, but I don't remember the doors ever getting locked. That's...odd.

Through the wire screen I see a shadowy figure step into the priest's side of the confessional.

"It's time to confess your sins, little fox."

The voice is deep and familiar.

It's the same sinfully sexy voice I remember the goat masked man having. The nickname little fox makes me tremble, but my traitorous pussy warms at the words.

Chapter 4
Felix

"It's time to confess your sins, little fox". I growl.

Last night I overheard Ronnie and Leah making plans to come to Haunted Hollow tonight, and I couldn't pass up the opportunity to tag along. From a distance, of course. I knew from my conversation with Ronnie that she loved stuff like this, but I wanted to see how much. I needed to see how far I could push her, and how deeply depraved she really is.

Her panting breaths on the other side of the confessional make me rock hard. Earlier tonight when I found her in Camp Killer, she tried to act so tough, it was cute. But then I told her to run and she did. And man, I fucking love the chase. I've been following her ever since, hiding just out of sight. But I can't resist anymore.

"Are you going to confess, or do I need to come over there and force your confession out of you?" I taunt. Oh, I hope she chooses the latter. I so want to break her.

"This isn't a normal part of The Chapel." Ronnie replies, her voice unsure.

"I didn't say it was. Confess." I demand.

"I don't know what you're asking of me." She replies shakily. "What do you want?"

"I want you to give into your most depraved desires." I shrug. "Tell me how wet your cunt is from me toying with you all night. Tell me how much you love me chasing you. Tell me how badly you want me to catch you and fuck you."

Ronnie inhales sharply at my words, and a small moan escapes her throat.

"You love the fear, the danger, the thrill." I whisper, quiet enough that she learns forward to hear me better. "You want me to wrap my hand around your throat and squeeze while I pound into your wet little cunt. Or maybe I'll fuck your tight ass. Or cum down your throat."

Her breathing is heavy now, and she whimpers.

"Would you like that?" I ask, already knowing the answer. I've seen the way she's reacted to me tonight, the way her pupils dilate when I tease her.

"Yes." She whispers, barely audible.

I growl. I whip my door open, unlock her side and push my way into the small space with her. There's barely room for us to move, making it so my body is pressed tightly against hers. I can feel her chest heaving, her round tits moving in time with her breaths.

I use the flat of my knife to raise her chin until her eyes meet mine. She won't be able to see them behind the mesh of the mask, but I can see hers. Her beautiful hazel eyes gaze at me, her pupils dilated. Her painted black plump lips are open slightly, her sweet breath mingling with mine.

I push my body closer to hers, my hands slamming against the wall above her head, the knife clattering against the wood. I press my hard cock into her soft stomach, grinding against her, and making soft moans fall from her lips. Her hands fly up to my chest, gripping the fabric of my hoodie in her tiny fists.

"I don't even know who you are…" She whispers through her small moans and pants.

"Does that matter?" I question, already knowing the answer. Honestly, I think she'd react the same way to me without the mask, but it adds more thrill to our encounter.

Ronnie offers a small shake of her head.

Dropping my knife hand, I press the cold steel against her throat. The blunt side is against her skin, since I don't want to hurt my girl, yet. I trail the fingers of my other hand down her soft body, brushing them along the hem of her nun dress. The dress barely covers her ass, and all I've been able to think about since I saw her in this outfit was bending her over and fucking her sweet cunt.

Flipping her around, I press her ass into my cock and grind against her. I slip my hand underneath her dress, finding the edge of her panties and moving them aside. My fingers run through her slickness, and I groan. I'm desperate for my little fox. I want to taste, touch, and fuck her in every way imaginable. I want to watch her break for me. She needs to be mine.

Ronnie pushes back into me, moving her hips to grind against me harder. Her moans become deeper and more needy as I slide my fingers up, finding her pulsing clit and rubbing tight circles around it.

Loud bangs hit the door to the confessional.

"Hello?!?" I hear a female voice call from the other side.

"Shit, that's Leah." Ronnie rasps. "It's okay! I'm fine. The ummm…door to get out of here is jammed. Someone's coming to get me out right now. Hang tight."

"That's my sly little fox." I murmur, still circling her clit. "Better come quick before Leah gets more suspicious."

Ronnie eagerly nods as I push two fingers from my other hand into her wet pussy. She rides my fingers, moving her hips quickly as she chases her orgasm.

"You're a filthy little fox, aren't you?" I trail my lips down the side of her neck. "Are you going to cum on a stranger's hand?"

"Yes." Ronnie whimpers, moving faster.

Her walls tighten and flutter against my fingers, and her wetness leaks down my palm and coats her thighs. I can tell she's close. My fingers curl, stroking that sweet spot inside her tight cunt over and over as her legs begin to shake.

"Fuck!" She cries, her orgasm wracking through her body.

I don't let up, rubbing her clit and stroking her g-spot as the waves of her orgasm hit her. My dick is so fucking hard, all I want to do is sink into her sweet little pussy, but I know we don't have the time tonight.

She comes down from her high, panting and covered in sweat. Her body shakes from the force of her orgasm. I hate to leave her like this, but we'll be caught any second.

I pull my fingers out, feeling her pussy clench as they slip from inside of her. Before she knows it, I'm slipping out of the confessional door, leaving it unlocked for her. As I leave, I slip my wet fingers into my mouth, savoring Ronnie's taste.

Chapter 5
Ronnie

My pants fill the air as I slowly open my eyes to find myself alone in the confessional. It's dark, and the air is significantly colder now that I'm alone. Even though he's gone, I can still smell him in the air. He smelled masculine and intoxicating, like wood and citrus. Fixing my clothes, I brush out any wrinkles and wipe the sweat from my forehead. I can't believe what just happened. I've never done anything like that in my life, but something about that man just drew me in.

A bang sounds on the confessional door again, followed by Leah's voice. "Yo, Ronnie? Are you still in there?"

I realize that there's a small lock that's been slid shut, making it so Leah wasn't able to come in. I grip the handle of the lock, sliding it back out and swing open the door. Candlelight fills the confessional, only part of it blocked by Leah's shadow.

"Are you okay?" Leah's eyes are wide with worry. "You look…flushed and…sweaty…"

"Yeah, I'm alright." I try to come off and breezy and cool. Inside, I feel anything but. "You know how I hate confined spaces."

"Sure…yeah. I guess." Leah sounds skeptical, but there's no way she has any clue what just went down in that confessional, right?

"Let's get out of here." I need another drink or three so I don't have to continue rethinking my life choices. Afterall, why should I feel guilty about getting freaky with the weird goat-masked man? I'll never see him again anyway.

***

The rest of our time at Haunted Hollow was decidedly less exciting than my encounter in The Chapel. We ended up hitting all of the haunts plus the hayride, but I never saw the masked man again. A part of me was disappointed that I didn't run into him, but another part was filled with relief. It's probably better for it to just have been a freaky one-time thing. Additional encounters probably wouldn't live up the same way anyway.

This morning, I woke up with a raging hangover. After The Chapel I decided to have a shot…or three…of straight tequila. Horrible, bad, atrocious idea. Luckily, I'm off of work today. The other autopsy tech, Elena, works today. I slept until noon, hoping the hangover would ease up. When that didn't help it was time for my trusty friends, a stick of Liquid IV and a fat stack of pancakes, followed by a steamy shower.

My shower turned into an everything shower. I needed to shave every last hair from my body until I was soft like a baby. My date with Felix is tonight, and while I usually don't put out on first dates, I might find myself unable to resist his sexiness. Legs shaved? Check. Pits shaved? Check. Pussy shaved? Double check.

My little romp last night is kind of turning me into a horny fiend. I'm slightly ashamed by it, but it was so incredibly hot. I'm drooling just thinking about the way that man's fingers worked me. Snap out of it! I'm about to go on a date with

Felix, and I should not be daydreaming about some rando in a mask with magic fingers. I'll never see mask man again anyway, and who knows, I bet Felix has some magic of his own. Something about Felix screams "I know how to fuck a woman so good she forgets her own name!"

I've got about ten minutes before my Uber comes to pick me up. Usually, I would just take my motorcycle, but I actually spent time styling my hair into loose waves. And there is no way I'm going to rock helmet hair to my date with Felix. My face has my signature makeup, including black lipstick. Sure, we're going to a fancy ass restaurant, but that doesn't mean I can't be myself.

I slip into a dark green velvet bodycon dress, it's tight and hugs my curves in all the right places. The top has a sweetheart neckline and two straps that tie atop my shoulders. I'm short, and I consider myself thick, but I love my curves. I like how my tummy, thighs, tits make me look soft. My heels are killer, high black stilettos covered in sparkles, making the muscles in my calves and thighs pop.

Not to mention the five-inch heels add to my short five-foot two height.

The restaurant, Sage, is in a ritzy part of downtown Westmound. It's surrounded by luxury stores, expensive apartments, and other Michelin star restaurants. I'm not one to usually wander to this part of town simply because I'm just not the type of girl who needs twelve hundred dollar Louis Vuitton heels or Chanel bags.

I wrung my hands the entire ride to the restaurant. My palms are sweaty, my knees are weak, and butterflies threaten to send my stomach into an upheaval as I step out of the Uber. I'm usually a very confident woman, but the idea of this date with Felix has me all sorts of nervous. Something about him seems different from other men I've dated.

I steel myself, take a deep breath, and stride forward. My chin is high, and I force myself to look confident. I'm about the pull the door open when a tattooed hand reaches out and pulls it open for me.

"Thank you—" I begin to say as I turn to find Felix holding the door for me.

He flashes a heart-stopping smile, before giving me a wink. Felix wears a fitted black suit, with a tie that almost perfectly matches the green of my dress. Although he's dressed immaculately, his wavy black hair is slightly messy. His green eyes sparkle as he looks me over.

"After you, Ronnie." Felix purrs my name.

My name rolling of his tongue sounds like sin. I want to hear him say it again and again. How can a man just saying my name make my panties damp? What kind of sorcery is this?

My skin heats, and a blush creeps across my cheeks. I nod in response, making my way into the opulent restaurant. The sound of the live violinist and pianist rings pleasantly through the high-ceilinged space. The floors are polished marble, and crystal chandeliers hang throughout the open room. People chatter quietly, with the occasional clinks of glasses and silverware chiming throughout the restaurant.

Felix steps in beside me and leads the way to the hostess. She's pretty, long auburn hair with brown eyes, but her face is cold and calculating. There's not an ounce of warmth about her.

"Good evening, sir. Do you have a reservation?" The hostess asks with a seductive smile. Her eyes gleam as she looks Felix up and down, acting as if I'm not standing right next to him. She bats her eyelashes at him.

"Yes, it's under Felix Drakos. It's for two, myself and my gorgeous date." Felix says the last sentence with a no-nonsense tone, effectively shutting down any thoughts the hostess had about trying to flirt with him. In the process he slings his arm around my waist, pulling me in closer.

As he does, I notice that his scent is familiar, but I can't quite place it. He smells like wood and citrus.

She clears her throat, uncomfortable and clearly not used to being turned down. "Yes, sir. Right this way."

The hostess leads us through Sage, and I can't help but notice how everyone is dressed up as if they're going to a gala. Suddenly my velvet bodycon dress feels too tight, and once again my confidence wains. I knew this restaurant would be too fancy for me. Places like this are way out of my comfort zone. Take me to a haunted house, or a coffee shop, or a Sleep Token concert and I fit right in. But Sage is like none of those things. The restaurant is made for the upper echelons of society.

We're led to a small table near the back of the room. It's less crowded back here, and far enough from the musicians that we'll be able to talk without raising our voices over the noise of the restaurant.

Felix pulls out my chair, gesturing for me to sit before sliding it back in for me and taking his own seat across the table.

"Thank you." I say quietly. Although we're out of sight from most of the other patrons, I still feel wildly out of place.

"So, Ronnie, how is your new job treating you? I hope Terrance isn't giving you any trouble." Felix grins.

"Terrance?" I question. "Oh, you mean Dr. Vargas? He's been very kind so far." I take a small sip of water.

"How did you get into your line of work?" Felix gazes at me intently.

"Oh, ummm. It's kind of a long story, I guess. I've been interested in the death industry since I was a child." I break eye contact, suddenly embarrassed about my morbid fascination. Though, I doubt I have reason to feel ashamed, seeing as Felix works in the industry as well. "What about you? How does one become a body transport technician?"

"My interest in the field started around five years ago." He answers, appearing lost in thought for a moment before continuing. "That's when I decided to start my company. Originally, we just did transport, but now I have a team that does crime scene cleanup as well."

"Something traumatic happened, no doubt." I say without even stopping to think. "Fuck…I mean…shit…sorry. That's definitely not first date conversation material." My face feels like an inferno, and now I swear I'm going to actually die from embarrassment. You don't start talking about trauma with someone you've talked to for ten whole minutes of your life. "I just meant...usually when you work with death there's a reason for it."

Felix just laughs, the sound like a balm to my ears. "It's okay. Everyone has some type of baggage or trauma, no?"

He's so incredibly charming. Felix turns my cringey moments into more palatable situations.

"Have you eaten here before?" He changes the subject gracefully.

"No...it's not a place I could afford, especially not when I was a broke college student. And certainly not on my autopsy tech salary." I reply.

"I suppose not. To be honest, I haven't been here either. I only brought you here to impress you." He says with a chuckle.

"Hah. Next time we don't need to get so fancy. Take me to a horror movie or to get some coffee and books. I'll be good to go. I'm not the type who's impressed by wealth."

"Noted." He smirks playfully. "I should've gleaned that by your personality, since you don't seem like the gold digger type. But you know what they say, don't judge a book by its cover and all that."

"Frankly, sometimes I feel like the only way to judge a book is by the cover." I reply before wincing. "Oof, that sounded harsh. Sorry, I've been on a lot of dates and usually the attractive ones have nothing worthwhile on the inside."

"So, you're saying that either A. you find me attractive but think I have nothing going on inside or B. I'm ugly, but have an awesome personality." He teases.

"Actually, I was going to say that you might be the first book that I shouldn't judge just from looks." I muse. "We both know you're fucking hot as hell. And you're intriguing and charming. But honestly, I'm a little skeptical. There's got to be something wrong with you. Literally no one is perfect." As I talk, I squint my eyes, pretending to examine him.

"Hmmm. Hot as hell, huh? Intriguing and charming? You're right, there definitely has to be something wrong with me." Felix laughs, but I also get the sense that there's a kernel of truth there.

"But that means there's also something wrong with you, seeing as you meet those three criteria as well."

"A girl never reveals her secrets on the first date." I wink, trying to sound cavalier.

"Next time, then." Felix flashes that award-winning smile again.

I don't know that it's actually won any awards, but it has in my book. Number one sexiest smile that makes my panties fall right off.

We share a bottle of chardonnay over dinner. I order this amazing butternut squash ravioli with cream sauce and pancetta. Felix gets mushroom risotto. Before long my anxiety over the date melts away, and I'm left feeling on cloud nine from the wine. I'm usually not a wine drinker, but it really is the best kind of drunk to be. It makes me giggly and happy.

Before long, we're wrapping up dinner. After the wine started flowing the conversation became easier and more relaxed. We talked about anything and everything, from our favorite bands, to our favorite horror movies, even our favorite foods. Felix and I share a lot of similar interests. Although that was probably obvious from our shared interest in the death industry.

After he pays the bill, he gently pulls me to my feet, lacing his fingers with mine. Felix's hands are large and warm, but also strong. I look down and admire the tattoo peeking out from underneath his sleeve. On his right hand he has vines trailing down his wrist and wrapping around his hand.

My body hums at the skin contact. My small hand fits perfectly with his, and I never want to let go.

"I want to show you something." Felix says, holding my hand the entire way out of the restaurant. "That is, if you're okay with this night continuing." His voice in confident, as if he can tell I'm not ready to go home yet.

He looks at me with those entrancing green eyes and I nod, squeezing his hand tighter. His grin is devastating as he looks at me. My body comes alive at the sight of him gazing at me with that happy twinkle in his eyes. We've only met, but the look he gives me makes me feel like he really sees me, right into the depths of my depraved soul, and likes it.

Chapter 6
Felix

God, she's fucking stunning. Her hand is in mine as we stand outside the restaurant. I can't stop looking at her. My heart has been on fire since I first saw her standing outside Sage tonight. And I swear she's looking at me with the same hunger I look at her with.

Last night at Haunted Hollow I got my first feel of her, but I need more. I desperately want to drag her into the alleyway and throw her up against the wall. I want to taste all of her. I need to be inside of her. Every time I look at her my cock jumps in excitement.

I can tell she has darkness inside of her soul, just like I do. I want to open her up and see every piece of her, every last bit of her from the inside out. Not that I want to kill her though, because that would mean that my time with her would be over. I need to own her, body, mind and soul.

I lead Ronnie to my sleek black Jaguar F-type, pulling the passenger door open for her to slide into the black leather seat. Rounding the hood, I slide into my own seat next to her. She said before that she isn't impressed by wealth, but I can tell from the astounded look in her eyes that she likes the jag. What's not to like? It's a fucking sexy car.

Farewell II Flesh by Ice Nine Kills filters through the speakers once I start the car. I turn the volume down enough so we can still hear the music but be able to have a conversation at the same time. In my periphery I see Ronnie smile, and hear her hum along to the chorus. I had a feeling she'd like Ice Nine Kills, their whole shtick is writing songs about horror movies after all.

"You like INK?" I comment.

"They're top five for sure." Ronnie turns to face me, her smile melting my heart.

I'd give anything to keep her smile for myself. I'm definitely not considering chaining her up in my bedroom and keeping her there forever…at least not seriously considering it…yet. I'm so fucked for this woman.

"Their early work was a little too scene for me." I quote one of their songs to her. "But when

The Silver Scream came out, I think they really came into their own. Commercially and artistically."

"The whole album has a refined melodic sensibility that really makes it a cut above the rest." She finishes the lyric for me with a giggle.

Fuck, I think I'm in love.

I'm having a really hard time focusing on the road as I drive because I can't keep my eyes off of her. The dress she's wearing hugs every fucking curve of her body. Her legs are out in full force, and her creamy thighs are begging to be wrapped around my head. And she can definitely keep those heels on while I'm in between them.

My dick aches just looking at her. It's jealous of the fingers I had inside of her last night. She was so fucking tight, her pussy clenching my fingers like it didn't want to let them go. Fuck, I have to think about something else. My cock can't take the strain. *Royce Mill's tiny limp dick. Wrinkly grandpa balls. Uhhh, fuck...baseball.* Well, that eased the boner a little bit.

"Where are we going?" Ronnie quietly asks, breaking me out of my own head.

"Somewhere special. You'll love it, I promise." I've never taken anyone to this spot before. It's a place I usually go alone to think. Ronnie is the first person I've wanted to share it with.

I pull up to one of my families' buildings. My parents are pretty well off, owning several luxury high-rise apartment buildings around the country. This one is my favorite because of the views it gives of the city surrounding us, the mountain range to the east, and the ocean to the west. I own the penthouse, acquiring it a few years ago. The reason I picked this building above all others was because of the access to the roof from the penthouse.

"Drakos Luxury Apartments on 5th…" Ronnie reads the sign on the building aloud. "Drakos…didn't you tell the hostess your name was Felix Drakos?"

"Yeah…uh…it is." I wince. I really don't want her to think I'm trying to impress her with money again.

"So…you own the building?" She asks hesitantly.

"No, my parents do. But my apartment is on the top floor." Now I sound like a spoiled rich boy. Great.

"You brought me here to show me your luxury apartment? That's what you said I'd *love*?" Ronnie scoffs.

Shit. I should have eased her into the whole billionaire parents thing. Too late now.

"No, I promise." I try to sound confident and smooth. "I didn't bring you here to brag about my apartment. I wanted to take you somewhere special to me, the roof. I've never shown it to anyone else, and it's my favorite place in the city. A lot of my spare time is spent up there thinking. Please, give it a chance." I'm practically begging now. I really don't want to have to seriously consider chaining her up, but I can't fucking let her go. I'm spiraling down a dark path of obsession and borderline madness over Veronic Woods.

"Okay, fine. I've had a great time with you tonight, so I'm going out on a limb here and trust you. Don't fuck it up, Felix." She sighs.

I'm not sure that she should trust me. I'm a little unhinged, okay, a lot unhinged, and becoming more so each second I'm with her. But I'm not going to tell her that because she'll run for the hills, which honestly is probably what she should be doing.

"I won't!" I'm way too excited right now, and my voice betrays my emotions, but luckily Ronnie just giggles.

I wrench open my car door and leap out, running around the hood to open Ronnie's door for her before she can even blink. I'm like a kid in a candy store right now. Or like someone who just snorted a shit ton of coke.

Ronnie takes my outstretched hand and steps out of the car. I intertwine our fingers, loving the way her small ones fit perfectly in between mine. Her skin is soft and smooth. Like me, she's covered in tattoos. Her left arm is a sleeve comprised of horror movie characters and references. Her chest is adorned with an ornamental piece with flowers and a ram's skull. Ronnie's right leg is also decorated with tattoos with an enchanted forest theme.

Entering the building, I greet the night guard, Greg, before leading Ronnie to the elevators. In order to reach the penthouse I have to use a special key card, otherwise the elevator only goes up to floor twenty-one.

As we ride the elevator, Ronnie's scent fills my nose. She smells like vanilla and patchouli. Earthy, yet sweet. I want to bury my face in her neck and inhale her delicious scent. Maybe later, if I'm lucky and win her over with the views from the roof.

The elevator dings and the doors slide open, revealing the foyer of my penthouse. When it was originally built it was very modern, with clean and minimalistic designs. That's definitely not my style, so I had it renovated. Now it resembles a gothic castle, with dark wood and stone. Iron accents linger throughout the apartment, as well as pops of dark green. I prefer the ambiance of candlelight and torches, so all harsh lighting was replaced with bulbs that resemble real fire.

Ronnie steps into the room with a gasp. "Wow...this is gorgeous. This is like my dream house."

"Mine too." I smile, looking at her awe-stricken face. I'm already thinking about a future with this woman, imagining what it would be like if this was her home too. "Can I get you a drink? And then maybe a tour before we head up to the roof?"

"That sounds fan-fucking-tastic." She replies, still a little tipsy from the wine at dinner.

I lead the way into the kitchen. The appliances are all state of the art. I love to cook, but when it's just me eating I find that I don't spend the time on it that I'd like to. But for Ronnie, I'd cook all day and every day. Anything to make her happy.

I pull down two copper mugs, setting them on the black marble countertop. When we were at Club Profile I noticed that she was drinking a Moscow mule, so I bought all the ingredients for them and worked on my recipe for them this morning.

Using a shaker, I mix the vodka, ginger beer, lime and ice. After pouring the mixed drink into a copper mug, I garnish it with a slice of lime and a sprig of mint.

"Here you go, little fox." I hand the mug to her, realizing my mistake after it's slipped from my mouth. I called her little fox. That's what I called her last night at Haunted Hollow. Fuck, play it cool.

An odd look passes over Ronnie's face. "Thanks…"

I'm almost positive she caught the nickname and is putting the puzzle pieces together, but she doesn't say anything about it. I get to work on my own drink, acting calm and collected.

Ronnie lifts the mug and take a sip, humming her approval. "You make a mean Moscow mule, Felix."

"Thank you." Fuck, I want to hear her screaming my name as she comes. "Shall we continue the tour?"

Ronnie follows as I lead her through the rest of the penthouse. The style is the same throughout, giving dark gothic vibes. When we get to my theater her jaw drops. The room is painted all black, with a 4K projector shining against one wall. There's a large deep seated sectional in the middle of the room, with an ottoman that can make the couch into a bed. I have a minibar in the theater, as well as a real theater popcorn machine. Surround sound tops off the room.

"We'll have to watch a movie in here next time." Ronnie says with awe.

"Oh, so you're already planning a second date? You are *so* into me." I jest.

Even in the darkened room I can see Ronnie's cheeks flush. It's the cutest fucking thing I've ever seen. I wonder if her cheeks flushed last night when I made her come.

"Ready to see the rooftop?" I change the subject to spare her. Although I'm liking the way she reacts to me, I don't want her to run just yet.

"What about your bedroom?" She asks before pausing, her cheeks flaring even brighter than before.

"Ronnie, Ronnie, Ronnie…" I tsk. "Coming onto me on a first date? How delightfully naughty of you."

"That's not what I meant!" She squeaks. Adorable.

"Mhm. Well, maybe after the rooftop you'll get to see my bedroom. If you're a good girl, that is." I purr.

Her body language shifts. I think Ronnie might have a praise kink. She rubs her thighs together, as if trying to get any amount of friction possible. Don't worry, love. I'll be more than happy to sate your appetite.

I move in closer to her, resting my hand on the small of her back. She shivers against me, but it's not from being cold. She likes the feel of my touch.

We head to the stairs that will lead to my rooftop terrace. When I first moved in, the rooftop was barren. But I instantly fell in love with the space and paid a contractor to turn in into my sanctuary. I hope Ronnie loves it as much as I do.

Chapter 7
Ronnie

As Felix leads me up the stairs with his hand resting on the small of my back, my mind keeps darting to him calling me 'little fox' earlier. Surely, it's a coincidence, right? But then again, what are the chances that both he and the masked man called me the same pet name. And it's not even a common one at that. I've never heard anyone call someone else 'little fox' before.

But maybe I'm overthinking it. Maybe I have foxlike features? I do have a more heart shaped face and thinner nose with wide eyes. I could just ask Felix why he called me that. But what if he really is the masked man? Would he admit it or just brush it off? That's it, I'm overthinking it. It's just a coincidence.

Felix opens the door to the rooftop, and I'm immediately blown away. The space is illuminated by fairy lights, and it's designed to be a cozy place. I could picture myself reading up here under the stars. In the middle of the roof there's a gas firepit surrounded by cushy looking chairs and one loveseat. On the left side of the roof there's a small wet bar area and a hot tub. On the right, there is a hanging egg chair wide and deep enough to hold two people. There are various plants and shrubs placed throughout the rooftop terrace.

Not only is the terrace itself stunning, but the views it provides are unreal. To the east the mountain range that borders our city can be seen. To the west lies the ocean. And all around us the city of Westmound sparkles and lights up the night.

"Wow. I understand now why you like this place so much. It's breathtaking." My eyes keep jumping to take everything in.

"The only breathtaking thing here is you." Felix murmurs, stepping in front of me while wrapping one hand around my waist while the other cups my cheek.

His thumb strokes my face as his lips hover inches away from my mouth.

"That line was so fucking cheesy." I giggle.

"Yeah, it was pretty bad." Felix agrees, his warm breath brushing across my lips.

"That's okay. I like cheesy." I close the gap, pressing my lips softly to Felix's. His lips are soft, warm, and inviting. He tastes like mint. I fucking love mint already, but now it might be my favorite flavor.

I find my hands raising to his chest, gripping the fabric of the black button-up beneath his unbuttoned suit coat. His chest his hard and lined with muscle beneath my fingers. Felix's hand moves to the nape of my neck and his fingers tangle in my hair. Although he's gentle about it, he has an air of authority as he tugs my head back using his grip in my waves.

Using the new angle, he deepens the kiss, tracing his tongue across the seam of my lips. A small moan escapes me as I open for him, allowing our tongues to collide. Fucccck. He tastes so fucking good. And he's an incredible kisser. My breaths become shallower as the kiss continues, and I feel dampness gathering in my lacey black thong.

Our lips part, breaking from the best kiss of my life. so we can both still our fluttering hearts and panting breaths. Felix's heart thunders beneath my palm. Though most of the time he seems cool and collected, I can tell that that kiss got under his skin as much as it did mine.

We stand there, gripping each other and staring into one another's eyes. I feel like I can see the entire universe in his emerald green gaze. This is only our first date, but something about him is pulling me into the deep end, and I don't have the will to swim.

I dive back in, wrapping my hands around the back of his neck and crashing my lips against him. This time the kiss isn't gentle or tentative, it's hungry. Felix kisses back with matched fervor, devouring me whole. My body feels like it's on fire.

His hands slide down until he cups the back of my thighs. Without breaking our kiss, he lifts them and I instinctively wrap them around his waist, locking my ankles. I've never had a man pick me up like this before, and it's insanely hot. Felix walks us over to the loveseat by the firepit, sitting down on the plush green cushion so I'm straddling his thighs.

Felix's hands cup my ass, as his tongue works against mine. His intoxicating wood and citrus scent swirls around me, and his taste makes me never want to stop kissing. I can feel his hard cock pressing against me, and I can't help but grind against it. What is with me the past couple of days? I was feral for the masked man last night, and now with Felix tonight.

Before now making out and sex have been okay, but honestly largely disappointing. Now, I never want to stop. He presses up into me with a groan as I continue to grind my hips slowly against him. Felix's cock is so fucking hard, and I can tell it's big.

Felix wraps my hair around his fist and pulls my head to the side, exposing my neck. He buries his face into the spot between my shoulder and neck, inhaling my scent before running his tongue along my pulse. The sensation has an unabashed moan slipping through my lips.

"You like that, little fox?" Felix whispers against my neck, kissing my pulse point.

"Mmmm." I moan and nod.

I'm so wrapped up in the tingles his lips and tongue ignite against my skin that it takes me a moment to process the pet name.

"Was it you?" I try to pull back to look at his face, but Felix's grip is tight on my hair.

"Was what me, baby?" Felix's hands bunch the fabric of my dress up, exposing my thighs and thong to the night air.

"Last night?" I question, my pulse skyrocketing.

"I'm not sure what you mean." He replies, his hands sliding underneath my dress, trailing up my stomach.

Either Felix is a really fucking good actor, or I'm overthinking the similarities between him and the masked man.

"You keep calling me little fox…" I pull my hands from around his neck and place them against his, stilling his hands from moving further up my torso.

"Do you not like it?" Felix's thumbs rub against the skin beneath my breasts in lazy circles. His mouth still presses kisses along my neck.

"No, I don't mind it…it just reminds me of someone else." Okay, I'm definitely overthinking this. Now I sound like a lunatic.

"That's not something a man wants to hear when you're grinding against his cock." Felix finally releases his hold on my hair and pulls his mouth away from me.

Fuck. I just fucked this up, didn't I? "Sorry, I didn't mean it like that." This is the first time I've felt this way just from kissing another person, and I'm fucking it up. Panic rises in my throat, replacing the lust that was there before. "Someone else called me little fox once, that's all. I didn't mean that I was thinking about someone else while with you. All I'm thinking of is you. I've never felt like this when kissing someone. I don't want to stop. Shit. Now I'm digging myself deeper. Fuck, sorry." As I ramble on my hands fly up to cover my eyes in embarrassment. Time to throw myself off this building. World, it was nice knowing you.

Felix's hands wrap around my wrists gently as he pulls my hands away from my face. My skin is burning hot with shame. He's so fucking hot and I just put my foot in my mouth big time. This date has been fantastic, and we have so much in common. But all confidence and calm I usually have has been thrown out the window tonight. Looks like there won't be a second date with Felix in my future. I'm fucking spiraling, and fast.

"Ronnie." Felix's tone is soft, but I can't bear to look at him.

"Veronica. Look at me." He uses two fingers to tilt my chin up, forcing my eyes on his. "It's okay. I understand what you meant. There's no need to freak out. I'm feeling the same things you are right now. I don't want to stop. I need this night to keep going. I need to feel your perfect fucking body against mine." His eyes blaze as his gaze sears into mine before he leans forward and kisses me again.

I melt against him and I can feel tears lining my lashes. The panic subsides and is replaced once again with lust. Fuck it. He said he wants me.

My hands find the lapels of his jacket, and I pull them to the side and slide the suit coat down his shoulders until he shrugs out of it. His hands wrap around my hips and he uses his strength to grind me against his still hard cock. My fingers fly to the buttons of this shirt, popping them open one by one until his torso is exposed. I break from his lips to take in the sight before me. His olive skin is tight across his pecs and abs. I run my fingers across the dips of his muscles, reveling in the feel of his skin beneath me. Leaning in, I run my lips along his chest, tasting him with my tongue and nipping at his skin.

He groans below me before flipping us so I'm sitting on the couch and he's kneeling in front of me. Felix uses his strong, warm hands to spread my thighs wide. He bends down, trailing his fingers higher up my thighs while planting kisses along the insides of them. His mouth moves upwards as he fingers the edge of my thong before slipping his fingers inside to find me absolutely soaking for him.

"Fuck." He growls, sliding a finger through my slit.

I pant needily, desperate for him to go further.

"I need to taste you." Felix's voice is a rumble.

His hands grasp the sides of my thong, slithering it down my thighs and calves before he lifts each foot, pulling it off of me completely. I watch as he tucks the black lace into the pocket of his pants with a delicious smirk. Using two fingers he spreads my pussy open, his eyes feral as he looks at my glistening cunt. Then he moves his mouth in, licking me from the bottom to the top slowly. I shudder at the feeling.

His mouth cups my clit, sucking it into his mouth as his tongue flicks across the sensitive bud. My hips jerk in response as I cry with pleasure. I feel his mouth turn up into a grin as he continues sucking, licking, even nibbling on me. Two of his fingers slide into my entrance, curling on the way out against my g-spot. My body shakes in response as my hips jerk each time his curled digits pass over that wonderful spot inside of me. Unholy sounds escape from my mouth between pants. Soon my hips are moving in tandem with him, riding his fingers and mouth.

My vision blackens as the waves of my orgasm flood my system. "Felix!" I scream at the orgasm crests and he continues to work my clit with his tongue and teeth, thrusting his fingers in and out of me at a brutal pace. My vision fills with stars, before I slowly start coming back down.

"Fuck, baby. That was beautiful." Felix purrs in between long licks up my slit.

My body is languid, all tension having melted away. The only time I've come remotely close to feeling like that was with the masked man in the confessional.

"That was…intense." I sigh, content and spent.

"I'm not done with you yet, love." Felix growls, moving up my body until his lips hover over mine.

His green eyes have darkened, and his pupils are dilated. Pressing down, Felix's lips meet mine in a rough, heated kiss. His mouth tastes like me, his lips wet with my arousal. Felix takes my bottom lip between his teeth, biting until it stings before licking away the pain. His hands wrap around my thighs and he hoists me up into his arms. My legs naturally lock around his hips, my arms circling his neck. Felix continues kissing, licking, sucking, and biting as he carries me back to the doorway leading down into his penthouse.

"I want you in my bed, Ronnie." He kisses me again. "I want my sheets to be soaked by you." Felix's mouth moves to the fluttering pulse in my neck. "I need to feel you coming around my cock."

He bites down on my pulse and I let out a gasp of shock and pain, but it quickly turns into a moan as I feel a gush of wetness dripping down my pussy.

Felix's strong hands grip my thighs as he pushes my back up against a doorway that must lead to his bedroom. I can feel his thick length grinding against my core. My wetness is soaking his suit pants, and I'm sure he can feel it.

Felix thrusts against me, and I can feel the head of his cock rubbing against my clit. I groan while he continues to slowly and firmly thrust up against me, my back pushed flush with the door. Suddenly, his left hand leaves my thigh and grips the doorhandle, swinging the door open behind me. For a moment my heart drops as the support of the door unexpectedly vanishes, but Felix's grip on me is still tight, and my ankles and arms are locked around him.

Felix drops me back on the bed. It's clad in cool black Egyptian cotton sheets and topped with a dark green duvet. He follows me down, pushing apart my legs with his muscular thighs and planting his hands on either side of my head. Felix smirks down at me devilishly, his eyes dark and sparkling. He's quite possibly the most attractive person I've ever seen. And he wants me. The hard length that presses against my core proves that.

His hands skim my thighs, before trailing up and gripping the hem of my dress which is still pushed up around my waist. He leans back, giving me room to lift up off the bed while he pulls my dress over my head. Felix tosses it to the floor, leaving me in only my black lacy bra. A second later, he's unclasping the back and pulling that off of me too. I lie there, completely exposed to his hungry gaze as he drags his eyes down my body.

My heart races, thudding in my ears as he looks down at me. My body is curvy, with thick thighs and a soft stomach. Worry and nervousness creeps into my mind, wonder if he's disappointed in what he sees. The longer he stares at me, the more uncomfortable I get. My hands drift up and clasp, covering my tummy. I'm usually so much more confident, but I think I might actually like Felix, and I'm scared that he won't want me anymore after seeing me bare.

I gulp, before whispering to break the tension. "We don't have to…" My eyes begin to water, and panic edges in. Why do I care so much if he doesn't like my body? This is our first date. If he doesn't like the way I look, he can get bent. Or at least, that's how I try to assure myself.

His eyes snap up to mine. "You don't want to?"

"I do…I just…you keep looking at my body and I…" I bite my lip. Fuck. I really don't want to say this out loud. "I'mworriedyoudon'tlikeit." I rush out, looking away from Felix's face.

His fingers grip my chin. "Look at me." He demands.

Oh no. I can feel a tear starting to fall down my cheek. Why am I letting what he thinks bother me so much? I've never cared about what anyone else thinks.

His fingers move to brush away the stray tear, before cupping my cheek and caressing my skin with his thumb. "Veronica. Please, look at me." Felix's voice softens.

I drag my gaze back to his, and his eyes are full of intensity. Felix rolls his hips into me, rubbing against my naked core, his dick still bulging and hard.

"You're fucking perfect." Thrust. "You're the most beautiful thing I've ever seen." Another thrust. "Does this feel like I don't want to fuck you, baby?" Another thrust, his heated gaze still locked with mine.

I shake my head no.

"Say it." He demands, grinding against me again without looking away from me.

I whimper at the stimulation. "It feels like you want to fuck me." I say quietly, my cheeks flushing.

"That's right, baby." Felix praises. "And I'm going to fuck you. I'm going to make you scream my name while you unravel on my cock. Each time I pound into that pretty pink cunt of yours, your big beautiful tits are going to bounce. I'm going to fill you with my cum until it's leaking out of your pussy and dripping down your thighs. You're going to take every last fucking drop of me, and once I'm done you'll be begging for more."

My body warms from his words, my pussy pulsing and soaked with arousal. The way he talks to me is unlike anyone else I've ever been with. His dirty words make me feral, and I grind myself against his trousers, desperate for him to fulfill his promises.

Felix slides off the bed, stripping his shirt and suit pants off. He stands there in his briefs, and my jaw drops as I see the outline of his cock. I knew it was big when I felt it against me, but holy fucking shit. Felix's thumbs hook around the waistband of his briefs, slowly sliding them down until they fall at his feet. His dick bounces free, and it's long, wide and covered in veins. My mouth begins to water at the sight.

Felix's fist wraps around his length, and it makes his hand look small by comparison. There is no fucking way that thing is going to fit in me. Zero percent chance.

"You like what you see, Veronica?" He growls. I could listen to him say my name forever. His hand pumps slowly up and down his length as he prowls towards me, crawling over the bed until he kneels between my spread legs.

My gulp is audible as I reach out to touch him, wrapping my own hand around his cock. He must be at least nine inches long, and my hand isn't able to wrap around him fully.

"I don't think I can take you." I whisper, staring at his length in my hand.

Pre-cum gathers around the slit, and I slide my thumb over it, eliciting a shudder from Felix.

"You can, and you will. You'll take every last fucking inch of me into your sweet cunt." Felix replies in a gravelly tone.

His eyes are filled with lust as he watches my fingers moving over his velvety soft skin. He looks like a god while kneeling before me.

"Condom?" I ask.

"I'm clean." Felix replies. "I don't sleep around, and I haven't been with anyone in six months. Are you on birth control?"

I'm surprised, and it shows on my face. "You're joking right? People have got to be throwing themselves at you left and right."

"That doesn't mean I sleep with them." He shrugs. "I'm very…selective."

"Hmmm. Interesting." My thoughts swirl as I consider his words.

Felix seemed sincere. And the thought of him cumming inside of me has me wild. I am on birth control too…is this stupid? The answer is yes, it fucking is. Do I care right now? Fuck no.

"I'm clean too. And I take the pill." I answer.

We're basically strangers who are taking each other's words. This is insanely fucking dumb on both our parts. Never try this at home, people.

The grin that spreads across Felix's face is lascivious.

Chapter 8
Felix

Veronica Woods must be fucking blind if she can't see that she's a goddess sent from the heavens to bless humanity. Not that I believe in heaven, or gods and goddesses, but you get the point.

She's sprawled out before me, with her perky tits, pierced nipples and glistening pussy, which tastes fucking divine by the way. I just can't fathom that she thought I was turned off by seeing her naked body. Did someone say that to her at some point? If I find out who made her feel that way, I'll fucking kill them. Honestly, I feel like killing anyone who has been with her before me. No one has the right to remember what my girl looks like naked.

Okay, Felix, focus. No more thoughts of death and destruction. Not when you have heaven at your fingertips, just waiting for you to make your move. I will absolutely ruin Ronnie. She'll never be able to fuck anyone else. Not that I'd let her out of my sight long enough for that to happen anyway. I've already decided that she's mine, now and forever.

Now, I know what you're thinking. You're thinking 'Felix, my guy, you met this girl two days ago and you're already dangerously obsessed with her. Chill.' But once you find your dream, you can't just let it slip away.

You're also probably thinking 'Well, you don't know a thing about her. How can she be your dream?' And you're most likely rolling your eyes. Well, counterpoint, do you believe in love at first sight? Because I sure as fuck didn't, hell I didn't even believe in love, until I saw Veronica Woods. Second counterpoint, I've had two full days to learn everything about Ronnie. I'm excellent at deep diving into people's pasts, I hunt down vile pieces of shit as a hobby, after all. I'm a certified stalker, and I'm not ashamed to admit it. And Ronnie has become my number one target.

Her birthday is October 29th, which is in a few weeks, and she'll be turning twenty-three. Her favorite color is emerald green. Her best friend,

Leah Crawford, has been in her life since fourth grade. Leah's parents adopted Ronnie when she was in eighth grade. Her birth parents were murdered, and the sick son of a bitch who killed them has been added to my list. Her favorite movie is Hereditary. Her favorite band is Ghost. She has a fascination with death, and her therapist thinks it's due to her parents being slaughtered in front of her. Do I need to go on? The point is I memorized every fact about Ronnie that I could find online.

Of course there are things about her that I can't learn online. Like how she sounds when my cock is pounding into her, which is why we're both here in my bed naked. Her hand is small and soft, her fingers gently and tentatively moving over my hard dick. She's obviously very worried about my size, but I can see the hunger in her eyes as her fingers move over my skin. If she's this nervous about me fucking her pussy, I can't imagine how she'll feel when I take her ass, but that's an adventure for another day.

Pushing Ronnie's legs up so they bend at the knee, I pin her knees to my chest before bending down to kiss her again. Her tongue tastes sweet and minty. I drag my lips from her mouth down her jaw, and then kiss and suck the pulse point in her neck. My girl loves it when I tease that spot on her neck, her breathy moans filling the air and making my cock twitch.

With my left hand braced by her head, I use my right to cup her breast. Her tits are fucking gorgeous, and her hard pink nipples are pierced with gold barbells. I brush a finger across her right nipple before pinching it with my thumb and forefinger. Ronnie gasps below me, rocking her hips needily. My right fist wraps around my cock, pumping it firmly while I pull her nipple into my mouth, tugging on the barbell of her piercing. Her breath comes out quicker now, and her moans grow louder.

I rub the head of my dick through her folds, stopping to rub it against her clit, before dragging it back down through her wetness. My little fox wants me so bad she's writhing beneath me, pushing her dripping wet cunt against me. She feels the same way I do; I know it. She's becoming just as obsessed with me as I am with her.

And Ronnie is too fucking smart. She already put two and two together when I accidentally called her little fox earlier. I had to play it cool and mislead her. I feel guilty about gaslighting her, but I'm not ready to let go of our little game yet. Her time with the masked version of me isn't going to end any time soon. I want to see just how depraved I can make her.

Lining the head of my cock up with her entrance, I push the tip in with a groan. "Fuck baby, you're so tight."

Ronnie's hands fly to my shoulders, her nails digging into my skin, as I push in further. She gasps at the stretch of her pussy around my cock. Even though she's fucking soaked I can tell it's uncomfortable for her, and I don't blame her. She was stupefied when she saw how huge my erection was, and I'm going to take a wild guess that she's never had anyone my size. But I know she can take it. She's fucking made for me.

My fingers move to circle her clit, drawing moans from Ronnie between the gasps as I push deeper into her.

"F-fuck...Felix...I can't..." Ronnie pants.

"Yes, you can. Look at how well you're doing, baby. You're going to take every fucking inch of me into that sweet pussy of yours." I praise, pushing my thumb against her clit firmly while sliding in the rest of the way.

I can feel the walls of her pussy like a vise around my cock. My thumb rubs tight circles around her clit while my dick rests inside of her, allowing her to get used to my size. Her pussy gets wetter as I tease, and after a minute she starts grinding her hips, pulling me in at a deeper angle. I groan before sliding out to the tip and then slowly thrusting back in until I hit the back of her.

She's so wet that there's little resistance as I slide in and out. All traces of discomfort are gone from her beautiful face, and they've been replaced with a look of pure pleasure while I drive into her relentlessly, still stroking my thumb across her clit.

The walls of her cunt pulse and flutter around me as she draws nearer to an orgasm.

"Are you going to come on my cock, Veronica?" I growl, pounding harder.

She fervently nods, her mouth open in an o, moans pouring from her.

"That's it, baby. Look at me when you come." I demand, thrusting deeply and hard enough to shake the bed and make her exquisite tits bounce.

Her eyes lock on mine, and her pupils are blown from how good she feels. Her pussy squeezes me so tight I can barely move, and then she's coming unraveled while holding my gaze. Ronnie's moans echo through my bedroom, unabashedly loud. In between moans and pants, she chants my name and I've never heard a sound so heavenly.

I thrust as deeply as I can one last time before spilling inside of her.

After a minute, I roll to the side, collapsing on the bed, my breaths coming out in pants. Ronnie lies next to me, humming contentedly and a small smile on her face. Turning on my side, I face her. She's divinity in the flesh. Breathtaking.

"I should probably go home." Ronnie whispers, breaking our comfortable silence.

My heart hurts at the thought. I don't want her to leave, now or ever. I want her to be mine. "Stay." I respond firmly, letting her know that I actually want her to, not that I'm just playing games.

She looks at me then, her doe eyes connecting with mine. "That's very forward…but sweet." She pats my arm, trying to placate me. "But I barely know you Felix, and I don't want to impose. I don't want to be that person who overstays their welcome."

"It's not overstaying if I want you here." I'm near begging at this point. I've never been desperate for anyone like this. Thoughts of cuffing her to my bed return.

Ronnie kisses my cheek, and then rolls out of bed. Clasping her bra, she pulls it into place before pulling her dress on as well. She looks around for her panties, before remembering that I took them.

"Can I have my underwear?" Ronnie's cheeks are red, and she asks like she's embarrassed.

"Nope."

Her jaw drops, her innocent doe eyes trained on me and the smirk that I'm wearing. "Felix!" Ronnie squeals.

"I'm keeping them." I say smugly. If she won't stay the night with me, at least I'll have something that smells like her.

"What, do you have some perverted obsession with collecting panties?" She scoffs.

"No. I have a perverted obsession with you." I admit.

Ronnie guffaws. "Right, okay." She walks out of my bedroom, likely looking for her purse.

She left it on my kitchen counter while I made drinks, but I don't tell her that. The longer she spends searching, the longer she stays with me. That's a pretty fucked up and desperate thought. I've fallen low, and it's sad, but I'm having a hard time giving a shit. I'd get on my knees and crawl for this woman if she asked me to.

"Aha!" Ronnie finds her purse triumphantly. "I'll order an Uber and be out of your hair." She calls out, not realizing I'm standing in the kitchen doorway behind her.

Ronnie turns and spots me, her eyes trailing up and down my body. Did I mention that I didn't put on any clothes yet? She seems to enjoy the way I look, and maybe if she sees me like this again, she won't be able to resist.

"Something on your mind?" I purr, giving her a wink.

"Nope. Not at all." She clears her throat. "Uh…I'm just going to go. Thank you for a wonderful night. Maybe we can do it again sometime?"

"Tomorrow?"

"Woah, Felix. Slow down. Let's cool off for a couple of days and then see where we're at. I'm sure I'll see you at work." Ronnie moves to the front door, pushing past me.

Damn, this woman is made of stone. She's committed to the idea of going home tonight. And maybe I'm pushing her too hard. I don't want her to get freaked out and run away. So fine, I'll let her go, for now.

"At least let me drive you home." I'd be a dick to make her take an Uber this late at night. And honestly, the driver could be anyone. What if he's a creep?

"That's okay, the Uber should be here in a couple of minutes. Thanks again, Felix."

And just like that, the love of my life walks out my door.

***

It's probably a good thing that Veronica and I haven't exchanged numbers yet. Sure, I could easily do some digging and find it out, but then I'd be texting her constantly and she'd probably get scared and block me. We can't have that. I'm obsessed, but she doesn't need to know how much just yet.

And anyway, I need to focus. I can't have my little fox distracting me while I'm hunting. That's just a recipe for disaster, and I don't have any wishes to end up behind bars or dead.

It's Tuesday now, and it's been three excruciating days without seeing my girl. Well, I shouldn't say I haven't seen her because every minute I have available I'm tailing her, she just doesn't know it. What I really meant is it's been three days since I've spent time with her in a capacity where she knows I'm there. It's been a slow week in the body pickup department, so I haven't even been called to the M.E.'s office yet. But once I'm done with tonight's escapades, there'll be a call tomorrow.

I'm sitting in the back of a rundown bar called The Well. Its name comes from the fact that they only serve the cheapest of beers and spirits. Well drinks, all around. If I'm being honest, this bar is complete ass. The booths and stools are covered in duct tape to keep the foam of the cushions in place. The tables are permanently sticky and discolored, and the floors look like haven't been mopped in the last decade. It's a shithole, and should've been condemned years ago.

But apparently some people like it enough to be regulars here. It's pretty quiet, which is lucky for me because it makes eavesdropping on my target much easier. Trinity Giles is sitting at the bar, giggling away as she talks with the bearded man next to her. The guy probably thinks she's talking shit, trying to seem tough, but I've learned enough about Trinity to know that she's not just blowing smoke.

Trinity isn't even trying to be discreet anymore, and that's what really pisses me off. She's actively bragging about getting off on the charges against her, putting all the blame on her waste of space boyfriend, Warner Hill. Although Warner wasn't a tough enough name for the guy, so he goes by Diesel, like a fucking tool.

See, Trinity and Diesel are absolute vile trash. It all started a few years ago when Trinity decided to let Diesel use her daughter, Hannah, at his plaything. I can't even consider Trinity as a mother to the poor girl, only the hole that Hannah came out of. Hannah is fifteen, and was twelve when it all started.

Then Trinity and Diesel had the idea to make money off of Hannah. They started inviting others over, letting them pay to destroy Hannah's body, mind, and soul. I guess they invited the wrong person, because word got out and the police and CPS got involved. Hannah was removed from their care, but when everything went to trial, it was pinned on Diesel alone. Trinity got off without a mark on her name. The only saving grace is that Hannah hasn't been returned to Trinity as of yet. And she won't ever be, after tonight.

The plan is simple, follow Trinity out of The Well, use my handy dandy syringe of ketamine, torture and kill her, and then deposit her carcass somewhere in the city. If I was really sick in the head I'd give Trinity the same treatment she subjected Hannah to over the last three years, but I'm not getting within ten feet of that creature's rotten pussy. No fucking thanks. So, the regular routine of torture will have to suffice.

It's after one in the morning when Trinity finally decides to take her slimy ass back to whatever hole she calls home. I slip out into the night behind her, pulling my hood low over my head and slapping on my goat skull mask. My boots are heavy, but I don't even try to mask my steps. Trinity is blitzed out of her mind, stumbling over her own feet as she heads down the sidewalk. This street is dead, with not another soul in sight. Perfect for my date with Trinity.

I slip up behind her, wrap one arm around her middle and in the next second I'm plunging the syringe into her neck and it's lights out. Well, not really lights out. Ketamine doesn't knock people out completely; it just renders them in a state of pliability. Trinity will be very unaware of her surroundings and not able to fight back.

My jag is parked just ahead, and from here it's just a matter of keeping her propped up and walking to my car. If anyone were to pass by, not that they would because it's like a ghost town out here, they'd think that Trinity was just wasted and I was helping take her home. And the lack of cameras in this part of town works in my favor. Opening the passenger door, I shove Trinity inside. Her movements are stilted and stuttering, which means the ketamine has taken full effect now. She won't be able to control her body movements any longer.

The amount of ketamine I pumped into her system will keep her docile long enough for us to drive to the abandoned house I've commandeered out in the forested hills outside of Westmound. The drive is about half an hour, which I spend blasting music and singing along. I don't have the best singing voice, but that doesn't mean I can't jam out. And besides, Trinity is in no condition to comment on it anyway, not like I'd give a fuck about her opinion.

The farm I've taken over is still technically abandoned, I don't want it traced back to my name if it's ever discovered. The house is in shambles, but the barn is in good enough shape that I was able to convert it into a torture chamber of sorts. The road to the property has long since been abandoned as well, so I can only drive so far. It's about a mile walk through the woods to get to the actual property, which works for me because it's secluded and hard to stumble upon.

The shitty part about it being a mile walk is getting my victims from the car to the barn. The forest is overgrown, this area not inhabited for years. If I cared about the wellbeing of my 'clients' I'd worry about it, but I just use this as another torture method. Not that they're lucid enough to fully experience it. I bind Trinity in rope, wrapping her arms and legs tightly. Here's the fun part, I've learned how to fashion two straps that attach to the arm bindings. She's almost like a fucked-up backpack now. Slinging the straps over my shoulders, I pull her limp body behind me as I trek through the forest. She'll be all sorts of banged up after the journey.

I don't bother avoiding branches as rocks as I walk, enjoying the sound of her skull thudding off of them. I really should work on the dosage of ketamine I use. It'd be so satisfying for them to be more lucid during this part of the torture. I'm too wound up to do any experimenting on Trinity tonight though. I want her disposed of by morning. That way I'll get called by Terrance to pick up her body, and I'll get to see my girl in her element at the M.E.'s office.

I have just enough time to get her strung up before she begins to wake. I've installed two metal cuffs on chains into the floors, as well at two from the ceiling. Once I strap her in, her arms are yanked above her head and her leads are spread apart. The chains are pulled taut enough so it hurts as her limbs are pulled in different directions.

There's a hose with a pressure washer attachment coiled up on the floor. Gripping it, I turn the valve until the freezing cold water is at full strength and blasting from the end of the pressure washer attachment. Trinity is coming to, but not fast enough for my liking. Holding the hose, I aim the powerful spray at her ugly face. The water hits her mouth, the force knocking her head back as she gurgles and gasps.

I continue spraying her mouth for another thirty seconds, filling her lungs with water as she struggles to breathe. Drowning like this would be a horrible way to die, but it's not her time yet. I want her to know who is killing her and why. Twisting the valve, the harsh spray of pressurized water stops.

Trinity's head falls forward, agonized gasps and groans ripping from her throat as water drips from her mouth. She coughs out water before gagging and then vomiting, a slurry of water and booze flying from her mouth, remnants dripping down her chin and chest.

"That was fucking disgusting. Good evening to you too, Trinity Giles." I sneer. Torture truly is a disgusting business, but someone's gotta do it.

She mumbles incoherently in response.

"Oh no, that's okay. No need to respond. I don't give a fuck what you have to say anyway." I shrug, stalking towards her hanging body.

As I approach, she tries to lift her head but fails several times.

"Ketamine and alcohol, not a good mix. Not for you, anyway. For me, it's perfect." I get right in her face, gripping her chin to tilt it until her eyes are on mine.

Her pupils are blown wide, and her eyes are unfocused, flitting back and forth in her sockets. Trinity's body twitches and pulls at the chains, but it's no use. There's no escaping me.

"Trinity…Trinity…Trinity…" I sing-song. "You thought that you had gotten away with it, so much so that you bragged about your deeds to anyone willing to listen at The Well. You truly are a vapid bitch." Tsking, I circle her.

"Wuhhh." Trinity slurs, drool dripping down her chin.

Lining one wall of the barn I have various weapons and torture tools hanging. From the reports, Hannah was severely beaten by the various abusers who paid to 'spend time' with her. I said I wouldn't go near Trinity's nasty pussy, so instead I'll beat her just like she let people beat her daughter.

I grab a claw hammer from the wall, swinging it idly in my hands as I make my way back over to Trinity. She's more alert now, her eyes becoming more focused and her head no longer lolling.

Her eyes rake over me, taking in my sadistic smirk and the hammer in my hands.

"Wuhhtt the fuckkk?" Trinity garbles, still nearly incoherent from the drugs and alcohol in her system.

"Trinity Giles." My voice is loud, echoing through the barn. "You allowed your boyfriend, Warner Hill, to violate your daughter on countless occasions. And then, you allowed people to pay you to violate her. Once you were caught, you had the audacity to deny your guilt and pin it all on Warner, or Diesel, as the fuckwad likes to be called. And instead of getting the fuck out of dodge and escaping while you had the chance, you started bragging about your role in the torture of Hannah to anyone who would listen."

"No…no…" Trinity cries, rattling her chains.

"Oh, yes…yes…" I grin. "Luckily for me, I love a little vigilante justice. Unlucky for you, that means I'm going to torture and kill you. I wish I could inflict every ounce of pain onto you that you allowed your daughter to endure, but unfortunately, we don't have time for that. So, you'll only be experiencing a fraction of what Hannah Giles experienced. Starting…now!" And with that, I swing the blunt side of the claw hammer into her left knee.

The force of my blow bows her knee backwards. Trinity's screams of agony are the sweetest symphony…but I can make her squeal more than she currently is. Moving to the other leg, my hammer hits her right knee from the side with a resounding crack.

"Fucccckk!" Trinity screeches, spit flying from her mouth.

"How many broken bones did Hannah suffer over the last few years?" I swing the hammer again, this time stopping it an inch from hitting Trinity in the ribs.

She flinches and cries, her eyes tracking my movements as I continue circling her.

"There were five records of her being brought to the hospital with various fractures. But we both know that there were times you didn't bother bringing her." I'm behind her now, out of her line of sight.

Flipping the hammer in my palm, I swing the claw side into Trinity's calf, planting the sharp claws deep into her muscle before wrenching it free. Blood gushes from the wound, dripping down her leg and forming a puddle on the floor. Trinity sobs, snot bubbling in her nose.

"What is with all of you and the fucking snot? Royce Mills did the same shit. Fucking gross."

I can handle the blood, guts, and gore, but fucking snot man. Disgusting. "Makes me want to puke."

"P-p-please…" Trinity cries, her breaths shaky.

"Skipping right past denial and anger, huh? Straight to bargaining. Honestly, that's fine with me because I don't want to spend more time with you than needed. I've gotta see my girl after this, so might as well keep the ball rolling." *Crack.* The blunt end collides with Trinity's ribs.

"If you believe in God, you better start praying. Although, there's no fucking chance for redemption at this point. Maybe begging the Devil for mercy would be the better route." And with that, I get to work. The time for talking is over.

Chapter 9
Ronnie

"We've got a fresh one coming in today, Ronnie." Dr. Vargas says, stepping into the autopsy suite. "Trinity Giles, age thirty-nine. Found in an alleyway downtown, body discarded near a dumpster. Whoever killed her put her through the ringer first."

"That name sounds familiar..." I think aloud.

"It should." Vargas confirms. "She was part of a big case recently. Her boyfriend, Warner Hill, was found guilty for sexually exploiting Trinity's daughter, Hannah Giles. Trinity was acquitted, but if you ask me, I think she was guilty as sin."

"Sounds like our vigilante killer struck again then. Can't say I'm too heartbroken over it, good riddance Trinity." I scoff.

Our justice system is so corrupt. People who should be behind bars get off all the time. And innocent people are imprisoned constantly. At least someone has the balls to enact justice when the system fails.

"Felix and Sav should be here soon with the cadaver." Vargas stands at the sink, scrubbing his hands in preparation for handling Trinity's corpse.

My heart races at the thought of seeing Felix. I haven't heard from him or seen him since Saturday. That night was…incredible. Every night since I've been under the covers, fantasizing about his hands and lips on my body. But I also want to take it slow. I don't want to seem clingy or needy, and I'm scared to get too close to him too quickly. I've been in one long-term relationship in my life, and the experience was crushing. That's one of the reasons I've only been casually hooking up here and there. But with Felix, I feel like it could be more than a casual fling, and that terrifies me.

The opening of the metal double doors into the autopsy suite pulls me from my thoughts. Sav walks in backwards, pulling the gurney with him. Felix pushes the other end, guiding it into the suite. Parking it next to the autopsy table, they put the brakes on. Felix's gaze meets mine, his eyes lighting up and a heartbreaking smile gracing his full lips.

"Hey, Veronica." Felix winks before trailing his hungry gaze up and down my body with a sinful smirk.

"Hi." I squeak.

"Hello! I'm here too. Geesh." Sav interjects, rolling his eyes.

"Everyone can see your big dumb face dude, no need to announce your presence." Felix jokes.

"Your mom didn't think my face was dumb when she was riding it last night." Sav quips back.

"Boys. This is a professional work setting, and you're in the presence of a lady." Dr. Vargas scolds both the boys, but the corner of his mouth is curved slightly and his eyes are crinkled at the edges.

"Sorry, Terrance." Felix and Sav reply at the same time.

Getting to work, Felix and Sav heave the deceased onto the autopsy table.

"This one looked pretty brutal. Hope you aren't squeamish, Ronnie!" Sav jokes.

"This would be the wrong job for me if I got queasy at a little gore." I sigh. I can tell Sav is a goofball, comparable to a golden retriever. He even kind of looks like one.

"Well anyway, we should probably head out. See ya, Terry!" Sav salutes Dr. Vargas before turning back to me with a smirk. "Hope you don't puke, Ronnie."

Felix grips Sav's shoulder, shoving him towards the door. "Alright, meathead. Let the professionals get back to work." Felix scolds Sav, winking over his shoulder back at me. "See you around, Veronica."

I stare after Felix, long after the doors have swung shut.

Dr. Vargas clears his throat. "Careful with that one, Veronica. He's not the settling down type. I'd hate for you to get your heart broken."

My cheeks flush in embarrassment. "Nothing's going on with us."

Terrance gives me a pointed look that tells me he knows I'm lying.

"It was just one date. One excellent, dreamy, date…" My thoughts drift back to that night and how badly I want it to happen again. It doesn't need to be anything serious, but I would like to spend more time with Felix. And people can change, right? So, what if he's never dated seriously before, maybe he'll change his mind with me. He seemed very into me. The guy practically begged me to stay the night with him. People don't do that if they aren't into you.

I clear my throat, changing the subject. "Anyway...should we get to cracking Trinity open?"

Unzipping the body bag, I let out a gasp. Sav wasn't kidding when he said this one was rough. Trinity's face and neck are mottled with bruises that look like they came from an immense amount of pressure.

There are stab wounds in various places on her body, her calves, her neck, her back. All of the stab wounds are in sets of two punctures, so whatever instrument was used must have been two pronged. She's also covered in contusions from a round, blunt object.

Dr. Vargas and I document numerous punctures and contusions all over Trinity's body. Her left leg is bent backwards at an odd angle, and her right kneecap has been shattered and blown the to the side. While the injuries are countless, none would have been fatal.

"Any ideas on cause of death?" I ask Dr. Vargas.

"None of the external injuries, that's certain." He answers, looking over the body once again. "While the external injuries are numerous, none were enough to cause a fatality. Our answer will most likely be discovered during the internal examination."

Terrance makes the y-shaped incision across the corpse's chest. Peeling back the skin, we begin examining her internal organs for signs of damage.

"Her lungs are filled with water." I note. "However, her body isn't bloated and her skin doesn't appear like she was in a body of water. Where was she found again?"

"In an alleyway downtown." Vargas confirms. "I agree that she most likely wasn't submerged. I do find the bruising around her mouth and neck interesting though. Let's examine her throat for bruising as well."

We confirm that there are an extensive number of contusions inside the victim's throat. It appears as if she was drowned, but not submerged.

"This seems odd but...could she have been waterboarded? Either that or forced to drink an ungodly amount of water. But drinking that amount shouldn't lead to this much bruising..." I ponder aloud.

"You may be onto something there." Vargas nods, his eyes glinting proudly at my deduction. "I've seen one other waterboarding victim during my years, and the damage is similar. Although that cadaver didn't have nearly this much bruising. The water source used in this case was likely high pressure."

***

As the hot water runs over me in the locker room shower, I keep thinking about Trinity Giles. On my break I looked up the case she was involved in. Trinity was acquitted, but Terrance said that she was most likely guilty. Whoever killed her must have thought the same, seeing as she was obviously tortured and then drowned.

Trinity marks the second case since I've started where the victim wasn't actually a victim at all. The second case where it seems vigilante justice was enacted. It definitely could be coincidence, but something tells me it isn't. Honestly, if Trinity was as guilty as Terrance believed, she deserved every minute of pain she was dealt. Whoever the vigilante is, I hope they don't get caught. They're making the city a safer place.

I promised Leah that we'd have a girl's night tomorrow. She's been so busy working nights I haven't seen her much lately. She happens to have a night off, and it's been way too long since we've been able to hang out just the two of us. And from the texts we've been exchanging, it sounds like she's got some news.

Even though we live together it's like we're on separate planes of existence. Our schedules are opposite. In one way, it's kind of nice because it feels like I live alone, but sometimes it gets lonely. I miss gossiping with my best friend over a bottle of wine, which is exactly what we plan to do tomorrow night.

I wrap my leather jacket tighter around my chest as I step out into the brisk evening air. The nights are getting cooler. Soon I'll have to switch from riding my bike to work to taking the subway. I hate winter. It takes away the freeing feeling of riding my motorcycle through the city. The only adrenaline rush I get from riding the subway is the apprehension that someone might grope me. I can't afford a car, and even if I could, trying to park that and my bike would be extremely expensive.

Our apartment is small, with two bedrooms, one bathroom, and a small living area and kitchen. Since Leah and I are never here at the same time, the small space isn't so bad. It's not in the nicest area of Westmound, and the building itself is dingy and outdated, but it works for us.

The inside decor is an eclectic mix of girly and gothic. Most of our furniture is antique, from thrift stores and flea markets. There's constant noise from the street below, and the flashing of a neon open sign for the pharmacy across the street, but you get used to both. And the only reason the sign is flashing is because the lights are dying in it, and management hasn't bothered to replace them. That's what they make noise canceling headphones and blackout curtains for anyway.

I throw my keys and helmet onto the table inside the entryway, shuffling my combat boots and leather jacket off with a sigh. The apartment itself is quiet. Sometimes I debate on getting a dog just to have something to come home to. Leah wouldn't mind, but she's definitely more of a cat person. I walk through the dark entryway, making my way to the kitchen for a glass of water.

When I go to flick on the kitchen light, the switch clicks but the room remains dark. I flip it a couple more times, with no luck.

"Fuck. Did we forget to pay the electric bill?" I mutter. I really don't want to spend my evening alone in the dark.

Rubbing my temples, I head towards the living room, trying light switches as I go. I pull out my phone to text Leah. Her reply comes quickly, meaning it must not be busy at the club.

'Bills paid. Power was on when I was there. (shrug emoji)' Leah's text says.

Well shit. The lights were on in the hall, and I can see the flashing neon open sign for the pharmacy across the street, so it must just be our apartment. I was really looking forward to curling up on the couch to watch the new true crime documentary on the River Reaper, a famous serial killer from the area. Looks like my hopes for a relaxing night have been dashed.

I exhale sharply out of my nose, annoyed at my situation. I decide to head out to Club Profile for the night instead. I'll call maintenance once I get there, and hopefully they can sort this out before long.

I'm wearing black skinny jeans and a ratty old band tee. Club Profile has a dress code, and while I know the bouncer would let me in anyway because he knows me, I would feel out of place. I trudge to my room and into my closet, using my phone's flashlight to illuminate the row of tops I have hanging up. I find a form fitting black lace bodysuit.

Shutting off my phone's flashlight, I turn as I yank the band tee over my head. I'm facing my bed now, but it's so dark without my phone that I can't see much. I begin to unbutton my jeans when I think see movement out of the corner of my eye. I squint, trying to make out the shape but shake my head, thinking that my eyes are playing tricks on me in the dark.

You know when you're lying in bed with your eyes open in the darkness, and you swear you can see static in the air or see shadows moving? That's how it felt just now.

"Great Ronnie, now you're seeing shit too." I grumble.

As I slide off my jeans, I think I hear a footstep and freeze. My jeans hang around my knees and my heart thunders in my ears as I try to listen for more movement, but don't hear anything else. The power being out is really messing with my head. I giggle aloud at how much of a scaredy-cat I'm being.

I step the rest of the way out of my jeans, standing in just my panties and bra. Goosebumps fill my arms, and the hairs on the back of my neck prickle, but neither is from the cold. It almost feels like someone is watching me. I quickly spin on my heel to where I feel the eyes, but even when illuminating the space with my flashlight I see nothing.

As I turn to my right, still looking behind me with the illumination from my phone, I feel a warm breath caress the left side of my neck and trail down my shoulder. The breath sends a shiver coursing through me.

I whip my head to the left just in time to see an all black goat skull mask peering over my shoulder. Hands with black leather gloves wrap around my hips, and a black clad body presses against my near naked back.

"What the fu—" I begin to screech, but one of the gloved hands shoots up and covers my mouth.

"Shhh…little fox." A dark, gravelly voice says, trying to soothe me. "We had so much fun at Haunted Hollow but I need more. I'm nowhere near finished with you yet."

I listen to the masked man's voice closely, trying to determine if I recognize it, but he speaks deeply and quietly, making it impossible to be sure. During my night with Felix, I was becoming so sure that he was the masked man, but then he made me doubt myself. Maybe tonight I can find out for sure.

"I'm going to uncover your mouth. Promise not to scream?" He whispers in my ear.

I nod, gazing at the blackened eye holes in his mask. It's so dark I can't make out what the masked man's eyes look like. He could be anyone under there. I breathe in deeply, trying to fill my nostrils with his scent. Felix smelled of wood and citrus, but this man smells spicy with notes of vanilla. His body is muscular, warm and slightly familiar. But now I don't know if it's because it reminds me of Felix's, or if I'm just remembering how the masked man felt against me in The Chapel.

"That's my good girl." He purrs.

"How did you find out where I live? Lurking in my house is pretty stalkerish." I jab.

"Maybe I am a stalker." He replies nonchalantly.

I huff an unamused laugh. "That's not usually something people brag about…"

"I'm not a usual person. Thought you would've figured that out by now. I did cut your power and break into your house after all."

"You were the one who fucked with my power?!" I yell, turning to face the man.

His thumb brushes my bottom lip before pulling it down. "Shhh…little fox. It's time to play."

Although I can't see his features, I can feel the heat in his gaze and hear the smile that plays on his lips. I should be scared of him. This is the start to many horror movies and true crime cases. Woman is stalked by masked stranger, woman is murdered by stalker, woman's lifeless body is dumped in the river. But surprisingly, I'm not scared enough to make a break for it. His presence is soothing in an odd way. I feel like I know him and can trust him.

"Who are you?" I ask, searching in the dark for the glint of his eyes, but only seeing the black holes of the mask.

I reach up, intending to lift the mask, but he grips my wrist hard and stops me.

"No." He growls.

"You can't expect me to play with you when you're a complete stranger." I grumble.

"You did in the confessional." He releases my wrist, instead running his fingers down my cheek, jaw, and then dropping to gently caress my collarbone. "And I know you enjoyed it. You enjoyed me following you around Haunted Hollow. You like me cornering you, scaring you and then making you cum. And I bet you're dripping wet right now, the thought of some stranger breaking into your home and waiting for you. Waiting to tease and fuck you."

I suck in a sharp breath. He isn't wrong. The night at The Chapel was one of my top two sexual experiences ever, right along with my night spent with Felix. Does that make me fucked up? Most definitely. But I never claimed to be normal. And besides, don't stalkers and serial killers usually get off on the other person's fear? This man sure doesn't. He wants to bring me pleasure, and maybe a little bit of fear and pain, but I don't think he truly wants to hurt or kill me.

"Your boyfriend doesn't have to know. If that's what you're worried about." The man's tone is impassionate and dismissive.

"I don't have a boyfriend." I spit back.

"Hmmm. Interesting." He replies.

Does he actually find that interesting? Does he think I'm lying? Felix and I have only been on one date. That doesn't mean we're in a relationship. But if my stalker watched my date with Felix, he might think my relationship with him is more than it really is. It's strictly casual, for now. Just like this rendezvous with my masked stalker. Oh great, now I'm thinking of him as mine.

Before I know what's happening, his fingers find the clasp of my bra, unhooking it and pulling it swiftly off my body. He bends, shimmying my jeans down the rest of the way.

My breasts spring free, my nipples pebbling in the cool air, and he literally growls at the sight. Picking my up by my thighs, he flings me onto my bed. The air whooshes out of my lungs as I land.

His body lands over mine, hovering above me with his hands braced on either side of my head. His dark presence looms over me, blocking everything but him out of my sight.

He pushes my thighs to the side with his knees, aligning his hips with mine until I feel his hard length pressing against my core. He grinds it against me, and I can feel the ridge of his cock rub through my panties and against my clit. The masked man was right when he bet I would be wet. Moisture clings to the cloth as he grinds against me. The friction makes me moan and writhe beneath him.

"My filthy little fox. I can feel how wet you are through my clothes." He breathes in my ear.

His hand trails between us, the leather of his gloves creaking as his fingers pull my panties to the side. The masked man's index finger presses against my clit, causing me to buck against him at the pressure. The pressure eases as he starts slowly circling the bundle of nerves, barely making contact with my skin. I lift my hips, trying to get more stimulation, but the masked man leans back on his heels, then holds my hips down with one hand while continuing his feather light teasing on my clit. The lack of friction is driving me mad, but the masked man just chuckles at my attempts to wriggle against him.

"You have such a needy little cunt for me, don't you?" He purrs.

I nod fervently. "Please. More." I beg.

He lifts his hand and shakes a finger at me, tsking behind his mask. "Good girls get rewarded. Are you going to be a good girl for me?"

"Yes." I desperately rasp. In the span on ten minutes this man has reduced me to a begging mess, longing for any attention he'll give me.

Getting to his knees, he crawls over me until he's seated on my chest. He doesn't put his entire body weight down, but it's enough to where I can't move. His fingers flick open the button of his black jeans before sliding his zipper down. The masked man pushes his pants down his hips before pulling his hard cock out of his boxers.

It's too dark for me to see much except the outline of his cock looming above me. His gloved fist wraps around the base, and it's wide enough where his fingers just barely meet each other. The goat masked man taps the tip against my lips, covering them in the salty taste of his pre-cum.

My tongue darts out, licking my lips before swiveling over the slit on his dick. A small moan escapes my lips at his taste, and he groans in response.

"Open your mouth and stick out your tongue, little fox." He commands, still gripping the base of his cock tightly.

I obey, opening my jaw as wide as I can and sticking my wet tongue out. He rubs his head against my tongue, wetting it before shoving into my mouth and filling me with his shaft. He pushes all the way back until the tip hits the back of my throat. I gag at the intrusion, which only makes the masked man groan and push deeper until he removes his hand from his cock and slides it all the way in to the base. It's so deep that I can't breathe, and I begin to panic. My hands fly up to his hips, gripping them and trying to tug him away.

"Relax your throat and breathe through your nose, baby." He coos.

I listen, letting my throat and mouth relax and taking a deep inhale through my nose. The panic ebbs.

"Good girl." The man praises, sliding back out until only his tip remains in my mouth.

He slips back in gently, but seating himself just as deep as before. This time I'm prepared for it and more relaxed. I've given blowjobs before but I've never deep-throated or been mouth fucked like the masked man is doing. He's in complete control of everything as he pins me down and pumps himself into my mouth and down my throat. His hips move faster, snapping back and forth, fucking my mouth.

The longer he fucks me, the more aroused I become. Giving up my control and letting this man use me as his personal toy is freeing. I don't have to worry about making it a performance, I can just let him take me however he wants. His pants and moans turn me on. I've never heard a man be so vocal during sex, and it's the fucking hottest thing I've ever heard.

Soon I'm reaching down to rub my clit as he fucks my throat. My moans vibrate around his pounding cock as I circle faster and barrel towards my own release. With his dick deeply down my throat my orgasm seizes my entire being. My free hand grips the man's hip, my fingers scratching and digging into his skin. My body tenses and my vision fades to black while my hips buck wildly through each waves of my release.

The masked stranger's release quickly follows mine. Spurts of his hot cum flow into my mouth and down my throat. I try to swallow as much as I can, but soon cum is leaking from my lips and down my chin. His thrusts become less controlled and his groans become louder. He stills for a moment before sliding his cock out of my mouth.

"Such a good little cum slut for me." His fingers trace my lips and then down my chin, catching the escaped cum. With two fingers, he wipes the cum from my face and presses it into my mouth and against my tongue, forcing me to taste him again. Once he's satisfied and I've swallowed every drop, he climbs off of me, slipping his still hard cock back into his jeans.

He strides for my bedroom door, calling out to me over his shoulder. "I'll see you again soon, little fox." Then disappears into the night, like nothing happened between us at all.

Chapter 10
Ronnie

As soon as the apartment door clicked shut and the lock slid into place, the power whirred back on. I laid in bed unmoving for a while, trying to process what the fuck just happened. The goat masked man snuck into my apartment, cut my power, and waited for me to come home. And instead of screaming and running for my life, I let him take control of me and cum in my mouth. And not only that, but I fucking *liked* it. That's some sick and twisted shit, even for me.

I felt intrinsically able to trust him with my body and my life. Very similar to how I felt when I was with Felix. But maybe that's because a huge part of me hopes that it is Felix. If it is, he's giving me everything I never knew I wanted. If it isn't him, things are getting more complicated than I would like.

How do I even go about figuring out if Felix is my masked stalker? I can't just go ask him, because if he isn't that would be a fucking uncomfortable conversation. And if he is my masked man, would he even admit it? The masked man wouldn't tell me who he is, and wouldn't let me take off his mask. He likes that I don't know his identity, and while it's driving me nuts, I also kind of like the mystery too.

Leah knows I'm a little crazy, but even this is a stretch for me. I feel the need to tell her and get her advice, but she's going to freak out. I'll have ply her with several glasses of wine before broaching the subject.

On the way home from work I stop at the liquor store for two huge bottles of wine. I prefer sweet white wines, but Leah enjoys full bodied reds. Picking out a Riesling for myself and a malbec for Leah, I secure the goods in my backpack before heading back to our apartment. Leah's in charge of ordering our Thai food for dinner. We almost always order Thai from the same place.

"Honey, I'm hommmeee!" I call out as soon as I step into the apartment.

"Perfect timing, babe. Food just got here!" Leah calls back, her voice coming from our kitchen.

I head into my bedroom to change into a comfy outfit, but pause as I look at my bed. On top of my pillow is a sleek black box wrapped in a velvet green ribbon. Secured in the ribbon is a deep plum colored snapdragon, my favorite flower.

"Leah, did you get me a gift?" I yell out to her.

"Nah, why would I get you a gift when my presence is a gift itself?" She jests.

Is this from the masked man? It has to be. He obviously has the means to get into our apartment undetected. I pick up the package, letting my fingers trail over the petals of the snapdragon before rubbing the green velvet ribbon in my fingers. How did he know that snapdragons are my favorite flower?

Untying the bow, I gently slip the flower out of it and lift it to my nose, inhaling it's sweet and fruity scent. One of the reasons that snapdragons are my favorite is because when they wither and die, the leftover seed pods resemble tiny skulls, and that's fucking badass and adorable. Another is what they represent. On one hand they're said to represent strength and grace, but on the other they represent deviousness, deception and magic. I wonder if the masked man chose this flower not only because of my love for them, but because they represent his deviousness and deception.

I set the flower on my nightstand, intending to keep it in a vase until it withers. And then maybe I'll take the withered flower and make it into an art piece, pressing it into a frame for my wall. The top of the sleek black gift box slides off easily, revealing emerald green tissue paper underneath. Underneath the tissue paper a gown sparkles in the fading sunlight. Pulling the gown from the box, I gasp. It's gorgeous. As I hold up the dress, a notecard flutters to the ground.

'Wear this to your birthday party for me, little fox.'
Your masked man

Well, that answers the question of who left the gift for me. I lay out the gown across my bed, taking in the glittering black bodice with a deep v neckline. It's a sleeveless dress, with a fitted bodice and then a black and emerald green tulle skirt. It truly is a ballgown, and I've never worn anything like it. It looks to be expensive. Still inside of the gift box is a set of glittering black stilettos.

"Woah, where'd you get that?!" Leah says from the doorway.

I jump; having completely forgotten she was home with me for our girl's night.

She strides over, picking up the notecard and snapdragon. "Your masked man?" Her eyebrow quirks, and her hand lands on her hip.

"Ummm yeah…about that…" I was hoping to have her well and truly drunk before revealing my encounters with the masked man. Too late now.

I regale her with the tales of my run-ins with my masked stalker. Her jaw is unhinged, hanging open wide as she listens to me. She doesn't even try to interrupt, which is almost unheard of for Leah. She must be in shock. Once I'm done, the silence stretches between us for several minutes.

Suddenly Leah's gaze collides with mine, and she squeals, "You little bitch! I knew something was off with your 'story' of getting trapped in that confessional!" finally breaking her silence. "And last night while I was at work you were here getting mauled by some masked stranger?! You let the dude cum in your mouth, Ronnie!"

"I don't think it's a stranger." I whisper, shrugging shoulders. I have no concrete evidence; in fact, I have evidence to the contrary. Felix and the masked man smelled nothing alike. Although both Felix and the masked man have called me little fox, but that doesn't necessarily prove anything.

"And?" Leah taps her foot impatiently.

"Well, I don't have any proof but…I have a feeling that the masked man is Felix." I chew on my lip, waiting for her reaction.

"Do you feel that way or are you just hopeful that's the truth?" Leah calls me out. She knows me all too well.

"Probably a bit of both. But now that I've revealed my dark secret to you, you can help me find clues to his identity!" I grip her shoulders, a wide smile on my face.

"And how the fuck are we going to do that?"

"I was hoping you'd have an idea." I mutter.

Leah rolls her eyes in response. "Okay well, I'm going to need some Thai food and a lot of wine to process this whole situation."

"Agreed."

We settle into our thrifted and worn in couch. It's a relic from some grandma's house, covered in a hideous floral print, but it's comfortable. I dive face first into my chicken pad Thai, yes, I'm basic, while Leah munches on her tofu green curry. I pour us each a full glass of our chosen wines. In the background the TV quietly plays a re-run of Buffy the Vampire Slayer.

"You said you had some sort of news?" I say after taking a large gulp of Riesling.

Leah huffs out a sigh. "Yeah, you know Micah?"

"Uh, bartender at Club Profile? Never heard of him." I answer sarcastically.

"Har har. Well, he's been crushing on me forever."

I choke on my noodles. "You knew that? You seemed so oblivious to his obvious puppy love for you."

"Yeah well, I tried to ignore it." She sips her malbec. "He's cute and all, but he's too much of a 'nice guy'. Anyway, I finally gave in and let him take me on a date."

"WHAT?! When?!" I screech.

"Chill, girl. It's not that serious." Leah rolls her eyes so often I'm surprised they haven't rolled right out her head. "He took me to an early dinner on Tuesday night, before our shifts at the club."

"And his puppy dog ways won your heart? You're getting married next month? You've already named your future children?" I tease.

"Uhm, yeah…no." She scoffs. "Don't get me wrong, he's a nice guy and super cute, but he's fucking B. O. R. I. N. G. It was a snooze fest. It was like talking to a cardboard box. So no, I won't be going on a date with Micah again."

"Really?" I'm shocked. "I guess I don't talk to him much, but I thought for sure the two of you would hit it off. Think of how cute your babies would've been. It's a shame that such good genes were wasted on a dud."

"No kidding." Leah sighs.

She doesn't get out much on dates, simply because her work schedule doesn't often align with other peoples. Leah is a catch, and any man would be lucky to have her.

"Maybe I can set you up with Sav, Felix's friend." I think aloud. "He's a golden retriever, but I have a feeling there's more to him than just being a goofy nice guy. He gives off some dark vibes."

"Let's invite him to your birthday party at the club." Leah smirks, a plan formulating in her brain as she talks. "I'm willing to take just about any dick I can get at this point. That is, any but Micah's. I'm afraid I'll fall asleep during."

"Oof, fucking harsh. But yeah, next time I see Felix I'll invite him and Sav." I agree.

My birthday is October 29th, and it happens to fall on a Saturday night. Leah was able to secure the private room of the club for us to celebrate. The party is going to be masquerade themed, in honor of Halloween being a few days after. The dress my mystery man got me will work perfectly with my mask for the party. He must've seen it when he was snooping in my room.

What I'm not sure about is how he knew of my upcoming party. We haven't even sent the invites yet. I wonder if this means he'll be showing up to the club in his goat mask.

"I think the masked man plans on attending the party, based on the note he left." I muse. "The gown matches the colors of my masquerade mask perfectly. It might be a great opportunity to see if Felix is behind the mask. He can't be in two places at once, so if we see both Felix and the masked man, we'll know it isn't him."

"Time for us to become amateur sleuths." Leah grins manically.

Chapter 11
Felix

"Why are we going to see your girlfriend at this club again?" Sav asks for the third time tonight.

"She's not my girlfriend, yet, at least." You'd think I was pulling teeth with how hard Sav is fighting me on this. "And because I haven't seen her since dropping off Trinity Giles at the M.E. And I want to exchange phone numbers. And you and I never go out anymore. It'll be good for you to see the world."

"And the world is at Club Profile?" He asks sardonically.

"Ronnie's hot friend Leah tends bar there. Maybe you can flirt with her."

"Why didn't you mention the hot friend sooner? I would've driven us there in half the time." Sav waggles his eyebrows.

Sav is a good person, but he's also a chronic playboy. A new lady on his arm every night of the week, and I haven't seen the same one more than twice. I used to be similar, but then the chase became monotonous and boring, so I gave up. Until I met Veronica Woods, that is. It might be a mistake to try and set him up with Leah. If he humps and dumps her like he usually does, it might make things strained between Ronnie and me.

"Listen, Sav." I side-eye him in the passenger seat of my jag. "Don't fuck with Leah. You can flirt all you want, but if you plan on taking her out at least take it seriously. I don't want you to fuck up my chances with Ronnie."

"When have I ever not taken a woman seriously?" Sav responds with mock abhorrence. "Pussy is very serious business, Lix."

"You know what I mean." I reply, my voice steely. "Actually, maybe you should stay away from Leah completely."

"Hey let's not take any drastic measures here. I'll be a good boy, I promise." Sav bats his eyelashes at me, a sickly sweet smile spread across his face.

"Don't make me regret bringing you." I seethe. I hope this isn't a giant fucking mistake.

It's Saturday night, and from the conversation I overhead between Ronnie and Leah in their apartment on Thursday it sounded like Ronnie would be at Club Profile tonight. The cameras I planted around Ronnie's apartment on Wednesday have really come in handy. I snuck into the apartment an hour before she was due home from work, planting cameras in the living room, kitchen, and her bedroom. They have sound and night vision, and it's made stalking her much easier.

The cameras are linked to my phone, available for my viewing pleasure 24/7. From them I watched Ronnie open the gift I left on her bed, a gown and heels for her to wear to her birthday party. I heard her and Leah discussing Ronnie's masked stalker, AKA me, Felix Drakos. I even overhead them talking about inviting me and Sav to Veronica's birthday at Club Profile, and Ronnie setting Leah up with Sav.

I've got to say, Ronnie and Leah's plan to find out if I'm the masked man is clever. Unfortunately for them, I'll be one step ahead. I'm not ready to give up the game between my little fox and her masked man. That's why I'm paying a stand in to help me be in two places at once. Ronnie will think she's seeing myself and the masked man at the same time, but really, she'll only be seeing Felix's double while I'm in the masked man's disguise. It'll really throw her off, and I can't fucking wait.

Just as I expected, I see Ronnie sitting at the bar, chatting with Leah. It's still early in the night, only seven o'clock, so Club Profile isn't super crowded yet. The lovesick puppy, Micah, hovers near Leah, stealing furtive glances in her direction. Leah told Ronnie all about her disastrous date with Mr. Cardboard, but clearly the dude didn't get the hint that she wasn't interested.

Leah glances in my direction, a smirk playing on her lips once she recognizes me. Her eyes dart to Sav standing next to me and her jaw drops. I can practically see her salivating from here. Micah notices Leah staring at Sav, and an angry expression crosses his face.

We both stalk up to the bar. I slide onto the stool to the left of Ronnie, and Sav slides onto the stool to the right.

"Oh, hi!" Ronnie squeaks, her eyes wide as she turns to me.

A pretty pink blush fills her cheeks. She's adorable, and I love the way she gets flustered in my presence. My hand floats to her thigh, gently gripping it as I smile at her.

"Hey, Ronnie." I wink at her and she melts in response. She's like putty in my hands. "Hi Leah. Leah, meet Sav. Sav, meet Leah." As I look at Sav I give him a warning glare, to which he just smirks in response.

"Hi Sav. Nice to meet you." Leah smile at Sav coyly. "What can I get you boys to drink?"

"Beer, the cheaper the better." Sav replies.

"My kind of guy. Unpretentious. And for you, Felix?" Leah asks.

"Gin and tonic, please." I reply.

"A little more pretentious than your friend here, huh?" Leah laughs.

"Yeah, well you know, Sav's kind of a basic white man. I'm a little more sophisticated." I quip, earning a laugh from Ronnie and Leah, but a scowl from Sav.

"I don't need to be sophisticated when I'm this hot." Sav grumbles.

Micah stands nearby, glowering at the four of us. The guy has no clue that he blew his chance with Leah, and is actually getting jealous of her interacting with Sav and I. How pathetic. An older woman at the other end of the bar calls him away, and he begrudgingly breaks his glaring gaze away from our group to take her order.

Leah hands Sav and I our drinks, and then refills Ronnie's glass of wine. Once she's done, she leans over the bar, her elbows resting on the glass top and one finger twirling her blonde ponytail, while she begins chatting away with Sav.

"Hey so—" Ronnie begins at the same time as I start saying '*Can I—*'

"Sorry, go ahead." Her cheeks flame pink once again.

"I wanted to exchange phone numbers. It's hard to set up a second date without a way to contact you." I say smoothly, pulling my phone out of my jacket pocket.

"Oh! Sure." Ronnie fumbles inside of her purse, locating her phone and handing it to me. "Go ahead and put yours in there. I'll put mine in yours too!" She says excitedly.

This is the perfect opportunity to install the app that will allow me to track her phone's GPS, as long as the download goes quickly. I rapidly click through, installing the app and logging in, then putting the app in a hidden folder. Afterwards I enter my phone number under the name 'Future Husband'. It's a joke, sort of.

"There we go!" She says, trading phones back with me. "It's perfect timing that you and Sav are here tonight. Leah is throwing me a birthday party here next Saturday, and I wanted to invite you both. It's masquerade themed, so dress up and bring a mask. Leah snagged the private room from nine until midnight." I can tell by the way Ronnie studies my expression that she's trying to see if I knew this already and am the one who sent her the gown.

I feign surprise. "Sounds like a great time. I'll be there, and I'll try and drag Sav along. Like I said, he's not super sophisticated so a masquerade ball might intimidate him." I laugh.

"Hey fucker, I heard that!" Sav reaches behind Ronnie to punch my bicep. "If Leah's there, I'll be there too." He winks at Leah.

I notice Micah hovering again, and his face turns into disgust at Sav's flirting. This guy is truly obsessed with Leah, and not in a good way. Sure, I'm obsessed with Ronnie but I at least make her life more fun. Micah is like an energy vampire, draining everyone in the room of all happiness. I hope he isn't working the night of the party, he'll be a real buzzkill.

Sav downs a couple more beers. I only finish off one gin and tonic before calling it, since I have to drive us home. Leah has kept Ronnie's wine glass full the entire hour we've been here, and I can tell she's very wine drunk by the way she giggles and squeezes my arm as she talks to me.

"Do you need a ride home, baby?" I ask her quietly. I don't want her driving her motorcycle after drinking this much.

"I loveeee it when you call me that. Babbby." She slurs.

Yep, she's fucked up.

"Come on, Ronnie." I stand up from my stool, pulling out my wallet and putting down enough bills to cover all of our drinks and a nice tip for Leah. "I'll drive you home. And then tomorrow when you're sober, I'll help you come get your bike. Sav, let's roll."

I help Ronnie off her seat, and she leans heavily against me. How much wine did Leah let her drink? It's honestly irresponsible of her. Unless this was her plan to have Ronnie ride home with me...

I wrap my arm around Veronica's waist, holding her tightly to my side so she doesn't stumble. Sav grumbles, but stands nonetheless to ride with me.

"Have a good rest of your night, Leah." I call over my shoulder.

Leah nods and mouths *'take care of her'* with a wink.

Getting Ronnie to the car in one piece is a challenge. So much so that I end up scooping her into my arms and carrying her through the parking lot to my car.

"My strong, sexy, stalker man." She says dreamily.

She is definitely too close to the truth. She's perceptive, and is easily putting the puzzle pieces together that tell her who her masked stranger really is. But once my plan plays out at her birthday party, she'll be rethinking everything.

One thing I forgot to consider is how I'm going to get both her and Sav home. My jaguar is a two-seater, and there's no way in hell I'm putting her in Sav's lap.

"I'll call an Uber. Take care of your girl, Lix." Sav pats my back gently, turning to head back into the club to wait for his ride.

"Thanks, man. Remember, be nice to Leah!" I call back, before carrying Veronica to my car and setting her against the passenger side fender. "Stay here for a second." I murmur.

I swing open the door and lay the passenger seat back for her. She sways on her feet as I lead her around the door and usher her into my car. Ronnie plops down in the seat, her head lolling to the side as I lean over and buckle her in. Underneath the smell of wine on her breath I can smell her intoxicating earth and vanilla scent. I stay there for a while, just observing her as her eyes flutter closed and she languidly lays in the seat. The thought of leaving her at home alone makes me feel guilty, especially when she's this out of it.

As I slide into the driver's seat, I consider my choices. I could take her home and then hang out at her apartment until Leah gets home, just to know that she's safe and isn't going to vomit all over herself or get hurt. Or I could bring her back to my penthouse, but she'll most likely freak out when she wakes up and wonders where she is. Although seeing her sleeping peacefully in my bed would be a bonus.

Taking my chances, I head towards my penthouse. I'll send a text from Ronnie's phone to let Leah know where she is, and then I'll take care of Ronnie tonight. Then maybe make her breakfast in the morning. Any extra time I get to spend with her, even if she's passed out, is a win for me.

***

Ronnie is still out while I carry her up to my penthouse. Even the jostling of her body in my arms doesn't make her stir. She's had far too much wine, and I'm definitely going to have a conversation with Leah about this. What if I was some psycho creep who wanted to do depraved things to Ronnie? Fine, that's not a good example because I am a psycho creep and I do want to do depraved things to my little fox, but not while she's passed out drunk. I want her to want me just as much as I want her.

I set her on my bed before rummaging through my closet for a t-shirt to slip her into. She's currently in a tight leather skirt, a tank top and her leather jacket. It feels…wrong…to undress her while she's passed out like this, but I want her to be comfortable. I fold up her clothes and place them on my dresser, before slipping my tee over her head. After tucking her into my bed, I place a cool glass of water on the nightstand along with some pain killers. She's going to need both of those come morning.

Settling into bed beside her, I flip open my laptop to do some research while Ronnie sleeps. I probably won't get much rest tonight myself because I want to keep an eye on her and make sure she doesn't get sick from drinking. I've decided that I'm going to dig more into her past and her parent's deaths. Her parents were murdered when she was nine, thirteen years ago.

I do a basic Google search for articles relating to the murders. *'Westmound, Washington. Woods murders, 2011.'* The articles that come up are about a serial killer who was leaving female victims in the forested hills surrounding the city. The killer has long since disappeared, presumed to be deceased. But I'm not interested in the Mountain Strangler right now. I narrow down my search, adding 'Veronica' in front of 'Woods', but it's no use. Newspapers aren't allowed to publish the names of minors involved in crimes. I'll need to find out who Veronica's parents were to get anywhere with this.

This time I search *Veronica Woods, Westmound Washington'*. This generates a lot of hits, including several social media profiles that belong to other women with the same name as my girl. The second page of results finally reveals my breakthrough. It's one of those 'free people search' websites that are honestly super creepy and sketchy, but I'll take what I can get.

Veronica E. Woods, Age 22, Westmound Washington.

May go by: Veronica Erin Woods
Addresses: Westmound, Washington
Relatives: Erin Woods, Dean Woods, Leah Crawford, Jake Crawford, Darcy Crawford

Bingo. The Crawfords are her adopted family, so that makes Erin and Dean Woods her biological parents. This time my Google search is more fruitful. *'Erin and Dean Woods murder, Westmound Washington, 2011'*.

The first article I click on in from the Westmound Tribune, discussing their bloody and brutal murders, but not in great detail. The article mentions that the couple had a child, not named by clearly Veronica, that was found covered in the blood of her parents. No wonder she has a fascination for death, she witnessed a violent one during her formative years. But this article doesn't give me the details I want. I need to know any information about the killer I can get. I know that there were suspects, but they all ended up being ruled out. I also know that no one was ever charged with the murders.

I was hoping that getting information would be as easy as a Google search, but clearly, I was mistaken. Frankly, I should have known better. Luckily, I have a way to crack into the Westmound Police Database, seeing as I've had to do this countless times while researching for my hobby.

It's going to be a long night, but I'd do anything for Veronica Woods.

Chapter 12
Ronnie

My eyes feel like they've been super-glued shut, and my head feels like one of those toy monkeys with the cymbals has been banging on it for hours. I let out a groan. Fuck, how much wine did I drink last night? I haven't been this hungover since my twenty-first birthday. Fucking Leah, refilling my glass all night. I love that girl, but Jesus fuck she'll be the death of me. But she can't shoulder all of the blame, I didn't have to keep drinking. Felix just makes me so nervous, I couldn't help it. Wine equals relaxed and chill Veronica.

It takes serious effort to lift my hands to my face in order to rub my eyes, it's as if someone strapped five pound paperweights to each one. My knuckles rub into my eyes, probably a little too harshly, for a minute before I can open my eyes. I'm groggy, and perhaps still a little drunk, and my surroundings don't make a lick of sense.

The massive bed I'm lying on smells like wood and citrus, and it's clad in black cotton sheets with a green duvet. The walls are painted a deep green, and a gothic chandelier hangs overhead. The room is familiar, but it's definitely not mine. I blink the sleep out of my eyes, trying to get them to focus while shifting my head to my right.

"WHAT IN THE FUCK" I shriek, seeing the form of a large body lying next to me. As my eyes trail up, I see a wide grin framed by supple lips, and sparkling green eyes staring right at me.

"Good morning, Veronica." A voice rumbles from those perfect lips, but my mind is not processing the situation clearly.

"What?" Is all I can manage to reply. My fists fly back up to my eyes, rubbing them furiously to rid them of this hallucination in front of me. "I must still be sleeping."

"Awww, do you dream of waking up next to me? That's so sweet. I can make that dream come true for you every day, baby, just say the word." The voice that sounds alarmingly similar to Felix's drawls.

"My dreams usually don't break the fourth wall, so this is a new development." I mumble.

Dream Felix's warm body crawls over me, his elbows and forearms framing my head. His thighs bracket mine, and he feels surprisingly real. Especially the hard length jutting against my core. Am I having a wet dream about Felix? There's no way this is real...

"It's real, baby." Dream Felix whispers, nuzzling his nose into my neck.

Did I say that out loud? I'm really losing it here. But the warmth of his breath along my jaw feels so nice. His scent envelops me, and his breath smells like mint, just like I remember. HIs lips trail along my jaw before moving to the corner of my mouth. This is the realest feeling dream I've ever had, and now I'm not so sure that I am dreaming.

I was at the club last night hanging with Leah when Felix and Sav joined me at the bar. We chatted for a while, and I progressively got drunker as Leah kept topping me off. I honestly don't even remember leaving Club Profile last night. Did I go home with Felix?

His lips collide with mine, pressing into me with warmth and intensity. I moan in response, letting my lips fall open enough for his tongue to slip inside. Felix's kisses have a unique taste, but I love it. Either my dream is extremely vivid and realistic, or this isn't a dream at all. I'm beginning to believe it's the latter.

I break our kiss, pulling back until there's a hairs width between us. "Wait." I breathe against his lips.

Felix pauses, his breathing heavy and his eyes darkened as he waits for me.

"I came home with you? Did we…you know?" I ask timidly.

"No, baby." Felix reassures me in his smooth voice. "You were beyond drunk last night and I offered to drive you home. But by the time we were leaving you were pretty much passed out, and I couldn't just drop you off at your apartment and leave you alone like that. So, I made the executive decision to bring you here for the night, so I could take care of you. And I would never take advantage of you. It's only fun when you want it as much as I do."

I breathe a sigh of relief. It's...sweet...that he brought me to his house to take care of me. Albeit, a little obsessive and overbearing, but no one besides Leah's family has ever cared for me like he does, and he barely knows me. But for some reason, I trust him. Which sounds insane, I know, but I'm usually able to read people pretty well and I feel good about him and where we might go. I can't believe I spent my first night with Felix and I was too drunk to remember it.

"Wait. Does Leah know where I am?" Panic suddenly grips my chest. What if Leah got home and discovered I wasn't there? She's probably freaking out.

"I texted her from your phone, she knows you're with me."

"Okay, good. So, uh...you must be really into me to go to all this trouble." I giggle awkwardly.

"I am, like *really really* into you." Felix replies in a silly voice before brushing another kiss against my lips. "And besides, how could I let you go home by yourself in that state? Anyway, do you want breakfast? I can make you something. I've also got pain killers and water for you, since I'm sure you're hungover as fuck."

"Yes, to all of the above." I nod.

***

Felix made me breakfast, waffles with eggs and bacon, before driving me back to the club for my bike and kissing me goodbye. He was a perfect gentleman, and even though I would've done more than just kiss him, he didn't push for anything. Which in hindsight was probably good because I was hungover as fuck. I spent the rest of the weekend on the couch, bingeing cheesy horror movies and nursing the pounding headache from drinking at the club.

The rest of the week went by quickly, although work was boring as hell, which I guess isn't a bad thing since that means there were no gruesome murders to take care of. When not taking care of a cadaver, I spend my time at the office reviewing files and making notes about them. One thing I've taken to doing is to look back at old files and see if I can figure out what the cause of death was. Doing so will help me with future cases.

I reviewed the cases for Trinity Giles and Royce Mills, and while both committed horrendous crimes and ended up dying brutally, nothing else connects the two cases. The modes of torture and death were vastly different. It could be that someone close to their victims decided to take justice into their own hands, but what's odd is that there was no evidence or DNA left behind by the killers. I doubt a random family member or friend of Chloe King and Hannah Giles would be capable of leaving the crime scene without a speck of evidence against them.

After digging through the files for the past year, I found a couple other cases that seemed to be related to vigilante justice, but like The Giles and Mills files, neither had evidence pointing to a perpetrator, and all four cases had different causes of death. Usually, serial killers will stick to the same modus operandi, eventually escalating to more violent crimes, before becoming sloppy and getting caught. But if this is one person pursuing vigilante justice, they're changing the style every time. In some cases, like Mills, the cause of death was similar to the way their victims died. In others, there was seemingly no relation between our cadaver's cause of death and their victims before them.

I plan on going back even further, trying to find other vigilante killings and see if there are any links. Maybe I'm just bored and looking for something to do, but I have a gut feeling that they're all connected in some way.

It's Saturday now, and my birthday party is tonight. This morning Felix had flowers delivered to my door, dark purple, pink and red snapdragons. Every time I look at them, I think back to the gift that was left on my bed with a purple snapdragon tied to it. I've never told Felix or my masked man that they're my favorite, and I don't think I've posted about it online either. Just like my gut feeling about the vigilante killings being connected, my instincts are telling me that Felix and my masked man are one in the same.

Tonight's the night to put it to the test. I know Felix will be there, and the masked man sent me my gown and asked me to wear it for him at my birthday party. While my instincts say they are the same guy, I'm still worried that they aren't. I don't know what I'll do if they're two separate people. In my heart, I know I would choose Felix over some masked stranger who has ambushed me a couple of times. But would the masked stranger be okay with that? I've never felt like he would hurt me, but would he if I asked him to leave me alone?

I need Felix and my masked man to be the same person. That's all there is to it.

My phone pings with a text from a contact named 'Future Husband'. 'Happy Birthday, Ronnie. Can't wait to see you tonight.' That's gotta be Felix. I want to say that I can't believe that he set his name as Future Husband, but it's so like him to do that.

Leah and I get ready together in our apartment. She curls my hair, the black and green tresses spiraling down my back. My eyeshadow is smokey black and deep green, and my lips are my signature black. Leah laughs when she sees my lips, teasing me about the shade.

"Oh, fuck off pretty pink princess." I roll my eyes and hold up both middle fingers while she cackles.

We're such polar opposites in our styles and personalities, and we're constantly teasing each other about it. Leah wears a bubblegum pink tulle mini dress, reminiscent of something from the '80s with a modern flair, and soft pink lipstick. Her blonde tresses are pulled up in a long, sleek pony.

Standing together, we look in the mirror and it's honestly hilarious how vastly different we look. People are shocked when they hear we're best friends, but I think our differences make us who we are together. We have different perspectives and are the yin to the other's yang.

"Whoever your mystery man is, he did a fucking fantastic job picking that dress. You look like you're going to a gala." Leah looks me up and down.

"It almost feels like too much, doesn't it?" Don't get me wrong, the gown is stunning, but I've never worn anything so lavish in my life. "It feels almost…wasteful." I frown.

"Nope. Don't go there. You look gorgeous, and it's your birthday." She waves me off.

"It's okay, maybe I'll just wear it every year on my birthday, and for my wedding, and every other big event after that. That way it'll get its use." I joke. Well, it's kind of a joke. I'm partially serious about it too.

It's quarter to nine by the time we step into our heels, grab our masks and purses, and get into our Uber. My heart pounds furiously. I'm nervous for tonight, seeing Felix and my masked man, and proving once and for all that they're the same person. At least, I hope that's what I prove.

Our ride drops us off in front of Club Profile, and Eric, tonight's bouncer, smiles wide and greets us.

"Happy Birthday, Ronnie!" He says, giving me a side hug before opening the door for us.

"Thanks, Eric!" I say, stepping into the pulsing building.

Eric is one of the bouncers that has worked at the club for years, but he only works Friday and Saturday nights now. I went on one date with him a year or so ago, but it didn't work out between us. The feeling was mutual, so there are no hard feelings and it's not awkward. And since we're friends, I know he'll have my back if anything weird ever goes down inside the club.

The private room is set up for us, with big black and green balloons filled with confetti and a big banner that says 'Happy Birthday Bitch!'. I giggle when I read the banner, knowing that it was Leah's doing.

"Thank you, Leah" I beam. I remember having birthday parties with my birth parents, but when I was in foster care my birthday was never celebrated. Once I moved in with the Crawfords they made a point to celebrate with me every year, and Leah has carried on the tradition. Those years in foster care were brutal, but Leah and her family brought me in at thirteen and treated me like family. Leah is truly my sister in everything but blood.

Leah pulls me in and hugs me tightly, squealing in my ear in excitement. "I love you, Ronnie. You're my best friend and my sister." Her voice cracks and her eyes become watery as she pulls back from me.

"I love you too." I kiss her cheek. "Now let's fucking party!"

I don't do well with other people's emotions. They make me uncomfortable, and my reaction is to automatically make a joke. The tender moment Leah shared with me was quickly ended by my statement, but after all these years she knows me. She knows how awkward I get when people become all teary-eyed around me, and doesn't take offense.

"Moscow mule?" She asks.

"You know it, bitch." I nod.

Leah walks out of the private room, presumably to the bar to get us some drinks. We're the first ones here, which was to be expected since it's only nine, so I find a seat and hang out on my phone while I wait for Leah to come back.

As I'm looking down at my phone, I see someone in my periphery walking towards me. I glance up, and a grin crosses my face as I see Felix walking towards me. He has a standard green masquerade mask on, just covering his eyes, but I know it's him by the hair, his stature, and those sinful lips.

Shoving my phone back into my purse, I stand to greet him.

"Look at you, birthday girl." Felix purrs, looking me up and down. "You look divine."

"You're not too bad yourself." I giggle. "Thank you for coming. Weren't you going to bring Sav too?"

"He's here. He saw Leah at the bar and wanted to help her with drinks." He replies, gesturing towards the door to the private room.

I'm about to reply when a group of five people walk into the private room. I don't have many friends, if I'm being honest, but Leah is always chatting with people who come into Club Profile, and she invited some of her regulars to the party.

"I should probably go say hi." I explain, excusing myself from talking with Felix.

As I walk over to the group, Felix grabs my hand and intertwines our fingers. I glance down at our connected hands, and then back at him to see him smirking at me. Well, he's certainly trying to make a statement to anyone who sees me tonight.

My introvert instincts tell me to hide away in a corner and let Leah do all the talking when she comes back, but I don't want to be rude. Felix and I meander towards the group, two girls and three guys. I recognize a couple of them from being at the club at the same time in the past, but I don't think I've ever had a conversation with them. Luckily Leah and Sav walk back into the room, bee-lining for us and saving me from this awkward encounter.

"Hey guys! Thanks for coming to my bestie's birthday! Everyone, this is Ronnie, the birthday girl!" Leah is bubbly as she introduces me. "And this is her...date...Felix." She gestures towards Felix, uncertain on whether or not to call him my date.

"Oh, we're not..." I try to correct her but Felix wraps an arm around my waist, pulling me close and interrupting me.

"Nice to meet you all." His eyes sparkle mischievously. "Well, if you'll excuse us, I want to spend some time with my girlfriend on her birthday." Felix winks.

Leah and I lock eyes, both of our mouths opening and closing silently. In my periphery I see Sav shaking, trying to contain his laughter. Felix moves his hand to the small of my back and leads me over to a sofa in the corner of the private room.

"You're welcome. I could tell you hated that." He says slyly.

"Th-thanks?" I stutter. I'm not sure what that was, but I definitely need a big swig of this Moscow mule before discussing it. The copper mug is cool in my hands as my fingers grip it tightly. My fingers shake slightly, making the drink slosh in the mug. After taking a hefty sip through the tiny straw, I set it down on the table in front of the sofa.

"Umm…so…" I clear my throat, not able to look at Felix. "Girlfriend? We've been on one date…" I grimace, realizing I sounded harsher than I meant to. "Don't get me wrong, that one date was fantastic…"

"I didn't even need one date with you to know that you're mine." He leans in, whispering.

His warm breath tickles my ear, sending a shiver down my spine.

My eyes are wide as I turn to him, but before I can say anything else he presses his lips to mine in a soft and sweet kiss. He tastes like mint and gin as he kisses me, and I melt into him. It's not that I don't want to be his girlfriend, but this feels like it's way too quick. And I need to find out who the masked man is first before this goes any further.

We break apart, my eyes closed still as his lips leave mine. I feel like I should come clean about the masked man. Maybe he'll admit that it's him and uncomplicate things. Or maybe he'll be pissed. But it's not like we've talked about being in a relationship before he dropped this 'you're mine' shit on me tonight.

My hands wring in my lap. I'm just going to fucking ask. I'm going to get this over with and hopefully untie this knot that's sitting in my chest.

"Felix." I turn my body towards him, and it feels like my heart is going to explode. "I need to know—"

Shouting from the entrance of the private room snaps my attention away from Felix. It looks like Sav and Leah are arguing with someone in the doorway, but I can't see from here. Leah sounds really upset and frustrated, which is unusual for her. I jump to my feet, moving around the crowd of people that came in at some point while I was talking with Felix.

I make my way through the crowd, just in time to see that it's Micah standing with Sav and Leah. He's poking Sav in the chest with his forefinger, fury lining his face. I've never seen Micah like this. Leah is gripping Sav's forearm, pleading with him to walk away. I'm about to step up to the group when Felix pulls me behind him and steps in.

"Sav, what the fuck is going on?" Felix tries to grab Sav's shoulder, but Sav shrugs him off.

"This fucker barged in on Leah and me while we were dancing." Sav spits. His silly golden retriever vibes nowhere to be seen. "He called her a whore. So, I'm going to fucking beat his pussy ass."

"What the fuck!" I step around Felix, getting right into Micah's face. While I would probably brush it off if someone said that about me, I have zero problems standing up for the people I love. "Micah, what the fuck is your problem." I shove my hands against his shoulder, making him stumble to the side.

"She fucking thinks that she can flirt and fuck anyone she wants? Not when she's seeing me." Micah snarls, regaining his balance.

"I'm not fucking seeing you, Micah." Leah shrieks. "We went on one date, and truthfully, it was fucking boring. We are not a *thing*, and we will never be a *thing*." Leah says the word 'thing' like leaves a bad taste in her mouth.

"We'll fucking see about that, Leah Crawford." Micah replies darkly. He gives one last burning look at Sav before turning and striding out of the room.

"Well, that was fucking weird." Felix mutters, and I huff a laugh in response.

I step up to Leah and wrap my arms around her in a tight hug. "You okay, babe?" I whisper against her ear.

She nods shakily, takes a deep breath and then steps out of our embrace. "I'm fine. Who knew Micah would be a clinger like that?" She laughs weakly. "I wouldn't have gone on a date with him if I knew he'd act like he owned me afterwards." Leah wipes angry tears from her eyes.

"Do you want to go sit, Leah?" Sav asks sweetly. Golden retriever persona reactivated. Leah nods and lets Sav lead her away.

"I don't like that guy." Felix says.

"Well, I hate to break it to you but you're kind of similar in your obsessions with girls you've only gone on one date with…" I joke.

Felix's face darkens. "Don't compare me to that prick. Leah clearly doesn't want his attention, and he isn't getting the hint. You on the other hand, I can tell you enjoy my attention. I wouldn't push otherwise."

"Calm down, it was a joke." Sort of, I think to myself. "Besides, you're right. I do enjoy your attention. I just…it feels too soon to be calling me your girlfriend." I bite my lip. Here goes nothing.

"And I have something to talk to you about before we go any further."

Chapter 13
Felix

Ronnie bites her lip, gnawing on it nervously. "And I have something to talk to you about before we go any further." She states.

Ah fuck, I know exactly where this is going. I'm going to have to lie right to Ronnie's face when she asks if I'm the masked man. That's going to suck balls, but I am not ready to give up our game yet. I didn't think she'd be able to put two and two together as well as she has, she's too smart for her own good. It brings me far too much pleasure, and I know that she's into it, even if she feels embarrassed by the taboo of it all.

I feel like shit about what I'm about to do, but I have to deal with Micah before he gets too far away. "Sorry, Ronnie, but can we pick up this conversation later? I need to deal with something quick." I feel like an absolute asshole cutting her off like this. But I'm not going to let that dickhead Micah get away with bullying my girl's best friend.

Ronnie looks taken aback and hurt, and I fucking hate it. "Oh...okay. Sure?" She replies.

"Sorry, I just...this is important. I'll be back soon." I lean down to kiss her cheek before pulling away.

As I pull away, I swear I hear her mumble "More important than my birthday?" and it's like she stabbed a knife into my heart. Fuck. I'm going to have to make it up to her somehow. But I can't tell her about my hobby or how my alter ego is going to beat the shit out of Micah and threaten him. We're not at that level of trust quite yet.

I exit the private room, trying to push past the ache in my chest from hurting Ronnie on her birthday. Micah isn't at the bar, but it's only been a couple of minutes since he stormed out. He wasn't wearing a work uniform, so he must've decided to come crash Ronnie's party on his night off.

I push through the crowded club, keeping an eye out for him, but he must've already left. Which is fine with me, better to catch him outside than trying to get him alone in the club. My ensemble tonight is a basic black suit, white undershirt and a black tie. I want it to be inconspicuous enough to where I don't have to change my outfit when I slip into my goat mask and approach Ronnie as her masked stalker.

It'll work for this too, there's no way Micah was paying enough attention to me to note what outfit I was wearing in the private room. I step into the night air, slipping my masquerade mask off and my goat mask on, effectively changing from Felix to the masked man. I really need to come up with a name for my alter ego. 'The Masked Man' is so dull. Goat man? Isn't that a demon that haunts some bridge? No….shit, now is not the time to be brainstorming vigilante names.

I'm pulling on my leather gloves, and it's then that I see Micah pacing in front of a beat up Ford Focus. His car is a piece of shit, just like him. I barely know Leah, but I already know that she deserves better than this loser. Micah's hands are gripping his golden brown hair and he's muttering under his breath.

I can't believe Ronnie compared me to this guy, even if she was joking. Micah's a fucking nutcase. Not that I'm one hundred percent sane, but this dude is on a whole other level of insanity.

I wait until Micah's back is turned before sneaking up to him and gripping the nape of his neck. The guy is tiny compared to me, and I easily throw him against the hood of his shitty Ford face first. His nose cracks against the metal, splattering blood as it breaks.

"Fuccckk!" Micah moans as I hold him down against the hood.

"Listen, motherfucker." I bend down until I'm right in his ear. "You're going to leave Leah Crawford alone."

"Or what?" He spits, trying to turn his head to the side to look at me.

With my hand still gripping the back of his neck, I slam him back down into the hood again. His nose crunches, the bones definitely obliterated by now.

"Or I'll fucking kill you." I snarl. "I don't give warnings, so you're fucking lucky that you're getting one. You should thank me for only beating your ass." I slam his face again, causing a pathetic wail to come from Micah's throat.

"In fact, I want you to say it. Say *'Thank you, sir, for beating my ass'*." My grip tightens.

"Fuck. You." Micah spits.

"Oh, still playing tough? I like that, it's more fun when I finally break you." I laugh. This bitch really thinks he's tough shit, doesn't he? Unfortunately for him, I fucking love proving pieces of shit like him wrong.

I pull a pair of handcuffs from my jacket pocket. Originally, I brought them to have a little kinky fun with Ronnie as my masked alter ego, but now they're going to serve a different purpose. Still holding Micah down by his neck, I click his left wrist into one of the cuffs, tightening it until the metal digs into his skin.

"Fuck man, that's too fucking tight." Micah whines.

"Too fucking bad, I don't care." I reply, clicking his right wrist into the remaining cuff, cinching it until it's a couple notches tighter than the left cuff. His hand begins to turn red immediately from the pressure of the metal digging into his wrist.

Once he's cuffed, I turn him around and push his back against the hood. His handcuffed wrists rest between his body and the metal, and I push down on his chest hard, pressing the cuffs deeper into his skin. Micah's pretty boy face is busted and covered in blood, tears, and spit. I'd almost be impressed that he hasn't given up yet, especially due to the state of his face, if he wasn't a pile of human garbage.

"Well, your nose is definitely fucked. Going to need some cosmetic surgery on that thing. Yikes." I shrug. With one hand still holding him against the hood, I swing my fist and connect with Micah's jaw, his head snapping to the side and blood flying out of his mouth. Was that a fucking tooth that just flew out too?

I don't give him a second to recover before I'm punching him again, this time with the opposite fist. After the second strike to his jaw, his head falls back limply against the car, gurgles and moans coming from him.

"Say it. Say thank you." I hit him again, this time with an uppercut that knocks his head forcefully back into the metal. His skull thunks loudly against the metal. It's at this point that I remember we're entirely in the open, and anyone could pass by and see us. I need to wrap this up.

Micah moans in response, his jaw hanging slack and most likely broken. He can't respond at this point.

"You're welcome. Next time you bother Leah, I'll fucking kill you." I shove him one more time before stepping away. As he slumps to the ground, I unlock the cuffs, slipping them back into my jacket pocket.

Micah would be an idiot to try anything with Leah again.

Now that I've taken care of that problem, it's time to pay a visit to my girl as her masked man. Would it be wrong for me to comfort her about 'Felix's' abrupt departure? That would definitely be playing with her feelings, and probably a step too far. I quickly push the idea out of my head.

Sure, I'm gaslighting her already about who the masked man is, but I'm not doing it to be mean. But what happens when the truth is eventually revealed? She's going to be hurt, and she might never trust me again. Shit. As much as I enjoy our time together as my alter ego, it's not worth losing her over. Maybe it's time for him to disappear from her life. Or maybe not. I don't fucking know at this point. For tonight, I think I'll leave the masked man behind.

I step into the alleyway on the other side of the building and switch my masks. After I pull off my gloves, I quickly realize that they're battered from my encounter with Micah. Fuck it, I'll have to keep the gloves on. Either way it's suspicious as hell, but maybe I can play it off and say that my hands are cold…shit, no…that's lame. Maybe I tripped and fell? Who the fuck trips, falls and lands in their fists? You know what, I'll just tell Ronnie that they got messed up at work and that's why I'm wearing the gloves.

The club is still crowded, bodies undulating to the pounding EDM coming from the speakers.

Stopping by the bar, I pick up another Moscow mule for Ronnie, and leave my credit card to cover her drinks for the entire night. It's the least I can do to make up for ditching her to deal with Micah. And of course, it's not all I plan on doing to make it up to her.

When I enter the private room, I see her dancing. Leah is sandwiched between Sav and Ronnie, with Sav at her back and Ronnie at her front. Sav's hands rest on Leah's waist as they grind to the music. Ronnie faces Leah, her arms wrapped around Leah's neck and one of Ronnie's thighs threaded between Leah's as they gyrate. I've got to admit, it's fucking hot, watching Ronnie move against Leah like that. They're so comfortable together that they have no qualms about touching and being as physically close as they are right now. I could never be like that with my friends, it must be a girl thing.

Sav and Leah look good together too. They'd make a cute couple, and Sav is a thousand times better than Micah. But if Sav fucks it up with Leah, I'll murder him. No one is going to get in the way of my relationship with Ronnie, especially not our best friends.

I approach the group, snagging Leah's attention first. Her eyes flick to me and then back to Ronnie, before she leans in and whispers in Ronnie's ear. Ronnie scowls, darting her eyes over to me.

"Can I steal Veronica away from you two?" I ask Leah.

"Don't ask me, ask Ronnie." Leah snaps, obviously on team Ronnie at this point.

My hand finds the small of Ronnie back. "Can I talk to you?" I ask, trying to put on my best sad puppy dog face.

"Fine." Ronnie retorts.

Sav flashes me a sympathetic look as I pull Ronnie away from him and Leah. Leah just continues glaring at me.

I lead Ronnie to a secluded corner of the private room, sitting with her on one of the red leather chaise lounges.

"Ronnie, Listen. I'm—"

"No, Felix. You listen to me." Ronnie turns to me, irritation lining her beautiful face. "You come in here on my birthday and call me your girlfriend in front of everyone. And then after Micah came in and caused a scene, you up and vanish? Where have you been for the past half an hour? What was so fucking important that you had to ditch me on my birthday?" She's shaking now, her voice raising an octave as she speaks. "You know what, I don't even know why I care. We've been on one fucking date." Ronnie sighs.

Fuck. I have to give her a sliver of the truth. I can't let her be angry with me like this, especially when all I was doing was protecting her best friend.

"I went to have a conversation with Micah…that's why I vanished." I rub my hand over my jaw. "It pissed me off how he came in here and treated Leah, and I felt compelled to let him know that it was unacceptable. Afterwards I took a breather to calm down."

"You went to talk to Micah? About Leah? Why?" At first Ronnie seems surprised, but then suspicion takes over her delicate features and she narrows her eyes behind her mask.

"Like I said, it was unacceptable. No one deserves to be treated that way, especially not your best friend. I told Micah to leave Leah alone, or else we'd have problems. That's it." And that's where the sliver of truth ends. I didn't only speak with Micah, I beat his face in. But Ronnie doesn't need to know that part.

Veronica's eyes soften as she looks at me. "Okay...That was kind of you, thank you." She exhales. "I'm sorry I went off on you. I'm not sure why it hurt me so much when you vanished. It shouldn't matter to me, I hardly know you."

"That's because you know that there's something special between us. What we have is different. It's...more." I watch as Ronnie's lips part slightly. I want to kiss her so fucking badly right now.

"You've gotta stop saying things like that." Ronnie's face flushes as she looks down at her hands.

"Why? Can't handle the truth?" I joke.

She laughs in response. "Maybe not."

"There's an ambulance outside and the cops are here, they're starting to close down the club and questioning people." Leah says breathlessly, having run over to us in her ridiculous high heels.

"What?!" Ronnie gasps.

It was bound to happen. You can't leave someone bloodied and beaten in a parking lot and expect no one to see. That's why I wear the goat mask, and hid from the cameras as well as I could. Well, except when I purposely flashed my mask at one of the cameras. I'm not one hundred percent sure why I did it. I never leave any traces to connect me to crimes, but I felt the need to connect myself to this one. Maybe it was for Ronnie. Maybe I wanted her to find out and connect her masked man to Micah's attack. Maybe I wanted her to know that he was watching out for her and her friends.

That's also why I wear leather gloves, no chance to leave DNA behind. Everything I do is for a reason. Although it is unlike me to leave witnesses, AKA Micah. Truthfully, I should have killed the fucker. I hope letting him live doesn't come back to bite me in the ass. Technically, he didn't do anything that really warranted being murdered, at least that's what I'm telling myself. Otherwise, I really don't know why I let him live.

The lights to the club flick on, and the sudden brightness is jarring. The music stops, leaving only the sounds of startled shouts and gasps from the crowd.

"Please remain calm. Club Profile is closing for the night. However, police are here to question all of you in regards to an incident that happened in the parking lot. Please remain inside until a uniformed officer excuses you. Thank you." A voice booms from the loudspeaker.

"What's happening?" Ronnie asks Sav and Leah.

"It sounds like they found someone outside who was severely beaten. There's an ambulance here to pick them up." Leah says.

"Do we know who?" Ronnie questions.

"Not yet." Sav answers.

Chapter 14
Ronnie

It's suspicious as fuck that Felix disappeared for half an hour, claiming that he was talking with Micah, and now there's someone who has been beaten to a pulp in the parking lot? Right after Felix returned from being outside? And not to mention the fucking leather gloves he's wearing now. He didn't have gloves on before. I'm starting to spiral. My mind is at war over Felix. I need to calm down, at least until more information is revealed. I don't even know for sure that the person found outside is Micah.

Several officers spread out through the club to question people. One comes to the private room, and as she makes her way through the crowd those that have been excused filter out the back door. After what feels like an eternity she makes her way over to our group.

"Good evening, folks. I'm Officer Halligan. I have some questions for each of you." The officer greets us.

"What's going on?" Sav asks.

"Who was in the ambulance?" Leah demands.

The officer narrows her eyes on our group. "I'll be asking the questions here." She points at Sav. "Since you're so eager, let's start with you. Follow me."

Sav and the officer walk away from us. She questions him for a few minutes before dismissing him. Officer Halligan takes Leah next, and then it's my turn.

Before I depart, I turn to Felix. "We'll wait outside for you?"

"See you there, baby." Felix winks. He's too nonchalant, especially when we're all being questioned by police.

"This way, miss." Officer Halligan directs me to an empty corner of the room. "Please state your name."

"Veronica Woods."

"Why are you here tonight, Veronica?" The officer questions.

"It's my birthday. My friend Leah rented this private room for us to celebrate." I reply, trying to remain calm. It's hard to stay collected when talking with the police, they always put me on edge.

"What time did you arrive? And have you left the building at all tonight?"

"Leah and I arrived together around nine. And no, neither of us left the club tonight." I answer.

"Do you know Micah Green?" She asks.

My eyes widen. "It was Micah in the ambulance?" I whisper. If it was Micah who was found outside, does that mean Felix did more than just talk with him? An image of the black leather gloves Felix is wearing flashes in my mind.

"Yes. Do you know him?" Officer Halligan presses.

"Sorry. Yes. He's a bartender here, like my friend Leah."

"Was Mr. Green working tonight?" The Officer asks.

"No. He wasn't working. He wasn't invited to my party either, but he showed up anyway." I'm sure she already knows the answer to this question, seeing as she spoke with Leah prior to me.

"And why would he do that?"

"He went on a date with Leah a week or so ago, and isn't happy that she doesn't want to pursue a relationship with him. He threatened her, and called her a whore. We told him to leave, and he did." I explain.

"He was angry as he left then? Did you see anyone leave with him?"

I don't have proof that Felix hurt Micah, and even if I did would I really want to tell the officer that? Micah deserved what happened to him after the way he treated Leah. And if it was Felix, I should be thankful that he cared enough to step in. Is that morally correct? Definitely not. But everything in this world is gray, and justice sometimes needs to be that way too.

"No, I did not." I lie.

"One last thing." Officer Halligan holds up a grainy black and white photo that looks like it was pulled from a security camera. "Do you recognize this person?"

She hands me the photo for inspection. I pull it closer, and realize it's a still from the security camera right outside the club. In it a man wearing a black suit, white button-up, black tie, and a black goat mask walks by. The timestamp says 10:34 p.m.. I try to school my face into an indifferent mask, but shock courses through me. I'd recognize that goat mask anywhere. It's my masked man.

"No. I don't recognize him and I didn't see anyone at my party with a mask like that." The first part is a lie, but the second isn't. I never saw my masked stalker here.

"This was taken around the time we believe Mr. Green was attacked. You're sure you didn't see this man?" The officer prods.

"No, ma'am. I'm sorry." Guilt claws at my insides. I hate being deceptive, and I'm doing it to a police officer. I'm covering for my masked man, who also might be Felix. I need to talk to him about this as soon as we're out of here.

"Okay. Thank you for your time. You're free to leave." Officer Halligan nods and points me to the back door.

As I open the door, I spare a glance over my shoulder at Felix. The officer is speaking with him now, and my heart seizes in my chest. If he did this, is he going to own up to it or lie to the officer's face just like I did?

Leah and Sav stand close together outside, Sav's arm wrapped around Leah's waist. They've been hitting it off tonight, and that makes me happy. So far Sav has been a perfect gentleman, and Leah deserves that. Besides the incident with Micah and the police, Leah has had a glittering smile on her face all night. She's usually a happy person, but this is beyond her normal level.

"Everything okay?" Sav asks once he notices me walking towards them.

"Yeah..." I'm not sure how to answer that. Is everything okay? Not really. My "boyfriend" might be my masked stalker, and he might be responsible for Micah going to the hospital. And I just lied to the police about all of it. But I think the thing that gets me the most is that while I feel a little guilty about lying, I don't feel as bad as I should. Why am I going out of my way to protect Felix

Drakos? What is it about him that pulls me in like a magnet?

The club's back door swings open, and Felix walks through unscathed and unconcerned. He struts over to us, smirking at me for a moment before schooling his face back into a blank expression.

"All good?" Sav asks.

"Yep. No problems here." Felix shrugs before wrapping an arm around my waist. "Would you three like to come back to my place? I feel bad that the party was cut short."

Leah looks at me in question, silently asking what I want to do. This might be the perfect opportunity to get to the bottom of the Micah and masked man situation. And maybe if I can spend the night at his penthouse, I can do some snooping, just in case he doesn't want to offer up any information.

"Let's do it. The night is still young." I plaster an easy-going smile to my face, but inside I feel torn.

"Unlike you." Leah snorts.

"You bitch! I'm only twenty-three!" I scoff, lightly punching her bicep.

Leah pouts her lip, acting like I hurt her, before bursting out into giggles.

***

Leah hops into Sav's car while I slide into Felix's. Being alone with him again makes me nervous, especially knowing that he might be the man who put Micah in the hospital. I've never seen the angry side to him, and I've never worried that he would hurt me, but now I'm not so sure.

I'm starting to second guess asking him about it while we're alone. If I ask him in the car, there's no escape if he becomes enraged. At least if we're at his penthouse, I could flee through the door. But there's no way in hell that I'm jumping out of a moving car. I take deep, calming breaths, trying to control my heart rate.

The first five minutes of the ride pass in silence. I gaze out the window, lost in thought. Everything in me screams that I should be scared of

Felix and scared of the masked man. But I'm not scared I'm just…nervous? I guess I'm more nervous of finding out the answers, whether I like them or not.

"What are you thinking about?" Felix asks, placing his hand on my thigh.

I unintentionally flinch at the contact, letting out a gasp.

"Are you okay?" He whispers, and I see his gaze fixed on me out of the corner of my eye.

"You should be looking at the road." I comment, which earns me a grunt in response. "I'm fine. I just…" Well, here goes nothing. I have to believe Felix won't hurt me. "Did you hurt Micah?"

"Why would you think that?" His voice is calm.

"Well, you went and had a 'talk' with him, and then not thirty minutes later he was being taken away in an ambulance after being beaten. It's not hard to come to the conclusion that you had something to do with it." There's no stopping now, might as well lay all my cards on the table. "You weren't wearing those gloves until after you came back from seeing him. And not to mention the picture Officer Halligan showed me of a man with your build, wearing the same clothes as you, in a goat mask right after the time they believe Micah was attacked."

Felix snorts, as if what I'm saying is absurd. "What does a goat mask have to do with any of this?" He acts as if the Officer didn't show him the still from the camera, when I know that she was showing everyone she spoke with.

"Don't treat me like I'm incompetent." Is he really trying to gaslight me right now? That's a sure-fire way to piss me the fuck off. "You saw the same picture I did. The officer was showing everyone she interviewed."

"Oh right. It's coincidence, that's all." He replies, his tone still level and not betraying a hint of any emotion.

"So, you're telling me that you talked to him, and after you left he happened to be attacked by someone else?" I'm in disbelief. Sure, is it possible that it was someone else that attacked Micah? Well, yes. Is it likely? Hell no. "And are you also telling me that you don't own a goat mask?"

"What are you talking about, Ronnie? Are you accusing me of something?" His voice has a hint of anger now, but I can't tell if it's real.

"Have you or have you not been stalking me while wearing a goat mask?" I ask point blank, looking straight at him and studying his reaction.

"What?!" He responds incredulously, his expression shocked.

"You didn't follow me around Haunted Hollow a few weeks ago? And you didn't break into my house, cut the power, and wait for me to get home?" My voice wavers. He's either a really good actor or...he knows nothing about my masked man.

Felix's eyes flash to me, concern lining his features. "Someone has been following you? And they broke into your house? Have you told anyone this?"

I gnaw on my lip, contemplating where to go from here. "Yes but...I thought it was you...and I've only told Leah, well, and you."

"Why would I stalk you when I can be with you anytime I want? Has this man hurt you?"

Oh, fuck. And now it's really complicated. I'll admit that I desperately hoped that Felix was the masked man, that we were playing a game together. I was so sure it was him. But the two men don't have the same scent. And the masked man's voice is deeper, darker. And now Felix is denying it. So, who is the masked man then? I've trusted him not to hurt me because I thought he was Felix. But if it's really some strange man, maybe he will hurt me. Maybe this is a game to him, just not one I want to play.

"No…he hasn't…ummm. I'm sorry. I'm very confused right now." I mutter, tears springing to my eyes.

Felix's hand grips my thigh tightly. "I don't like that some guy has been following you and has broken into your house. Do you have a security system?"

"No…"

"I'll buy you one. I'll have it installed first thing Monday. In the meantime, I think it's safer if you and Leah stay at my place." Felix's left fingers tap on the steering wheel while his right hand still tightly grips my thigh.

"Okay." I whisper.

I've fucked up.

Chapter 15
Felix

Well, I feel like a piece of shit. What was I thinking when I started stalking Veronica? How did I possibly think it would work out in any other way than breaking her trust and her heart? And the fucking fool that I am, I insisted on keeping up the ruse rather than just admitting my mistake. Because you know, the longer it goes on the easier it will be when the truth is revealed, right? Fucking not.

I think the worst part of it is how scared she is now. I can see her lip wobbling, tears forming in her eyes as she sits in the passenger seat next to me. But what can I do about it now? I can't just say 'Psych! I am your masked stalker.' and hope it all smooths over. My best course of action now is to leave my alter ego out of Ronnie's life. I'll pay to have the security system installed for her and Leah, and the masked man will slip out of her life forever. Then it will just be me and her.

We pull into the parking garage underneath my building. She unbuckles her seatbelt and goes to open the door when I stop her.

"Hey. I'm sorry about your stalker. If he shows up again, will you call me? I want to help you, and I don't want you getting hurt." Yikes. He will not be showing up again. Because I am him. But I want her to feel secure and safe again, even though I'm the one who took that away from her. Fuck, I'm an idiot and a major asshole.

Ronnie sniffles. "Okay, thank you." She inhales deeply, fidgeting with her fingers and staring down at her lap. "I'm sorry I accused you of all that. I guess I was hoping it was you…and I know that's fucked up and weird but as you're probably figuring out I am fucked up and weird so…"

"And you're probably figuring out that I like fucked up and weird. And it makes sense that you'd want for it to be me. Your brain wanted to make sense of the situation, and it's easier to think it's someone you know than a stranger." I reach over, taking her chin between my forefinger and thumb and turning her face to look at me. "It's okay. We'll get it sorted out. But no more tears, not on your birthday."

Ronnie nods, blinking the tears from her eyes and wiping her cheeks. "If Leah and I are staying here until Monday, we'll need to pack a couple of bags."

"Already one step ahead of you. Leah and Sav are swinging by your apartment first. She'll bring a bag for you."

"And you're sure that it's okay for us to stay? Leah and I can go back to our apartment, we don't want to put you out." She's looking down at her lap again.

"I'm positive. Now, let's go birthday girl. Let's finish the night off strong."

It's not long after we get inside my penthouse that Sav and Leah arrive. We all slip into more comfortable clothes before sitting on the couch in the theater room. Leah snuggles up to Sav, and Ronnie snuggles into my side. She decided she wanted to watch movies the rest of the night. And of course she picked some '80s horror classics.

Horror movies seem to be soothing for her, which might seem odd for others, but I understand it. When you're watching or reading horror, you know it's not happening to you. You get sucked into the story, wondering what's going to happen next. When will the killer show up again? Who's the next victim? For me, there's also something nostalgic about films like The Evil Dead and Carrie. I've seen them so many times that they've become a comfort, and Ronnie seems to feel the same.

Clearly, Leah does not agree. Her hands shield her face, her fingers spreading now and again so she can peak at the TV screen. Sav squeezes her tight, and every time she jumps from a scare he laughs but assures her it's okay.

Ronnie happily munches on popcorn, enthralled by the movie. Partway through she shifted so her back is against the armrest and her feet sprawl across my lap. I try to keep my eyes on Children of the Corn, but my attention keeps being drawn to Ronnie's face as she watches the movie. This is better than being at a party, or going out to a fancy restaurant, or even stalking her at Haunted Hollow. This is casual, and endearing, and something we both enjoy. I want to spend every Saturday night curled up like this with her.

It's nearing two in the morning when the movie wraps up and Leah stands up, stretching.

"Well, this has been riveting, but I think it's time to tuck in for the night." Leah walks over, giving Ronnie a hug and a peck on the cheek. "I love you, birthday girl." She saunters away, and I truly mean saunters, gazing back at Sav before heading down the hallway into the guest room.

"And that's my cue." Sav says, jumping up and practically running to catch up to Leah. The door shuts behind him, and the distinct sound of the lock clicks into place.

"They're totally going to fuck." Ronnie giggles.

"Oh, one hundred percent. I'll have to burn those sheets. Shame, because they're new."

"I'm happy for Leah. She deserves someone nice, and I think Sav might be good for her." Ronnie says, her face lit up with a brilliant smile.

"I hope so, I'd hate to have to rip his nuts off if he hurts her…" I mutter. Mainly because I'm worried that Sav hurting Leah would put a strain on my relationship with Ronnie. And I suppose I care about her, simply because Ronnie cares for her.

"Mmmm? Nut ripping? That's the sexiest thing you've ever said." Ronnie quips as she slides her thighs until they bracket mine and she sits on my lap facing me.

"Yeah? That get you going, huh? I'll talk about de-nutting men all night for you if you want." I purr, leaning forward to nuzzle into her neck.

"I'm good thanks. I'd much rather not do any talking at all." Ronnie grinds her hips down onto me, my already hard length growing even harder.

"Mmmm. Tell me what you want to do then." I run my tongue up her neck, settling in the spot below her ear and sucking her skin into my mouth, prompting Ronnie to gasp.

"Better yet, let me show you." Ronnie crawls off of my lap, pulling my hand for me to follow her towards my bedroom.

As soon as the bedroom door clicks shut behind us Ronnie sinks to her knees in front of me. She gazes up at me with a wickedly sexy grin, reaching up towards my sweatpants and toying with the waistband. I thought my dick couldn't get any harder, but seeing my little fox on her knees for me makes my cock painfully erect.

Ronnie slowly pulls my sweatpants down to find I'm not wearing boxers underneath. The fabric falls around my feet as my dick springs up in front of her. Her eyes are locked on my throbbing boner, a moan falling from her mouth as she bites her lip. Fuck, she's so unbelievably hot. I'm desperate to make her take my whole cock down her throat. I want to feel her moan around my length.

She braces her right hand on my thigh and grips the base of my cock with her left. Her grip is firm as she leans in to flick her tongue against the slit. My hips instinctively buck, seeking the wet heat of her mouth, but Ronnie just giggles in response, continuing to tease my tip with her tongue. She places a gentle kiss against the head of my cock before tracing her tongue on the underside of my shaft. I groan, this girl is going to fucking kill me.

"Ronnie..." I warn, about ready to pop her mouth open myself and force my cock down her throat.

"What, baby? Something wrong?" She replies teasingly, planting kisses along my length.

"I need you to wrap your pretty lips around my cock, little fox. I need to fuck your throat." I hiss, my dick twitching in response to her gentle touches.

Her eyes flash to mine when I call her little fox, but she doesn't comment on it.

Instead, she says "Beg."

Oh, fuck. I've never begged in my life for a blowjob. I've never begged for anything sexual, ever. I haven't ever needed to, and that's not just me being cocky. But for Ronnie? I'd crawl for her. I'd douse myself in gasoline and fucking light myself on fire for her.

"Please, Veronica. Please put my cock in your mouth." I plead, and I'm not even ashamed at how whiney I sound. I fucking need this.

"Good boy." She replies, wetting her lips, sticking out her tongue, and sliding my tip into her mouth.

"Mmmmfuccckkk." I groan. Did she just awaken a praise kink in me? I'd do anything to be her good boy.

Ronnie pops my tip out of her mouth and I'm about to protest when she moves back over me, taking me deeper inside. She continues, each time she takes my cock deeper into her mouth until I hit the back of her throat. She holds me there, tears forming in her pretty hazel eyes as she swallows around my cock. It feels so fucking good.

Ronnie slowly pulls back, letting my dick fall completely out of her mouth. "I want you to fuck my throat, Felix." Her voice is sultry.

I feel like I could cum just from hearing those words fall from her mouth. Her black lipstick is now smeared around her lips, and traces of it coat my dick.

"Open your mouth and stick out your tongue, love." My hand tightly grips my pulsing cock.

Ronnie does as I ask, bracing both of her hands on my thighs now with her mouth open wide and her wet pink tongue sticking out.

My hands wrap in her loose hair, dragging her head forward until my cock meets her lips. "First, I'm going to fuck your sweet mouth and throat, and then I'm going to coat you in my cum, pretty girl."

Ronnie moans in answer, her fingernails digging into my thighs as I slide my cock in, gently at first. I hold her there, letting her mouth and throat loosen around my size. After a minute, I can't wait anymore. I pull out to the tip, and then slam back in until I hit that back of her throat and she gags around me.

"You look so fucking pretty with your lips wrapped around my cock, tears streaming down your face." I pick up speed, relentlessly fucking her face as she moans around me. "Play with your clit, Veronica." I command.

One of her hands slips into her pajama shorts. The room fills with sounds of her wet mouth around my cock, her fingering her wet cunt, and both of us moaning. I watch as her fingers circle faster beneath her shorts, but I want to see it all.

"I want to see you naked, baby. Strip for me." I demand.

I watch as Ronnie stands, letting her shorts and panties fall around her ankles before stepping out of them. Next, she peels her t-shirt off, her perfect round tits dropping as the shirt releases them. I'm torn between continuing where we left off or throwing her on the bed and pounding into her swollen pussy.

Ronnie makes the decision for me. She drops back to her knees and wastes no time taking me back into her mouth while rubbing tight circles on her clit. I'm mesmerized watching Ronnie take my cock all the way to the base while frantically playing with her clit. She's a goddess.

Her free hand cups my balls, and it's game over. I'm panting and groaning, on the verge of unloading down her throat. But I want to cover her face and tits in my cum. I pull back, popping my dick out of her mouth. She looks up at me confused and stops playing with herself.

"Don't stop, Ronnie. Keep playing with yourself while I coat you in my cum." My hand wraps around my length, squeezing and pumping. Ronnie obeys, her jaw dropping wide and her tongue lolling out for me. "Fuck, you're beautiful."

I fuck my fist, pumping a few more times before my release finds me. I groan loudly as hot spurts of my cum paint Ronnie's mouth, chin, and chest. She moans loudly as my cum hits her, her body bucking and shuddering as her orgasm takes hold.

We both come down from our highs, panting. I rest my hands on the door above her while she leans back on her heels. Once my heart stills and my breaths stabilize, I scoop her into my arms and carry her lax body to my bed.

Her eyes flutter shut, and she breathes a moan of contentment.

"Let me clean you up, love." I leave to get a wet washcloth to clean her with, but by the time I get back she's already asleep. Soft sighs fall from her lips.

I wipe my cum from her, cleaning every drop. The primal part of me wants to rub it into her skin, mark her with my scent. Once she's clean, I pull the sheet and duvet over her naked body, slide into bed with her and pull her close to my chest.

Chapter 16
Ronnie

I'm having the best fucking dream. We're in Felix's bed and he's got my legs wrapped around his head, feasting on my pussy like he's starved. He licks and sucks my clit, teasing me until I'm panting and begging for more. I feel the vibrations as he groans against me, lapping at my arousal. I wish this was real. But it's only a wet dream, an incredibly fucking hot wet dream.

Two of his fingers trace my entrance, edging closer and closer as I buck and plead for him to shove them inside. I need his fingers in me like I need my next breath. He keeps me on edge until I'm a sobbing mess, pleading for mercy and release.

As his fingers finally slide home, my eyes snap open and I wake. But I can't fucking see anything. It's pitch black in here. I realize it wasn't a wet dream, I can hear the sounds of Felix's tongue flicking my clit, and his fingers pumping into my slick core.

I whimper. "Felix, I can't see…"

"You don't need to see baby, just feel." He replies in between nibbles.

My hands dart up, grasping my face. There's a cloth wrapped around my head. A blindfold. No…no…no…panic edges in. I try to breathe deeply, attempting to ground myself to the here and now with Felix instead of the there and then with my parents.

But it's no use.

"Felix…" I pant, my voice cracking in fear. "Please…stop…no, no, no!" I'm sobbing now, and the tears are soaking the fabric covering my eyes. It furthers my panic, reminding me of that night.

His mouth and fingers leave me as he crawls up my body, hovering over me. His palms grip my face. "What's wrong, Veronica?"

"The…blindfold…" I choke out. "Take it off. Take it off. Take it off!" I'm inconsolable now.

Flashes of my parents' dead bodies take over my mind. Blood. Gore. Piss. Tears. The sounds of screaming and pleading, met with laughter from the man who killed them.

Felix's deft hands reach behind my head, as he fumbles with the knot keeping the blindfold tied around my eyes.

My harsh breaths fill the air. "Please, Felix…please."

"Almost there, baby. Breathe for me, okay?" His voice is a soothing balm in the storm of my mind.

I try to focus on his voice, letting it anchor me in the present.

When the blindfold falls away, I see streaks of sunlight peeking through the heavy velvet curtains covering the windows of Felix's bedroom. The sunlight falls across Felix's face, suspended over me. His eyes are lined with concern.

I blink away the tears in my eyes. "S-sorry." I gasp out.

He cradles my cheek. "Don't apologize. I'm the one who should be sorry. I didn't know you'd react like that."

"Y-you couldn't h-have k-known…" I close my eyes, not able to look into his anxious green irises any longer. "The man who…killed my parents…he ummmm…he blindfolded me while he was hurting them."

"Jesus fuck…Ronnie. I never would have done that if I'd known. Shit…" He presses his forehead to mine.

I tremble underneath him. "It's okay…"

"No, it's really not." His body comes down next to me.

My eyes open to see him tugging at his hair as he stares at the ceiling.

I launch myself over him, gripping his wrists in my palms and staying his hands. Seeing him hurting himself in response to my distress snaps me out of my fog. "Hey…don't do that. It's not your fault."

His sad eyes meet mine, but he nods, accepting my words. His hands fall from his hair and land against my hips. I want to distract him from his unease. I want to erase the guilt and pain he feels on my behalf. I wish I was normal and not so fucking broken inside. Some other girl might've loved what he was doing. All he wanted was to surprised me and give me pleasure, but I had to freak out and ruin it.

"Thank you for trying...I'm sorry I'm such a mess. If it's any consolation, I really enjoyed it until I realized I was blindfolded." A blush creeps up my chest and cheeks. "I thought I was having the best wet dream ever."

My confession brings a smirk to Felix's face, lightening the heavy mood instantly.

"You can count on me to turn all of your dreams into reality, pretty girl." He winks.

I giggle. "That was super lame."

"Yeah, well, what can you do. Not all my lines can be bangers." He shrugs, his chest shaking underneath me as he laughs. "But maybe we can pick up where we left off...sans blindfold." He waggles his eyebrows.

"Mmmm...yeah, maybe we can." I bend down to kiss him, brushing my lips softly against him before letting my tongue flick against the seam of his lips.

Felix groans against my mouth, sliding his tongue along mine. I suck it into my mouth, biting softly as he pulls it away.

"Fuck, Ronnie…you make me so fucking hard." Felix growls, his eyes igniting with lust. Felix pulls my hips toward his face. "Sit on my face, baby."

"What? I'll suffocate you!" I push my palms against his chest, fighting his pull.

"And what a way to die." He grins. "Now. Sit. On my fucking face, Veronica." His voice turns into a demanding guttural growl.

His hands grip my ass, dragging it until I'm hovering on my knees over his mouth. I struggle against his hold, nervous about legitimately killing him if he makes me do this. But Felix doesn't seem to care as he pulls my thighs down until my pussy rests against his waiting tongue.

Felix strokes his tongue up my slit, parting my lips at it trails from my entrance to my clit. As he reaches the sensitive nub, my hips involuntarily grind against his face.

He pulls his head back enough to praise me. "That's it baby. Fucking suffocate me."

His lips wrap around my clit, pulling it into his mouth as he sucks hard. I throw my head back, crying out as the sensation rolls through me. I'm apparently still on edge from his earlier ministrations, because I'm already close to cumming. I shamelessly grind my hips on his tongue, seeking more friction, and Felix lets me. He flicks his tongue in time with my thrusts. I forget about everything else in world but the way his mouth feels as it devours me.

"I want you to drown me in your pussy, pretty girl." Felix moans, breaking away for a gasp of air.

I feel my cunt dripping onto his tongue as his words drive me closer to the edge. What pulls me over is the sound of him groaning as he feasts on me. He's feral, and enjoying this as much as I am.

"Fucking cum all over my face like the needy little slut you are." He bites down on my clit, and I explode.

My fingers dig into the headboard, my body rocking over Felix's mouth while he draws out every ounce of my orgasm. He moans into my pussy, lapping up the remains of my arousal and cum, treating it likes it's the nectar of the Gods. I've never had anyone go down on me like Felix does. He eats me like I'm his favorite meal, and it's absurdly fucking hot.

My body relaxes, crumbling down beside Felix while I try to catch my breath. "Oh my god." I mewl. "That was…"

"Fucking amazing? A religious experience? The best orgasm you've ever had?" Felix supplies, smugly.

"All of the above. You've converted me to the religion of Felix Drakos." I slap my palms together, as if in prayer.

"Welcome to my church, baby."

Chapter 17
Felix

Ronnie returned to her apartment a few days ago. Her place is secured now, with a top-of-the-line security system, that I also have access to. I've watched her walk around her apartment, eating dinner, watching TV. I've barely been sleeping, because I've spent the nights watching her rest peacefully in her bed. I know it's too soon for her, but I want her to move in with me. I want my bed to be hers. Watching her sleep feels like the closest thing to that.

It's the fourth night she's been back at her own apartment, and it feels like my lungs have been ripped out of my chest. It feels like I'm dying without her next to me. Leah works late, and once again Ronnie is alone at home. She shouldn't be alone, she should be with me. It frustrates me that I can't be with her every fucking second of the day. I'm obsessed. I've completely fucking lost it. Any sanity I had, out the window.

It's just after ten at night when Veronica turns off the living room TV, fills her water bottle, and heads into her bedroom. She strips out of her joggers, leaving her wearing only a baggy t-shirt and lacey panties. My mouth waters at the sight. Veronica is my wet dream, every fantasy I've ever had come to life. Ronnie pulls the duvet back and then scoots into bed, but doesn't cover herself with the sheets or blanket, which is unusual because she usually cocoons herself in them.

She lies there for a minute, staring at the ceiling, before sighing and sitting up. Her eyes dart to her bedroom door, making sure it's closed even though she's alone at home, and then she eases open the top drawer of her nightstand. Oh, fuck. I know what she keeps in that nightstand. This is unbelievably wrong for me to watch, but I can't peel my eyes away from the screen.

From the drawer, Ronnie pulls out her bright pink rabbit vibrator. She props up her pillows behind her, and leans back against them. Her bent legs fall to the side as she spreads them open wide, trailing her hand down over her panties. She uses two fingers to rub small circles over the fabric, right where her clit sits below. I can hear her breathing becoming heavier, accented by moans every now and again.

"Fuck, Veronica." I hiss, palming my throbbing cock over my sweatpants.

As if in response, Ronnie peels her panties down, flinging them to the floor. Although it's dark in her room, I can still see the wetness of her soaked pussy glistening in the moonlight that filters through her blinds. I wonder what she imagines when she takes care of herself like this. Does she think about me? God, I hope so. Because since I met her, every time I jerk off it's to images of my girl.

Ronnie clicks on the vibrator, both the rabbit ears and the dildo, slicking it through her folds. She holds the vibrating head against her clit, turning the power up even higher as her hips grind against it. She's impossibly sexy. I imagine burying my face in that sweet cunt, lapping up her arousal and making her scream my name. Pulling my dick out of my sweatpants, I fist it tightly, rubbing from base to tip.

Ronnie slips the toy into her entrance, and she's not gentle about it. She slams it all the way inside, pushing the vibrating rabbit ears around her clit while she bucks and moans. I grasp my cock even tighter, picturing it sliding into her warmth as she clenches tightly around me. A bead of precum gathers on my tip, and I swipe it down my length.

My girl gets up on her knees, riding the rabbit, impaling herself on it. She fucks it fast and hard, one hand holding the toy in place against the bed, while the other one crawls underneath her shirt to pinch a nipple.

"Yes, Felix. Yes, yes, yes, right there!" Ronnie cries out.

My movements stop, and the world feels like it's in slow motion. Did she just…say my name? While masturbating? Am I desperate enough to imagine that?

Ronnie's movements stutter and her body tenses, her orgasm wracking through her body. "FELIX!" She screams.

"Oh, shit!" Hearing her scream my name sends me over the edge, my own release rippling through me. Cum spurts, coating my hand and sweatpants. Once I come down from the high, I'm utterly shocked, but also pleased. She wants me. Ronnie imagined that it was me making her cum. Satisfaction rolls through me. Veronica Woods is fucking *mine*.

***

I lied. I'm a big enough man to admit my faults. When it comes to Ronnie, I'm weak. I know I said I would hang up my mask when it came to her. I promised myself that I wouldn't stalk her anymore. Well, no one is perfect, and I guess I'm a fucking liar.

So anyway, after the show she gave me earlier tonight, I couldn't help myself. How could I stay away when this beautiful woman was shrieking my name as she pleasured herself? The answer is that I couldn't. That leads to the here and now.

I'm sitting in the armchair she keeps in the corner of her room. Ronnie's usually very cleanly, but she had a stack of clothes taking up space on the chair. They didn't smell dirty, and I'm assuming she throws them there when she doesn't want to fold laundry. I did the favor of folding them, and putting them away for her. I might've also snagged a pair of green lace panties from her dirty laundry hamper, slipping them into my back pocket. I'm sick in the head, okay? Don't judge me.

Once my seat was cleared, I plopped down, kicking back to relax. And that's what I've been doing since. Ronnie snores softly, wrapped up like a burrito in the blanket with only her head peeking out. She's so goddamn cute. I'm dying to crawl into bed with her, just to hold her close. She's a pretty deep sleeper, and I could probably get away with it, but then I know I'd never want to leave her side. And it'd probably be pretty jarring for her to wake up in my arms with no memory of me being here before she went to sleep. I enjoy scaring Ronnie, but only when it's for sexy foreplay. Although, I did bring her home with me when she was drunk that one night and she reacted pretty well to waking up in my bed…

I watch a tendril of hair move with her breaths, blowing away from her face when she exhales, and settling against it again when she inhales. My body acts of its own volition as it carries me to the side of her bed. My hand reaches out and tucks the stray strand behind her ear gently. She sighs as my fingers trace her skin.

Bending down, I brush my lips across her cheek, and then her lips, featherlight to not wake her. "I love you, Veronica." I murmur. I can't tell her while she's awake yet, it'd only scare her away. But for my own sanity, I had to say it to her, even if she's unconscious.

"Felix…" She mumbles, shifting slightly, but still asleep.

I've infected her heart and soul, just as she has me. I'm glad I'm not the only one falling here, sinking into the depths of madness over my love for her.

I turn to leave. It's almost five in the morning, and Ronnie usually wakes up around six. I could stay a little longer, but it's best not to risk it. When I near the bedroom door, I'm reaching to turn the knob when I hear a whimper come from the bed.

"Help. Please…no…" Ronnie softly cries.

I whirl around, kneeling by her bedside once again. She's still deep asleep, but tears run down her cheeks and small whines escape her mouth. Ronnie's body thrashes to the side, kicking the covers off.

"Not the blindfold...please..." Ronnie wails. Her legs kick out, and her arms flail as if she's fighting someone off.

I can't sit here and watch her suffer. I have to take the chance that she'll wake and realize I'm here with her. I pull my hoodie over my head, tossing it to the floor, and slide into bed with her. Whatever she's dreaming of has my beautiful girl terrified. I need to comfort her. I lie on my side, wrapping my arms around her waist, pulling her back into my chest. She struggles against me, and I have to wrap one leg around hers to stop her from kicking me. I pin her arms underneath mine, holding her still.

"Why? Please don't kill my mom. Daddy, why aren't you helping her? Why are you quiet?" She whines, her chest rising and falling rapidly in her panic.

I nuzzle my nose into Ronnie's hair, whispering in her ear to calm her. "Shhhh...baby, it's okay. You're safe. It's not real, pretty girl. I've got you, always." My fingers stroke along her arms, rubbing soothing circles over her skin.

"Please...don't take them away." Her pleas are quieter now, her body relaxing a fraction.

"I won't, baby. No one's taking them away." I realize now that she must be dreaming of her parents, and the night they were murdered. I wonder how often she relives that night in her sleep.

I'll do anything I can to help her. Eventually I'll find the killer and serve him vengeance. He'll never hurt her or anyone else again, I'll make sure of it. But for now, all I can do is hold her.

I kiss her cheek, and then rest my face against hers. Ronnie's breathing calms, the tears drying on her face. Her arms and legs have gone still, and her whimpering has stopped. The nightmare has finally released its grip on her.

My arms relax, not needing to press as tightly to keep her safe and still. As soon as they do, Ronnie turns in my arms until she faces me. Her arms wrap around my waist, and her face snuggles into my bare chest. Even in sleep, she's finding comfort in my presence. My heart leaps to my throat, overjoyed with her reciprocation.

I let her cuddle into me for fifteen more minutes, but then I have to slink out of her grasp. Ronnie will be awake soon, and she can't find me here.

Chapter 18
Ronnie

The blaring of my alarm wakes me up with a jolt. I can tell I had the nightmare about my parents again, the sheets are soaked in sweat and so am I. I have the same nightmare pretty frequently, but it still bothers me each time I have it. I've spoken to therapists about it, but they said the nightmares are due to unprocessed trauma. How the fuck am I supposed to process the trauma of my parents literally being murdered in front of me?

I sigh, sitting up in bed. As I do I stiffen, noticing two things simultaneously. First, the smell of something woody with notes of citrus. It's familiar, reminding me of Felix. I did spend a few days at his house, maybe his scent rubbed off on me and that's why I smell him in the air.

The second thing that I notice is my chair that's usually littered with unfolded laundry is cleared off, and there's an imprint in the cushion like someone was sitting in it not too long ago. That's...odd...no one ever sits in that chair, I use it exclusively as a spot to dump my clean laundry. Maybe I put it away last night and I just don't remember? I've been super tired this week, so it's not out of the realm of possibility. And maybe the indent in the cushion is from the weight of the clothes that were piled on. It's also an old, thrifted armchair, so it could be that the indent has always been there and I never noticed.

I think to check the newly installed security cameras, when I remember that there weren't any installed in my bedroom. Scratching that idea off the list, I guess. Wait, I can check the cameras in the living room and entryway, just to see if anyone came in last night.

I log into the security app, and pull up the camera for the entryway. I speed through the footage, but nothing happens. The timestamps look correct, and no one comes into the apartment but Leah at one in the morning. The footage for the living room is exactly the same.

That means Felix wasn't here last night, and neither was my stalker. The scent must've been due to Felix's cologne on my clothes, and the indent on the chair must be because it's old. I haven't seen my stalker since my birthday party anyway, he must've grown bored with me and moved on. And what reason would Felix have for breaking into my apartment? If he wanted to come over all he'd have to do is ask.

I exhale loudly. Well, at least past me did the favor of putting my clothes away. Now I don't have to dig through the pile to find my outfit for the day. I don't bother showering, knowing that I'd have to do it all over again after work. I can't stand the scent of death that permeates the office and sticks to my hair, skin, and clothes.

Once my hair is in a bun and my teeth are brushed, I head out to the kitchen. Leah's usually asleep by now, but this morning she sits at our kitchen island, scrolling through her phone.

"What are you doing up?" I ask, walking over to our coffee maker.

"Ugh. Couldn't sleep. Kept thinking about what happened with Micah at your party." Leah sighs dramatically.

"You shouldn't waste your time and energy on him, babe." I scowl at her.

"I knowww…" She whines. "It just fucking bothers me, the whole situation. I went on one date with the guy and he treats me like he owns me? And then after he makes a scene at your party, he ends up getting beaten to a pulp in the parking lot? It's just…weird."

I don't tell her that the man in the picture was my stalker, and is the suspect connected to Micah's involuntary rearrangement of his facial features. If my stalker grew bored of me, why would he hurt Micah before abandoning me?

"I just worry." Leah nibbles on her lower lip. "What happens when he gets out of the hospital? Is he going to come after me again, or Sav? Am I putting you in danger? And it's all out of my fucking control. I had no idea what a nut Micah was before going on a date with him. If I had, I wouldn't have gone in the first place."

I round the island, wrapping my arms around her shoulders. "Leah. You can't control what Micah does or doesn't do. But I'm sure that he learned his lesson at my party. There's no way he's going to keep bothering you, he'd have to have a death wish." I kiss her cheek. "You need to sleep, babes. And I gotta get to work. Are you going to be okay?"

"Yeah, I'll be fine, Ronnie." Leah squares her shoulders and raises her chin confidently. "I'll probably take a couple gummies and try to sleep. Go play with corpses, or whatever you do at work, you little freak." She quips.

"You bitch." I gasp with theatrical flair. "Call me if you need me, Leah."

"I will." Leah calls over her shoulder as she saunters away to her bedroom.

***

Today's cadavers are Sally and Eddie Meyers. Husband and wife, cause of death looking like an apparent murder/suicide. These two were brought in by a different crew from Felix's company, and I can't help but be a little disappointed that I didn't get to see him today.

The bodies are laid flat on their backs on two separate autopsy tables. Dr. Vargas works on Eddie, while I work on Sally. The police officers at the scene were definitely leaning toward the murder/suicide angle, but our job is to simply state facts. These facts will help Terrance make a determination and pronounce a cause of death. Of course, we can never be one hundred percent sure what exactly happened to any of our cadavers, but their bodies will give us pretty big clues.

Sally's death was brutal. She was stabbed twenty-seven times. Five of those were in her neck, and the rest were in her chest and abdomen. Her skin is shredded, strips of flesh barely hanging on. It's gruesome and gory. Although it's hard to see, there are some ligature marks on her neck that look like handprints from a large male, possibly matching the size of her husband's hands, Eddie.

If it was Eddie who killed Sally, I wonder what caused this amount of rage. Oftentimes when there are this number of wounds, particularly stab wounds, as well as ligature marks, it's due to the perpetrator being enraged during the kill. In college, we're taught to distance ourselves from our humanity while working with the cadavers. We're not meant to ruminate on why someone died the way they did, or what made one human kill another. Our job is to deal in facts and hard evidence, not concocted stories.

And even though we're not supposed to think about the why's, I can't help myself. It's just like I can't help but wonder why my parents were murdered. Why our family? And why did the killer spare me? He must've planned it from the beginning, otherwise he wouldn't have blindfolded me to make himself unidentifiable to the sole survivor.

My mind wanders to that night as I work, documenting all the injuries to the outside of Sally Meyer's body. The smell of the living room, drenched in the metallic scent of blood and reeking odor of urine. I think about how my pajamas were soaked through because I wet myself, and I sat in my own pee until the police woman came and took me out of the house. I remember my mom's cries and screams. I remember my dad pleading with the man to stop. The sounds of squelching and dripping gore as my parents were sliced and stabbed. The man who killed them giggling one minute and threatening the next.

If I think hard enough, I can still feel the wetness of the blindfold pressing against my eyelids, soaked through with my tears. I can sense the man coming closer, smearing warm and wet blood on my cheeks, blood that he took from my parent's corpses.

And if I close my eyes, I can still see the moment when my blindfold was removed, and over the police woman's shoulder I saw my mom and dad. They were tied to chairs, their mouths cut into too large grins, dripping in blood.

"Veronica!" Dr. Vargas snaps, his gloved hands gripping my shoulders. The blood from Eddie's corpse leaving fingerprints on my scrubs.

I blink my eyes, focusing them on Terrance standing in front of me. I realize that I must've zoned out, standing here while staring into space instead of doing my job.

"Sorry...I..." I shake my head, willing the thoughts of that night away.

"It's okay, Ronnie." Dr. Vargas's eyes are kind as he looks me over. "You scared me, is all. Tell you what, I'll finish Sally up. Why don't you take a break. Maybe get some fresh air, go for a walk, clear your head. This job can get to the best of us sometimes."

I nod solemnly. It's that nightmare that put me in this headspace, I know it is. I try not to let them get to me, but I guess maybe seeing Sally's stab wounds triggered me. I've debated on going back to therapy, but none has helped so far. I'm not sure if I can be helped at this point.

Chapter 19
Felix

Leon Clark. Pedophile, predator, child groomer, murderer. I've been tracking this one for a while, following his screen name through the dark web, venonmousvixen_clarkxxx. Once I figured out who was behind the screen name, it was embarrassing how obvious it was. Dude didn't even try to hide himself. You'd think a predator would realize that putting his last name in his username was a bad idea.

He'd been trying to groom minors and often frequented the most depraved recesses of the internet. That's how he caught my attention. I track people in Westmound who visit these websites, and when I find out their identities, they make my hobby list. Unfortunately, I found his identity too late. Leon killed his first victim, Finn Hardt, a couples of months ago.

I've been toying with a new torture method, and I think old Leon here will be the perfect test subject. And even if my plan doesn't work, it'll still be painful for him and fun for me. Logistically, my new method is probably a one time deal. It was a lot of work taking care of the black widow spiders for the past two weeks. Black widows will eat each other if kept together, so I had to set up five different enclosures for them, and keep them well stocked with other insects to eat. The work associated with this has been time consuming, and it's been a pain in the ass. But hopefully it'll be entertaining.

He's currently strapped to the metal table I've got situated in a corner of my requisitioned barn. This guy was harder than most to get back to my torture chamber. He's almost as round as he is tall, and the stench of body odor coming off of the guy is gag worthy. His greasy hair is combed over his clearly balding head. The image he uses on the various chatrooms he frequents is of a young blonde woman in a cheerleading uniform, since he obviously couldn't advertise himself as a middle-aged man with subpar hygiene.

Right on cue, Leon begins moaning and shifting in his bindings. Rounding the table, I position myself behind his head, watching as his eyes begin to flutter. *Slap.* I swing my hand, colliding with his cheek and sending his face sideways against the table. Leon grunts, but still is in the space between asleep and awake. *Slap, slap.* Two hits in quick succession, making his right cheekbone smack against the metal table. This time Leon groans, his eyes slowly opening and trying to focus.

"Wake up, Leon." I lean down, whispering in his ear.

Now his eyes are snapped open wide and focusing on me.

"Finally. Thought you'd stay asleep all evening." I jest.

"Am I in the hospital?" Leon slurs, drool dripping from the corner of his mouth.

"Oh, no, buddy. You aren't." I pout. "You'll probably wish you were soon, but I'm not a genie so I can't grant your wishes."

"Who are you?" Leon is still confused and out of it.

"Call me V." Yes, I came up with a name for my alter ego. Yes, it's V as in vengeance. Lame?

Probably. But it's the best I could come up with so don't judge me. I'm not a creative guy, unless we're talking about torture methods that is.

"I'm excited that you're here, Leon Clark." I move a rolling cart until it's parked next to the table. "I have a special type of hell for you today, and it'll be thrilling to experience it together. So, let's just get started, shall we?"

Leon's eyes track my movements, watching as I pick up a hard rubber open-mouth gag.

"What the fuck? That better not be for me." Leon snips.

"It's cute that you think you have any say in this, seeing as you're strapped down and at my mercy." I mock.

"Are you some kind of freak? Does this get you off or something?" Leon sneers.

"Ironic." I hum, nonchalantly swinging the rubber o-ring of the gag around my finger. "You know how they say that cheaters usually accuse their partner of cheating due to their feelings of guilt? What's that called again, projection?"

"The fuck are you talking about? This isn't funny, you fucking freak." Leon's cheeks are red, he's becoming angrier with each passing second.

"It's not supposed to be funny, Leon. At least, not to you." I stand above him now, getting ready to strap the gag across his face. "Anyway, you're wasting your precious last moments trying to insult me. Don't you have anything you want to say? Any Gods you want to pray to?"

Leon's jaw clenches shut. It's almost as if he's pouting like a child who isn't getting his way.

I laugh and shrug, "Okay then. What a waste of your last words. Now, open wide!"

He jerks his head to the side, trying to hide his mouth. I was prepared for him to be uncooperative, I mean, what kind of person would just let a stranger gag them like this? Well, I'm sure there are people in the world who are totally into that, but I had an inkling that Leon wouldn't be one of them. I sigh, setting aside the gag in order to grab the leather strap to the side of Leon's forehead. The man is not strong, so it's easy for me to grip his head in my hand, turning it and using the leather strap to hold it in place.

"Good boy." I pat his cheek aggressively. "Now are you going to open up for me, or do I have to force your mouth open?"

Leon glares up at me. As he glares, I hear him gathering saliva in his throat, but as he spits it out at me I move out of the way. The loogie flies in the air and then splats back down, hitting his cheek.

"That worked out well for you, didn't it?" I cackle.

I truly didn't expect Leon to give in to my demands, which is why I brought a speculum. I slip the ring of the gag onto the speculum before pressing the cold metal against his lips. He fights me, cinching his lips together tightly, but I don't care if I have to cut off his lips to get this gag behind his teeth. The metal cuts into his lips, spots of blood pooling in the crease of his mouth.

Using my thumb and forefinger, I pry his lips apart, shoving the metal speculum against his teeth. "I'll knock your fucking front teeth out if I have to." I growl.

The speculum finally gets enough leverage to slip one of the metal clamps between his teeth. Holding it steady, I begin spreading his mouth wide, his bottom teeth being pushed down by the device. When his jaw is open enough, I fit the open-mouth gag behind his teeth.

"There we go. That wasn't so hard, was it?"

Leon's tongue flicks against the gag, saliva pooling in the back of his throat as he tries to push against the gag. He gurgles, trying to talk.

"You're so impatient, Leon." I chirp over his gurgling. "I know, I'm getting to it. You're going to fucking love this part." A wicked grin spreads across my face as I retrieve the small closed container with my black widows.

His eyes are wide and confused as he looks between me and the spiders.

"Did you know that female black widow bites are rarely fatal? Lucky for you, I have five males waiting for you." I hold the container up to his face, letting him examine the black widows. "And while one black widow bite from a male isn't fatal to the average, healthy person, I wonder what five will do?"

Leon whimpers.

"I've heard the bites are extremely painful." I muse. "I'm curious how it will feel to have them bite inside of your mouth and throat? Do you think your throat will swell shut and you'll suffocate? Or do you think the shock will kill you?"

Leon tries to shake his head no, pathetic whines coming from his throat.

"No, you don't think five bites will kill you? Pretty confident of you." I flip the container so the opening is over Leon's mouth. "Only one way to find out." The lid of the container slides open easily, allowing me to jam the open container into the hole in his gag. It only takes a couple of taps on the bottom of the container to have all five spiders fall into Leon's open mouth.

His eyes widen in panic as he feels the spiders land on his tongue. While the container is jammed in the o-ring, I unbuckle the gag. This is the tricky part. I have to remove the container and shut his mouth quickly, followed by wiring it shut. Don't want any of these black widows escaping. I feel bad for the little spiders, but I'd hate to have them bite my girl when she's autopsying this fuck. Once he's dead I'll burn his corpse, killing the black widows in the process.

Leon cries and gurgles, tears streaking down his face as the spiders crawl inside his mouth. By his wails, I'm guessing that they've started to bite. His body thrashes against the restraints, but it's no use. The container is shoved so far into his mouth that there's no chance of him spitting it out. At first his tongue worked, trying to push it away, but now I can see through the glass that it's beginning to swell. Maybe he will suffocate from his body reacting to the venom, swelling his throat closed. Sweat beads on his skin, and his face begins losing color. Leon's chest rises and falls rapidly. He's panicking.

Generally, I like to talk to my victims first, letting them beg and plead for mercy. But Leon Clark didn't give Finn Hardt any clemency when he strangled him to death. I gave Leon more of a chance to pray and contemplate his last words than he ever gave Finn. And honestly, I don't give a fuck what Leon has to say for himself.

I watch as Leon's throat starts to close and his swelling tongue fills his mouth. His audible howls have become quiet sobs. He shudders, his chest expanding but unable to bring any air into his lungs. I feel no remorse or sadness for Leon Clark. He met Finn Hardt online, pretending to be a blonde teenager named Sarah. Leon chatted with Finn for weeks, grooming him and convincing him to meet 'her' at a local park.

I'm not sure what Leon's plan was from there. What did he expect to happen when Finn realized that Sarah was actually a four hundred and fifty pound middle aged man named Leon? Did Leon always plan on murdering Finn and violating his body? Or did things get out of hand? Truthfully, I don't give a fuck what Leon's intentions were. No matter how you cut it, Leon spent copious amounts of time grooming Finn and ultimately killed him.

Leon Clark is a monster. As time went on, he delved deeper into the dark web, falling further and further into his pedophilic ways. My only regret is not catching him sooner and saving Finn's life. In the process of taking Finn Hardt from this world, Leon also destroyed Finn's father, Oliver. And while eliminating Leon won't ever fix things for Oliver, at least maybe it'll grant him some closure.

Clark finally stops moving, his body going from tense to slack. I wait five more minutes, watching the empty shell of the vile man in front of me. I need to make sure he's really gone before removing the glass container and gag. Checking his pulse, I verify there's nothing left inside of him. His eyes are wide and vacant. The rotten soul that once inhabited Leon Clark is gone, and if hell exists, he's there.

Once I remove the gag from his mouth, I slam his jaw shut and quickly wire it, trapping the black widows inside.

"I'm sorry, spiders. Sorry you have to die inside this piece of shit, but I can't let you hurt my girl." I feel guilty about my black widows. I've taken care of them for weeks now, and I guess I got a little attached. I was worried it might happen, that's why I decided against naming them.

The gas can in the corner of the barn is full, and I take my time dousing each inch of Leon's corpse, before striking a match and throwing it onto his body. The flames engulf him quickly, the fat underneath his skin bubbling and popping as it boils. The smell is putrid, so I don a gas mask I had tucked away on a shelf.

After his body is charred beyond recognition, and I'm sure that the black widows are deceased, I use the hose to extinguish the flames. I plan on dumping his body in the same park where Finn was found. Poetic justice.

***

I spent an hour in the shower after dealing with Leon Clark. I had to get the stench of his vileness off of my skin, scrubbing until my body was raw and pink. I'd never let anyone see me like this, except maybe Ronnie, but after a kill I always weep. Not for my victims, or for the pieces of my soul that chip away with each person I murder, but for the people who were hurt by my victims. Even though I do everything I can to enact justice, by the time I intervene it's too late. Someone has already been killed, hurt, or broken.

You might ask why I feel that it's my responsibility to take care of the injustice. Why is it Felix Drakos who needs to shoulder this burden? My answer is simple. If I don't, no one else will. I saw how Gwen was after her attack. My sister was shattered, everything sweet and innocent about her spoiled. She rotted and withered until she was just a shell. And although she's gone to therapy, been in in-patient care, and worked really hard to pick herself back up, she will never be the same Gwen Drakos that she was five years ago. That's what kills me.

She's terrified of men, all of them except myself, Sav and my father. She won't date, and hardly leaves her house except to work. And even though her rapist is dead, she still sees no peace. Her world has been altered, and no matter what we do I don't know if she'll ever come back to herself.

I called her tonight, after my shower. She said she was doing good, and that work was busy but interesting. But I could tell she had been crying. It's been five fucking years and that fucking piece of shit is still destroying her, long after his death. I told her that I worry about her. She doesn't talk to any of the friends she used to have. When she's not working, she's hidden away in her apartment. Gwen always tells me I'm being dramatic and that she's fine. I've asked her to move into my penthouse with me, that way I could see her more and keep an eye on her. She refused. But maybe I can convince her and Ronnie to spend some time together. She needs a friend.

I've been texting back and forth with Veronica. After my conversation with Gwen, I bounced the idea of Ronnie, Gwen and Leah having a girl's night. Ronnie is so sweet, she immediately said 'anytime' with a cute blushing smiley face emoji. Ronnie said she's excited to meet my sister and that she wants to get to know my family more. I guess that means that Veronica is getting more serious about our relationship.

Since exchanging numbers, Ronnie and I have been texting non-stop. Each morning, we check in with each other, and it's been really nice. If it were up to me, I'd spend every day with her. Hell, I'd have her already moved in with me. But she's taking things slow. She's not as obsessed with me as I am with her, but I'm working on fixing that problem. I need her to rely on me. I need her to need me just as much as I need her.

The drive to the shitty part of town takes me twenty minutes because of all the fucking stoplights. I had a cashier's check made out to Oliver Hardt in the sum of twenty-five thousand dollars. Oliver owns The Well, the dive bar where I picked up Trinity Giles not too long ago. The place has fallen deeply into disrepair, but I don't blame Oliver entirely for that. He's been through hell, and as a single father he's not exactly raking in the dough to keep The Well in top shape. I'm hoping that the donation helps him in some way.

I've scouted out the building prior to today, so I know that there is a back door that's left unlocked during business hours. I pull my jag into the alleyway, envelope with cashier's check in hand, and slip into the unlocked door to The Well. The office is to the left as soon as I step in. Fortunately, Oliver is working the bar tonight and the office is empty. It's a quick job. I sneak into the office, placing the envelope on the desk, and then sneak back out into the night.

Chapter 20
Ronnie

Have you ever smelled an incinerated cadaver? I hadn't either, until work today. Add that one to the list of fucked up shit I've seen in my lifetime. Even Terrance was phased by the stench and appearance of the husk that Felix and Sav delivered today. And Dr. Vargas has been doing this for thirty years. Now that's saying something. Next time I'm going to need to put some menthol vapor rub in my nostrils to block out the smell.

The cadaver was burned beyond recognition. We're waiting on the comparison between his teeth and local dental records to identify the body. We were able to determine based on the pelvic bones that the corpse was biologically male, but that's pretty much all we were able to determine. Whoever torched the guy got rid of all evidence, making it so the cause of death has to be ruled due to arson.

Last night Felix asked if Leah and I would be willing to have a girl's night with his sister, Gwen.

He sounded really worried about her, and made it seem like she doesn't hang out with other people much. It was endearing to hear about his love for her. It was nice to see another side of Felix, the one that cares about his family and would lay his life down for them.

It's Thursday night, and since Leah has the night off, we decided to invite Gwen over tonight. I'm really not sure what to expect. Felix described her as introverted and closed off, but I have a feeling that Leah will be able to get Gwen to open up. Leah is so bubbly and funny, she's usually able to charm just about anyone. Me on the other hand, I might be a little off-putting for Gwen. But I suppose Felix and I have a lot in common, so maybe she'll find spending time with me comfortable.

We plan on ordering pizza, wings, and then drinking liberal amounts of strawberry margaritas. I'm nervous to meet Gwen, and desperate for her to like me. Although I don't see Felix easing up on his obsession with me, I do worry that if Gwen dislikes me it'll put a damper on our relationship. Whatever our relationship is at this point. Felix is already calling me his girlfriend, but I'm moving at a slower pace. Yet, I feel my attachment to him growing at an alarming pace. He makes me feel like no one else has before, and it's terrifying.

Felix is protective of those he loves, and I'm definitely starting to feel like I'm being counted in that circle. And frankly, I'm into it. I like that he stood up for my best friend at my birthday party. No one has ever done anything like that for me before. And he did it simply because of my love for Leah.

Since Leah and I came back to our apartment Monday evening, after Felix had the new security system installed, Felix and I have been texting almost constantly. It's nice to wake up to a good morning text, and have him wish me sweet dreams before bed. He's even brought coffee and breakfast to my work each day this week. How he knew that I love croissant breakfast sandwiches and vanilla cold press coffees, I'll never know, but he nails it every time.

Dr. Vargas hasn't said anything else about the obvious thing between Felix and I, but he has been giving pointed looks after Felix drops off my breakfast and kisses me goodbye. I know that Terrance is just looking out for me, but I'm a big girl who can make her own decisions. And people can change. The Felix I'm getting to know doesn't seem like the type to pump and dump. He seems…committed.

Leah is working on mixing up the margaritas while I place the order for pizza and wings. Pepperoni with extra cheese and mushrooms? Yes, please. It seems like the three of us already have the type of pizza we like in common. As I hit submit on the online order, the new video doorbell that Felix had installed rings and sends an alert to my phone.

"Coming!" I call out, quickly heading to the front door.

New interior locks were installed, and it takes me a minute to unlock all of them before I can swing open the door to greet Gwen and Felix.

"Hey, baby." Felix grins, leaning in to kiss my cheek.

"Ewwww." I hear a feminine voice squeal from behind Felix. That must be Gwen.

Felix rolls his eyes before stepping aside. "This is my sister, Gwen. Gwen, this is Veronica."

Felix's sister looks similar to him. The same deep green eyes and black wavy hair that hits her collarbone. Her skin is a glowing olive tone, and she's breathtakingly gorgeous. She wears black jeans with a purple hoodie.

"Hi Gwen, come on in! Leah's working on her famous strawberry margs and I just ordered the food." I step aside, letting Gwen and Felix through the front door.

"Hey, girl!" Leah calls from the kitchen, peeking her head around the corner.

"Hi." Gwen replies, somewhat shyly. She was vocal about being grossed out at Felix kissing me, but now that she's past the threshold she's crawled back into her shell.

Leah saunters out of the kitchen, carrying a glass filled to the brim with alcohol. "Here you go, Gwennie. Come on, let's go sit on the couch and get comfy!"

Gwen turns and gives Felix a pleading look before Leah drags her away. She mouths 'Gwennie?!' at him, which only makes him laugh.

"Have fun, Gwennie!" He calls after her. Once Leah and Gwen round the corner, Felix turns to me and presses me against the wall of the hallway. "I wish I could stay with you all night." He says between kisses along my neck and collarbone.

I smile. "Sorry, it's girls' night. No stinky boys allowed."

Felix pulls away slightly, feigning hurt. "Me? A stinky boy?"

"Mhmmmm." I hum, smirking.

"That makes you a stinky boy liker, and that's just as bad as being a stinky boy. Maybe even worse, actually." He sticks his tongue out at me, then leans in and runs it up my cheek, leaving a wet trail behind.

I giggle and wipe his slobber away. "Gross."

"Ronnie, are you coming? Wait…don't answer that…I don't need to know what you and Felix are doing over there…" Leah calls from the living room.

I hear Gwen gasp and spit out a mouthful of her drink. "Ugh. Please don't make me picture Lix like that."

"Lix, huh? Fitting." I point to the spot on my cheek that he previously licked.

Felix waggles his eyebrows at me. "They call me Lix for a reason, baby. Maybe I could remind you of one of them quick."

I shove his chest playfully. I enjoy joking around with him, it feels comfortable and easy. "Alright Lix, you better get going. We'll take good care of Gwen, I promise."

"I know you will, baby." Felix tips my chin up and captures my lips in a soft and sweet kiss. "Have fun tonight." He tucks a loose strand of hair behind my ear, kissing me once again before reluctantly pulling away.

"Be good, Gwennie! Don't do anything that Leah would do!" He calls out before opening the door and leaving for the night.

As the night continues, Gwen loosens up more and more with each margarita. Leah's bubbly personality brings Gwen out of her shell. She's a sweet girl, but I can tell that there's some darkness inside of her too.

"So, Gwen, are you in college?" I ask. I want to get to know her and connect. Who knows, she might fit into our little circle perfectly.

"I'm taking online classes. I'm working as a secretary at a law firm, but I'm planning on going to school to be an attorney after my undergrad." Gwen explains.

"Ooh, fancy. What made you want to do that?" Leah's asks excitedly.

A sudden uncomfortable silence falls over the room. Gwen stares down at her margarita, her hands shaking slightly. Leah and I look at each other quizzically.

"Everything okay?" Leah reaches out to place a hand on Gwen's shoulder, but Gwen flinches away, spilling her drink over the sides of her glass with the sudden movement.

I jump up to grab a wet washcloth to help clean Gwen up. "Here, Gwen." I hand over the cloth. "We didn't mean to pry or upset you. We can talk about something else, or we can watch a movie, whatever you want to do."

Gwen wipes the spilled drink and sets down her glass with quivering hands. "I...ummm...I just went through something about five years ago and the law was not kind to me. I want to help others who went through a similar experience." Her voice wavers.

On our first date Felix mentioned starting his body transport business five years ago, and when I mentioned trauma, he agreed that he had baggage. It could be coincidence, or maybe Gwen's incident five years ago is the reason Felix started his business. But, it's none of my business and I'm not going to push her. Gwen barely knows us, and if she wanted to tell us about it she would.

"That's very brave of you, Gwen." Leah praises.

Conversation between the three of us dies down, but the discomfort from before slowly fades. We end up watching movies the rest of the night. Gwen and Leah are into romantic comedies, so we stream one after another until all of us eventually fall asleep on the couch.

***

"How was everything last night?" Felix asks, waiting for Gwen to finish packing up so he can drive her home.

"It was good. She was quiet at first but Leah got her to open up." I reply, then lean in and whisper "Although there was this odd moment where we asked about why she wanted to be a lawyer and she froze up."

Felix stiffens at my words, his face full of tension. "We don't talk about that."

"Yep. Definitely got that vibe from her." Yikes. Whatever it was must've been huge. I don't need to know, but I hope that someday Gwen feels comfortable enough to talk about it with me.

"Ready, Lix?" Gwen rounds the corner, surprising upbeat for the amount of alcohol we consumed last night.

Leah and I on the other hand, are hungover as fuck. I ended up calling in sick from work today, which Dr. Vargas was fine with seeing as we haven't gotten the results back from our incinerated cadaver, and we haven't gotten any new corpses since John Doe. Once Felix and Gwen leave, I'm heading straight back to the dark confines of my bedroom.

"Just a minute, Gwen. I gotta say goodbye to my girl." Felix's tension melts away and he returns to his usual flirty self.

Gwen rolls her eyes and lets out an audible 'ugh', heading back to the living room. "Call me when you're done playing tongue hockey!"

Felix grips the back of my thighs, lifting me and forcing me to wrap my legs around his waist as he pushes my back up against the wall. "I was thinking that we could hang out tonight? We could cook dinner, watch a movie, make out a little?"

I giggle. "Your house or mine? And I hope you're the one offering to cook for us."

"Will Leah be home tonight?" His lips brush against the shell of my ear.

"Nope." I pop the p.

"Let's be here then. I haven't stayed in your bed yet."

"Presumptuous of you, Mr. Drakos." I say slyly.

"It's not presumptuous if it's fact. I'll be keeping you company all night." His teeth graze my earlobe, before sinking into my skin gently and then letting his tongue swipe away the small hurt.

"It's a date." I sigh contentedly, arching my neck to the side for Felix to brush his mouth against it.

"See you soon, baby." He hesitantly sets me on my feet. "Let's go, Gwennie!"

Chapter 21
Felix

It hasn't even been a full week and I'm having serious withdrawals from not stalking Ronnie as V. Sure, I'm still vigilant about watching the cameras I installed every second she's home. And now I have access to her entire security system, including the few cameras the company installed, unbeknownst to Ronnie and Leah. When I had my guys install the system Ronnie was at work and Leah was still at my penthouse, so they have no idea that I set up access to it. Is that amoral?

It's taking every ounce of willpower I have to not don the mask and play with my little fox. I miss the thrill of it, but the thrill isn't worth losing her over. And I need to be more careful with my alter ego anyway. I lost it at her birthday party, not caring about the consequences of beating Micah to a pulp in the parking lot. I even fucking flashed my mask at the camera. What was I thinking? I wasn't, apparently. I was lucky that I remembered to wear my leather gloves during the crime, and even luckier that they shielded the impact enough that my hands weren't too battered afterwards.

When the officer questioned me, she was definitely suspicious of the gloves. She forced me to take them off, and I had to hold back a sigh of relief when I saw that my hands looked almost normal underneath. My hand tattoos also helped cover any bruising and cuts I had. The point is, I need to keep myself in check. Veronica makes me lose control, in the best and the worst ways.

To the law, it doesn't matter that the people I get rid of are the scum of the earth, murder is murder. And I can't keep cleaning this city if I'm behind bars. But I'd gladly give up my hobby to keep Ronnie in my life. Eventually she'll find out about what I do on the side, and although she's said she thinks the vigilante is doing a service to the city, I don't know how she'd react knowing that I'm the vigilante.

On the ride to Gwen's apartment, she chattered the whole way about how nice Leah and Ronnie were to her, and how much fun they had drinking margaritas and watching rom-coms. I'm happy that she was able to have a night out, and maybe the three of them will become friends. It's a big deal for me to trust Ronnie enough to take care of my sister. I've never introduced a girl to my family before. It might be time to bring her home to meet mom and dad. But shit, would Veronica think I'm moving too fast? It doesn't feel too fast for me. In fact, I'd have her move in with me and marry me right fucking now if she was down for it.

But I know she isn't there yet. And even if she was, she's too worried about societal standards to give in to me like that. Fuck society, and fuck the system, that's always been my motto. And it definitely applies to my relationship with Veronica Woods.

I've spent my afternoon watching the camera in Ronnie's bedroom. She hasn't moved from bed for hours. Gwen mentioned that they drank a lot of margaritas, so Ronnie is undoubtedly hungover. Hopefully she recovers in time for our date, but I have plans and they don't involve going easy on her.

My mom is Scottish and my dad is Greek, but I've never really enjoyed Scottish food (sorry Scotland!). I plan on making a Greek meal for Ronnie tonight. My dad has always been proud of his heritage, and is a fantastic cook, so Gwen and I grew up eating a lot of traditional Greek dishes. I stop by the store, picking up the ingredients for moussaka, dolmades, and spanakopita. There's a great little bakery that carries loukoumades and baklava, so I pick those up as well. I prepare all the dishes at home, that way I only have to finish cooking them tonight at Ronnie's apartment.

Ronnie rolls out of bed around four, and I follow her movements until she hits the bathroom to get ready for our date. And no, I didn't put any cameras in the bathroom. I may be obsessed and a little unhinged, but I'm not that far gone. She could stay in her cute oversized shirt and panties all night for all I care, she's beautiful without trying.

It's five when I pull up outside of Ronnie's building. I stopped watching the cameras after she went into the bathroom to get ready, wanting to be genuinely surprised and awed by her beauty in person. And when she opens the apartment door to let me in, I'm blown away. She's dressed casually, in a flowy black dress with long sleeves. Her hair is pulled up into a messy bun, and the only makeup she wears is her signature black lipstick and some mascara. She's ethereal.

"Wow...you look fucking out of this world, Veronica." I breathe. Fuck eating dinner, I'd rather eat her.

"You're not bad yourself, Felix." She replies, shyly looking me up and down. I'm in dark jeans, with a white t-shirt and my leather jacket. But even though she's dressed casually, she outshines me in every way. I'll never compare to her. "Come on in. I preheated the oven like you asked."

I pop the trays of food into the oven to heat up as Ronnie sits on the kitchen island, her legs swinging and her arms propped up behind her for support. Her black dress was mid-thigh when she was standing, but now that she's perched on the countertop it rides up her smooth, tattooed legs. She smiles at me as my eyes trail down her legs and then back up to her face. Using my palms, I spread her knees apart and stand between her thighs, leaning into her with my arms braced on either side of her ass on the counter.

I press my face into the crook of her neck, breathing in the scent that's uniquely Ronnie's. I'd happily bathe in her scent and have it surround me at all times. I want her surrounding me at all times. My thoughts turn dark as I consider what might happen if she ever tries to leave me. The answer is simple, I won't let her. I'd rather chain her to my bedroom wall than let her get away from me. There's no chance of this thing between us ever ending. She's my forever, even if she doesn't know it yet.

Fuck, I'm in so deep with Veronica Woods. Is it crazy that I've already started looking at rings for her? Before her I never even considered getting married, but now all I can think about is making her my wife. We haven't even said I love you, out loud that is, but I know she's my universe. There's no reality where she isn't mine.

My lips press against the pulse in her neck, and I feel it thumping wildly underneath them. I love the way she reacts to me. The way her heart reveals the truth to me even if her words won't. She's just as deep in this as I am. I work on her flesh, alternating between biting, sucking and licking. I'm not gentle, and I know that my mouth will leave a mark. The idea of her walking around marked by me makes my dick hard. I want to possess her, claim her.

Ronnie whimpers and moans beneath me, her breaths becoming heavier with each touch of my mouth to her skin. I move my way downwards, nipping her collarbone and leaving a series of marks across her pale, creamy flesh. She becomes putty in my hands, her hips moving as she tries to press her thighs together in search of friction.

My hands find her thighs and crawl upwards under the hem of her dress. I finger the lace of her panties, teasing my way underneath them before urging her to lift her ass off the counter as I slide them down her hips, thighs, and off her feet. Ronnie wore a red lace thong tonight, and as I hold it up, I can see a distinctive wet spot left by her glistening pussy.

Holding them up to her, I growl "Baby, look at the mess you made for me."

Ronnie's pupils are dilated, the black overtaking the hazel of her orbs. I set the panties aside and spread her legs even further. My fingers inch closer to her cunt, teasing and tickling along the insides of her thighs. While I tease with my hands, I continue to tease her neck and chest with my mouth. Ronnie is full on panting now, writhing and whimpering beneath me. My mouth meets hers, our tongues dancing when my hand finally brushes against her soft wetness.

"You're fucking soaked for me, Veronica." I groan, knowing that she's dripping and making a mess of her dress and the countertop.

She nods, pushing her hips forward into my fingers.

"Ah, ah, ah." I tsk. "Don't be greedy, baby. You'll take what I give you."

Ronnie whines in protest, desperate for more contact. Who am I to deny my girl what she needs? I push her down until her back hits the countertop, and then place her legs over my shoulders and lean my face until I'm close to her sweet pussy. Just like I suspected, her thighs are wet and the fabric of the dress that sits below her ass is soaked.

I hold her thighs apart with my hands, spreading her as wide as she can go, to the point where it's probably a little painful. My hot breath caresses her skin, and I feel her shiver in anticipation. I'm so fucking hard right now, looking at her dripping cunt, waiting for me to devour it. I run my tongue up the length of her slit, spreading her lips with it as I go. Her moans are breathy as I tease her with my tongue.

"Fuck baby, you taste so good." I moan, salivating at the sweetness of her.

My tongue works its way back up her slit, stopping to caress her clit. My cock feels like it's going to burst straight out of my fucking jeans. The zipper presses against it painfully. While my tongue flicks against her sensitive nub, causing her to buck against me and moan, I reach down to undo my jeans. I fist my hard length, needing to ease the pressure of my erection.

I feast on Ronnie like a man starved, laving, sucking and nibbling on her clit like it's my last meal. Sliding two fingers inside of her, I curl them against her g-spot and pump them in and out, bringing her closer and closer to the edge while I fist myself and spiral along with her.

"Oh, fuck! Fuckkkkk." Ronnie cries out, her back bowing off of the counter and her body tensing as she cums. I taste it on my tongue as it gushes out of her, and I can feel her walls fluttering around my fingers.

Seeing her lost in pleasure is my undoing. Quickly throwing her dress up, I expose her stomach in time to coat it with my cum. I groan as the warm jets hit her soft stomach, dripping down her sides. Her legs fall off my shoulders, and she places her heels on the edge of the countertop, still spread before me.

Grabbing the discarded red thong, I use it to wipe up the evidence of my orgasm. "I'll buy you a replacement pair." I pant.

"You better, those were my lucky panties." Ronnie replies in a serious tone, and for a second I feel like an asshole, until she giggles. "Just kidding."

"You little minx." I growl, slipping my arm underneath the small of her back and pulling her up towards me until our lips crash together.

Chapter 22
Ronnie

"Oh my god, Felix." I moan, my eyes rolling back into my head.

"I know, right?" He replies, taking another bite of the Greek donut-esque dessert that Felix said was called loukoumade.

"How'd you know that the way to my heart was through sweet treats?" I lick some of the sticky honey off my thumb.

"Hmmm…is that you admitting that your heart is mine, Veronica Woods?" Felix wears a devilish grin.

"TBD, Felix Drakos. You're definitely on the right track, but I don't give my love away so easily. It'll take a few more loukoumades for you to win that." I jest. In reality, he is winning my heart. I've never felt this way with any of my previous relationships, and that makes me scared. Falling in love is terrifying and leaves you vulnerable. What if I decide to go all in and end up diving head first into heartache?

I've been broken before, when my parents were murdered and then time and time again when foster families rejected me. But I fear the rejection of my previous foster families will have been nothing compared to what Felix could put me through. So instead of letting Felix in, and giving him a piece of me that I'd never get back, I laugh it off. Maybe someday I'll be ready for love, and I hope that it's with him, but today is not that day.

"I'll bring you these little treasures every day for the rest of my fucking life if that's what it takes to win your heart, Ronnie." Felix isn't joking when he says this. His eyes search mine, as if he's looking into my soul and trying to discern my feelings.

I fidget in my seat, suddenly uncomfortable with his attention. I'm not great with emotional stuff. I tell Leah I love her all the time, but it never goes beyond surface level. What I really feel is that she's my sister, and that I'd be lost without her, and I'd kill anyone who dares to hurt her. But to actually voice those feelings? Fucking forget it.

I clear my throat. "Well, dinner was great, Felix. I've had Greek food before but this was the best I've ever had. I wasn't aware that you could cook like this."

"The breakfasts I've cooked you in the past didn't reveal my cooking skills?" His serious expression melts away and is replaced with a smile and sparkling eyes.

"I mean yeah, they were good but this…" I pinch my fingers together and smooch the air in a chef's kiss. "Exquisite!"

He laughs, deep from his belly. "I'm glad you enjoyed it. My father is an even better cook than I am, I learned everything I know about it from him. He and his parents lived in Greece until they immigrated here in the late sixties. He was young when they came to the United States, so he doesn't remember much about living in Greece but his parents were adamant that he retains his heritage. My grandmother taught him to cook."

"That's amazing. Have they ever been back to Greece?" I ask, genuinely curious about his family's history.

"My grandparents passed before they got the chance. They weren't well off, and by the time my father made enough money to afford to take them, they were already deceased. The four of us, my sister, me, mom and dad, went when I was a teenager though. It was beautiful." He looks wistful, lost in memories of his family.

"I'd love to go someday. I've always wanted to travel, but have never had the luxury." I say.

He shakes his head as if shaking free of the memories. "Then I'll take you. Where ever you want to go."

I blush. "Okay Mr. Fancy Rich Man who can afford to take his hook-up to where ever she wants to go." There I go, brushing off the uncomfortable feelings again.

Felix grips my waist and pulls me into his lap, leading me to shriek in surprise.

"This is more than a 'hook-up' and you know it. You're mine." He holds my chin in his fingers, forcing me to make eye contact.

My heart squeezes and my breathing stutters. He makes me feel crazy when he tells me I'm his. I so badly want it to be true, but I'm too scared to give in.

I drop my eyes and slightly shake my head. "No." I whisper.

"Yes." He replies in a deep and gravelly tone. "You are mine, Veronica. Accept it, embrace it, and give into it. Now that I have you nothing will take you away from me. I will never let you go. Even if I have to chain you down and force you to be with me."

I shudder, not in fear, but in delight and arousal. Why did that turn me on? I know that I'm not normal by any means, but I feel like him threatening to chain me down should horrify me, not turn my insides to goo and my panties into a puddle.

"Tell me you're mine." He demands.

I can feel his stare penetrating me, but I can't meet his gaze. The emotions swirling inside of me are too much to handle, and I'm not equipped for them. "I can't."

"Yes, you can. Say it." His voice drops to a deadly whisper, promising wrath and punishment if I don't give in.

But maybe I want his wrath and punishment. Maybe I want to push him and see everything his dark heart as to offer me. So far, our sex has been fairly vanilla, but deep down I know there's something darker lurking inside of him. A beast waiting to be unleashed. And I want to be the one to unleash it. This man's entire persona screams 'KINKY!' and I want him to free that side of him and show me all that he is. And maybe this will be enough to distract him from trying to unearth the depth of my feelings.

So, I push back. "No." I hiss. "I am not yours, Felix. I don't belong to anyone but myself."

He growls, literally growls. It rumbles from his throat. "I'm not the type of man you can play games with, Ronnie. Don't fucking push me."

I muster the courage to glare directly at him, my eyes meeting his fiery orbs. "This isn't a game. You don't own me. I am not yours."

"You're going to regret fighting me." Felix promises.

"No, I don't think I will."

His chuckle is dark as he abruptly stands, his arms wrapped around me securely. Felix walks us to the leather jacket he slung over the recliner in the corner, fishing for something in the pocket. A glint of silver is all I see before I feel metal wrapping around my wrist and hear the click of a cuff locking into place. Felix presses me against his body so tightly that I'm unable to move the arm that's squished between us, and he easily snaps the other cuff into place on my trapped wrist.

"I wasn't kidding when I said I would chain you up." He walks us towards my bedroom. "By the end of the night you'll be screaming that you're mine and begging for my forgiveness. And maybe if you're a good girl I'll be merciful and unchain you. But only if you give in and tell me what I want to hear."

"Why should I give in? Why do I have to tell you that I'm yours when you haven't given the same to me? I'm not going to put myself out on a limb with no guarantee from you that I won't get hurt." I whisper.

His eyes soften a little as he stares down at me. "I thought it was obvious. You can't tell that you own me by how obsessed I am with you?" Felix tosses me down on the bed, my body bouncing as it lands. He crawls over me, gripping my bound wrists in one hand and holding them above my head. "There isn't a second of the day where I'm not thinking about you." He kisses me. "Craving you." Another kiss. "Needing you." This kiss is slow and sensual, stealing the breath from my lungs as he consumes me.

When he finally pulls away to look down at me, tears line my eyes as I whisper "You don't even know me, not really."

"Yes. I do." Felix growls. "I know everything about you. I'm obsessed with you baby, and I'm not exactly sane, but I know that you like that. You crave me too. You all but admitted your obsession with me when you told me you wished your stalker was me. Don't fight it." He's almost begging me now.

And the thing is, he's not even wrong. I did hope that he was my stalker. I want Felix to be obsessed with me. I want all his dark and depraved parts. I'm aching to feel like he needs me more than he needs air. The love I crave is all consuming, irrational, and dangerous. Right now, Felix is feeding into those fantasies, telling me he'll give me everything I want and need.

"I'm scared." I whisper. It's hard for me to admit feelings, to admit I have a weakness. He's the weakness.

"I know, baby. But I've got you. You won't fall alone, because I'm already there. Just fall with me, Ronnie." His gaze is locked with mine, and I see the sincerity in his eyes.

None of this is rational or logical, but isn't that what love is supposed to be like? You can't control love, it does what it wants without consideration. It's wild and messy. Love is about trusting the other person to catch you when you go down, and I know I can trust Felix with that. He's proven to me that he cares not just about me, but my family. That he'll do anything to protect me.

I nod, not able to voice my feelings yet.

Felix rumbles low in his throat with need, capturing my lips in a bruising kiss. "I'm still going to make you beg and scream for me, pretty girl. I've been gentle with you up until now, but I'm done playing nice. You'll embrace all parts of me, even my rough edges. You'll love that I scare you, take what I want, and give you what you need."

My chest rises and falls rapidly, fear igniting in my gut, but coiling with my lust for him.

"I'm going to uncuff you for a moment. When I do, I want you to take off your clothes, and then get on your hands and knees for me." Gone is any trace of softness from Felix's deep voice. "Do you trust me?"

"Yes." I squeak. And I do trust him. And I fucking want this.

"Good girl."

The cuff around my left wrist falls away. I immediately follow his earlier commands, slipping my dress over my head and unclasping my bra. I flip onto my stomach and rise until I'm on all fours in front of him. As soon as I settle, I feel his hand pressing down on my neck, forcing my ass into the air and my chest and face into the mattress.

"Hands behind your back." He demands.

He relocks my left wrist into the cuff, and now my hands are locked behind my back. I'm very vulnerable and open in this position. My ass and pussy bared to Felix.

"I will never hurt you in ways you don't like, do you understand?" He asks, one of his warm hands caressing my ass cheek.

"Yes." I whimper.

Smack. Felix's hand rears back and slaps my backside, stinging my skin and forcing me to gasp. *Smack*. His hand hits the other cheek, leaving a stinging sensation in its wake. *Smack*. *Smack*. Felix slaps each cheek forcefully in succession, and this time the sting it leaves behind isn't as jarring as before, but actually pleasurable. He begins rubbing my reddened cheeks, soothing away the ache from his spankings.

Felix groans gutturally as he rubs me. "You love this, don't you? And don't bother lying, I can see the way your pussy is dripping."

I nod as much as I can with my face still pressed into the mattress.

"My." *Slap.* "Dirty." *Smack.* "Little." *Slap.* "Fox." *Smack.* "Your ass is turning such a pretty shade of pink for me."

Felix leans in, skimming his lips across my buttcheeks while massaging them. I feel his fingers grip each cheek, pulling them apart and exposing my hole to him. He groans, angling down further, swirling his tongue from my pussy entrance, up my crack, and over my asshole. I suck in a sharp breath, surprised by his mouth and tongue moving around by puckered hole. I've never had a partner feast on me like this. I've experimented with anal on my own, and once with another partner, but it wasn't anything but painful and awkward.

My muscles clench, my cheeks tensing as I try to close myself off from Felix's advances. But his grasp on me is firm, and he holds me in place as I try to wriggle away. The more I try to fight him, the more adamant he becomes as his tongue flicks and circles my hole. A small part of me knows that it feels fucking amazing, but the larger part of me is too self-conscious and uncomfortable to enjoy it.

"Stop. Moving." Felix growls.

I turn my head to the side, "I can't. Please…"

"Yes, you can." Felix slips one finger inside of my pussy, working it in and out as he curls it against my g-spot. "Stay still and take it. Every part of you is mine to devour and use. I've claimed your pussy and mouth already, and tonight I'm claiming your ass."

"No, Felix." I cry out in pleasure as he slides another finger into my cunt while sliding the flat of his tongue slowly up my asshole. My body begins to loosen and relax into him as he plays with me. My mouth is telling him to stop, but my body is begging for him to keep going.

"Don't worry baby, I'm not going to hurt you. I promise you'll love everything I do to you." With that, he pulls back and I feel saliva dripping from his tongue and sliding down my crevice until it settles on my asshole.

Felix's two fingers keep pumping into me, slowly rubbing against that sweet spot inside of me and winding me tighter. I hear him sucking one of his fingers before it presses against my puckered opening. He applies more pressure, rubbing against it until I feel it sink into me. I gasp as the sensation of his finger sinking inside of me while his other two fingers thrust harder into my pussy. Felix's hands move in tandem, and before I know it, I'm rocking back against him, wanting him deeper inside of both of my holes.

"Are you ready for more, Veronica?" His voice is gravelly and low.

"Y-yes." I manage to moan.

His fingers leave me, and the sudden emptiness is unbearable. I whine, wondering what he's doing. Did he change his mind? Did I do something wrong?

As I begin to spiral into anxiety, I hear a cap snapping opening and the squeeze of a bottle behind me. Did Felix bring lube with him? He must've planned for this to happen tonight. Sly devil.

His fingers plunge their way back into my cunt, and I sigh with relief.

"Relax, baby." Felix croons, pushing the tips of his forefinger and middle finger against my asshole. As they slip inside and find the same rhythm as his other hand, he groans "Good girl."

"That f-feels s-so good" I moan, thrusting in time with his hands, pleading for more. I've never experience anal play like this, and I think a large part of the enjoyment for me is that it's Felix here with me. He makes me feel safe and comfortable, and when he works me into a frenzy like this, I'd do just about anything he asked of me.

I can feel my stomach tightening while the pleasure coils in my abdomen. Felix increases the pressure on my g-spot and picks up the pace, driving me further towards the edge.

"Fuck, Felix!" I cry out as I crash over the precipice, stars dancing behind my eyes while my heart races wildly.

Felix's fingers keep driving in and out of me, coaxing out each wave of my orgasm until it peaks, ripping a scream from my throat. When I finally come down and my vision returns to normal, I lay there panting, a sheen of sweat covering my skin. I've never cum like that before. Each time I think that I've reached the peak of orgasmic bliss with Felix, he brings something new to the table and turns up the heat.

Felix bends over me, pressing soft kisses against my spine. "Such a beautiful fucking girl. I love it when you cum for me."

"I love it too." I whisper, feeling boneless and awash in calm.

I hear the clicking of the cuffs as Felix unlocks them, and he rubs my wrists gently before letting them fall to my sides. He gives me a moment to breathe before his arms wrap around my waist and he flips me over onto my back.

"I need to see you when you cum with my cock filling your ass, Ronnie." Felix places his hands underneath my knees, pushing my legs to my chest until my lower back is curved and my ass is exposed to him and the ceiling above.

His hard cock bobs between my legs, and seeing it makes my insides clench with anxiety. "Felix...I don't think you'll fit in there..."

"Believe me, baby, my cock is going to fit perfectly in your tight little ass. Don't be nervous."

I gulp, but nod, letting myself trust him. Felix doesn't want to hurt me. He wouldn't do anything that I wouldn't like. "You've done this before?"

He gives me a pointed look. "Do you really want to talk about my past sexual experiences right now?"

"No." Felix is right, I really don't need to know who he's fucked and how.

Gripping his cock, he nudges his tip at my puckered entrance. I breathe in, willing my body to relax and trust him.

"Rub your clit for me, baby." Felix commands.

My fingers shake from nerves as they find the right spot and rhythm. I close my eyes and relax into the pleasure that sparks through me as I play with my clit.

"Eyes on me, Veronica. I need to see you come undone for me."

As our eyes lock, Felix slowly thrusts forward, shoving the head of his dick inside me. The stretch is intense as he pulls out and then moves back in, deeper with each thrust. His large cock fills my ass, snatching my breath from my lungs.

"Ahhhfuckkkk…" I whimper. "It feels sooo f-full."

Felix settles all the way inside of me with a grunt. "Fuck, baby, you're so tight."

Tears spring in my eyes from the sensation of his cock deep in my ass. It hurts, but in a good way and I want him to start moving again.

"Fuck my ass, Felix." I plead, still circling my clit.

Felix's eyes ignite with fiery lust as the black of his pupils expands and he breathes raggedly. Keeping his eyes locked on mine, he slowly pulls out to the tip before quickly sinking in deep again with a grunt, until his pelvis hits my cheeks.

I never knew it could feel this good. The harder he fucks my ass the more undone I become.

I pull him down to my lips, kissing, biting, sucking until we're both breathless and our lips are sure to bruise. My nails rake down his back, definitely leaving marks. We become feral together, like animals interacting on a primal level. The room is filled with the sounds of our moans and the slapping of skin on skin.

"Come for me, pretty girl." Felix moans, rutting into me ruthlessly.

His words send me over the precipice, and my eyes rolls back into my head as the shocks of my orgasm take hold of my body. My legs tremble and my fingers dig into his shoulder blades as he moves in and out of me, dragging my orgasm on and on. Fuck, it feels like I died and then reanimated. I've never known pleasure like this. I've never known someone as carnally and intimately as I do Felix Drakos. And I don't ever want to know anyone else like this, nor do I want Felix to experience this with anyone else ever again. I'm his.

I can feel Felix tensing above me, getting closer to his own release. I want nothing more than for him to fill me with it. I want everything he can give to me.

"Give me every fucking drop of your cum, baby." I whisper in his ear, taking the lobe between my teeth and flicking my tongue over it.

His movements stutter as a full body shudder takes hold of him. Felix lets out the sexiest fucking moan I've ever heard as I feel his cock swell. I feel him pulsing inside of me, my tight ass milking his cum. Pulse after pulse of his cum fills me, and I don't think either of us has ever cum as hard as we did from this. Felix's orgasm subsides, and his sweaty body comes down over me, caging me in with his muscular form. He rests his face in the crook of my neck, nuzzling me and planting soft kisses on my skin.

We lie there for several minutes, waiting for our hearts to stop racing and our lungs to begin working again. When our souls re-enter our bodies, he lifts himself up and pulls out of me. Resting on his side, head propped on his fist, he stares at me reverently. His free hand traces my neck, cheek, lips, like he can't help but touch me.

"You called me baby. You've never called me a pet-name before." He whispers in awe, his eyes shining.

"It felt right." I reply, turning onto my side to face him. I rest my palm on his cheek, moving closer until our lips touch. "You were right, by the way." I murmur against his mouth.

"About what?" He pulls back enough to see my face. His brows are drawn as his eyes dart back and forth between mine.

"I'm yours."

Chapter 23
Ronnie

Six weeks later...

Things with Felix have been...stellar. We've spent almost every night together since the night six weeks ago when I told him I was his. It's honestly been a whirlwind. I was afraid of moving too fast and getting hurt, but as time went on, I stopped fighting it. This thing between us feels inevitable.

I haven't seen the masked man since the police officer showed me his photo the night of my birthday party. And I'm glad for it. Whatever that was with the masked stranger is over, and I don't miss it one bit. Felix keeps me on my toes enough without some masked stalker pestering me. I'll always wonder who he was, but I guess I'll never know, and I can live with that.

Work has been steady, and since Leon Clark there haven't been any vigilante killings. Whoever was behind them just...stopped. Which either means the vigilante moved, was arrested, or killed. I mean it could also be that there haven't been any vile beings in need of slaughtering, but that would be a stretch. There are always sick pieces of shit in the world.

I do find it odd that the masked stalker and the vigilante disappeared around the same time. And it's super strange that the masked man seemed so obsessed with me and then disappeared off the face of the earth. Could they have been the same person? Possibly. But I'll have to put that one in the big book of 'Things I'll Never Have The Answers To'.

Tonight's a big night. Felix has been asking me to meet his parents for weeks now, and I agreed to attend the Winter Ball they throw at one of the buildings they own. It's apparently a charity event, the proceeds being donated to a nonprofit who supports survivors of abuse. It's a really great cause, and apparently his family has been hosting this event for the past four years.

To say I'm nervous would be an understatement. Gwen has become an integral part of our friend group, joining every girl's night Leah and I have. I'm not worried about Gwen, but I am worried about meeting *the* Mr. Andreas Drakos and Mrs. Elsie Drakos. Rich socialites who own a large portion of the city. Philanthropists who donate large sums to charity, and apparently Mrs. Drakos spends her free time volunteering around Westmound at various charities and nonprofits. Parents to my boyfriend. So basically, they're this amazing power couple who have graced the earth with their good deeds and God-like offspring.

Felix has told me that it's nothing to worry about. They'll love me, he said. They're down to earth and super cool, he said. But I think he forgets my track record with previous parental figures. Being bounced around to foster home after foster home made me see that I'm not exactly 'bring home to the fam' material. The only positive parental figures I've ever known are the Crawfords and my own deceased parents. All the other ones I've met were severely disappointed in me as a person. And that's the kind of shit that changes you forever, making you question your worth for the rest of your life.

Luckily Felix, Sav, Leah and Gwen will all be there as buffers for me. And I can always play the 'migraine' card if things get too intense and I need to bolt. Leah and I have made it a point to spend one night a week together, just us girls, since both of our relationships are growing more serious. She spends as much time with Sav as I do with Felix. They've hit it off, and honestly, they're so fucking cute together. Sav attends the Winter Ball every year, and this year he asked Leah to be his date.

Leah and I both found these beautiful vintage gowns at a secondhand store to wear tonight. Leah's is very flapper-esque, dark purple with fringe, lace, and a mermaid fit. Mine is more 1950's Audrey Hepburn, black with a fluttery cap sleeve top and full skirt. We took time doing each other's hair, both of us sporting elegant updos. I'm going without my signature black lipstick tonight, opting for a more subdued blush tone, to impress the parents.

I feel glamourous, like I'm about to walk a red carpet at some type of Hollywood film award ceremony. Seeing myself in this fit and flare gown, hugging my waist and accentuating my curves in all the right places, I feel confident. And hopefully that's enough of a boost to help me not make a fool of myself in front of the future in-laws.

Oh, woah, where did that come from? I'm getting ahead of myself. Future in-laws? Felix and I haven't even said I love you. I'm not even sure where that thought stemmed from. Sure, I've thought about what it would be like to become Mrs. Felix Drakos, but not seriously. We've only been together officially for six weeks, well according to me that is. If you were to ask Felix, he would tell you that we've been together since our first date.

Leah and I stand in the vestibule of our apartment building, waiting for Felix and Sav to pick us up. I'm scrolling through my phone when I hear Leah gasp.

"Uh, no fucking way!" She squeals.

It startles me so much that I drop my phone and hear a crack as it hits the tiled entryway.

She winces, "Shit…sorry!" Leah bends to pick it up, turning it to look at the now shattered screen. "Fuck, babe. I'll buy you a new one. But look, I think that limo is for us!" She jumps from foot to foot, handing my broken phone over to me before pointing to the road outside of our building.

"It's fine…I needed a new phone anyway…" I grumble. Not that I can really afford one right now. Even though we live in a shithole, it's still expensive in the city. And since I'm still new to my field, it's not like I'm raking in the dough. Buying a new phone will be a huge setback, and one I know Leah can't afford either. I swipe at the screen, trying to see if it still works at all, and luckily it does. Although I end up slicing my finger on the shattered glass.

"Fuck." I hiss, sucking my bleeding thumb into my mouth.

"Hey, gorgeous." I hear Felix's deep voice croon. He steps into me, and I look up at his beautiful face. "What happened?" He grabs my hand, examining my thumb.

"It's my fault. I spooked her and she dropped her phone." Leah admits.

"Ah shit. Cut yourself on the screen?" Felix asks, pulling my hand up to his face. "I don't think there's any glass in the cut, so you should be okay."

He kisses the cut gently, as if trying to heal it with a magic kiss.

"I'll be fine." I blush. "You look fantastic by the way." I look Felix up and down, taking in the way his suit clings to his muscles. My heels bring my height closer to his level, but I still have to get on my tippy toes to brush a kiss across his cheek. "You're fucking sexy in that suit." I whisper.

He pulls back and winks at me before threading his fingers through mine.

"We should get going, can't be late to my own families' party." He pulls me along with him, and I can't help but check out his delicious ass in his tight suit pants. God, this man is *divine*.

The three of us slide into the limo, where Sav is waiting for us with a bottle of champagne.

"You ladies ready to party?" Sav asks, waggling his eyebrows with a stupid grin.

"Guys, this is insane? A limo?!" Leah can't contain her excitement.

This is a first for both of us. Not only are we going to a charity ball where the cities' rich, powerful elite will be, but we're going to be arriving in a fucking limousine? I've never really cared about money or power, but I have to admit that it feels pretty freaking awesome to be treated like royalty tonight.

Sav pops the cork on the champagne, pouring the fizzy drink into flutes to hand to each of us.

I take a sip of mine with a shudder. Oof, that's dry as fuck. I don't believe anyone really likes champagne, they just drink it to be 'fancy'.

"Yikes. That's ummmm…" Leah smacks her lips after taking a drink. "I'm just gonna say it…champagne blows."

The four of us burst into a fit of laughter, all agreeing that champagne isn't our drink of choice.

"I've never felt as thirsty as I do after taking a sip of that. It literally evaporated the saliva out of my mouth." I'm joking, somewhat. My throat does feel significantly drier than before I had the champagne. "Still gonna drink it though. I need something to calm my nerves."

"Baby, please." Felix wraps his arm around my waist, tugging me closer to him on the bench seat. "Tonight will go great. My parents are excited to meet you. In fact, they're ecstatic that I'm finally bringing a girl to meet them."

"Yeah, Ronnie." Sav reassures me. "Elsie was starting to worry that Felix would never find someone to get serious with. She was about to auction him off for this charity event, just to drum up some interest!"

"Fuck you, Sav. She was not." Felix grimaces.

"She totally was." Sav leans in and whispers.

"So, Leah and Sav, when are you meeting each other's parents?" I butt in, trying to steer the topic away from me and Felix.

"Well, Sav has already met mine." Leah chimes in cheerfully.

"And my parents aren't worth my girl's time." Sav says darkly.

"What?! When did Sav meet your parents? And why wasn't I invited?" I pout. "I would've loved seeing that shit."

"A couple of weeks ago. You were too busy with Lix to tag along." Leah counters.

"Jake and Darcy lovvveeeddd me. I was the highlight of the evening." Sav laughs.

"No fucking way." I raise an eyebrow. "Jake Crawford has never liked any person Leah has brought home. There's no way in hell he liked you. Keep dreaming." I'm not saying this to be a dick, either. Jake is notorious for scaring off every person Leah has ever dated. She's his little princess and no one has ever been good enough. I like Sav, but I can't imagine Jake putting away the torch and pitchfork for him.

"It's true!" Leah's blue eyes are wide and animated when she speaks. "I was shocked. My dad has never liked anyone, except for me, my mom and Ronnie. It was…kind of twilight zoney. He even invited Sav over to watch football and have a beer with him sometime."

My jaw hits the floor. I'm happy for them, really. I never thought I'd see the day when Leah's partner got her father's approval. I thought she might end up being a lonely spinster with fourteen cats. And not by any choice of her own, mind you.

Leah is a fucking catch, but her parents are very protective of her.

"Well now you two can never break up, because if you do I think Jake will be devastated. He'll never let Leah date again. So, I guess it's time to start planning your wedding." I quip.

Leah laughs awkwardly, brushing off my comment, but a flicker of some unidentified emotion crosses Sav's face before he schools it back into a smile. Hmmm…interesting.

The limo comes to a stop, and I can hear a commotion outside. The door closest to the building opens up, and the driver peeks in.

"We have arrived." He announces, stepping out of the way to let us out.

My heart begins thumping, and my fingers shaking as I grip my clutch with an iron grasp. Felix slides out first, reaching his hand back into the limo to help me out. I stand on shaky feet as he wraps his arm around my waist and begins walking me toward the building. There is literally a red carpet on the walkway from the limo to the door way. And there are actual paparazzi photographing us as we make our way to the building.

"Umm...I didn't realize there would be a literal red carpet and paparazzi..." I hiss at Felix, feeling completely out of my element. It's one thing to attend an event like this, but another altogether to have it be high profile enough for fucking paparazzi!

"Sorry." Felix cringes. "I thought it would be better if you didn't know ahead of time. I didn't want you stressing about it."

I plaster a fake smile to my face, sucking air through my nostrils and forcing it through my teeth. I'm not sure if it's better to be surprised or not, but we're here now.

"Mr. Drakos! Can I get a picture of you and your date?" One of the paps calls out to us.

Felix looks at me questioningly, silently asking if it's okay. I hate getting my picture taken, I always have. Well, not always. But the day my parents were murdered, we took family photos for the first time. It wasn't something we did because it was an extra expense we couldn't afford, but my mom had really wanted a nice set of pictures. So, she scrounged up enough money to pay a professional photographer. The three of us got dolled up, dressed in our nicest clothes, and took family pictures in the fall leaves.

Later that night my entire world was shattered when a man broke in and terrorized our family, killing my parents and leaving me in their blood. Since then, I've been wary of photos, and a bit superstitious, I guess. I know that there's absolutely no way that getting our pictures taken as a family let to our demise, but it's a memory that sticks with me.

The thought of taking a photo with Felix has me panicking. Especially one that's as 'professional' as this. A selfie is one thing, but the idea of having a photographer do it sends me into a tizzy. Felix looks down at me, and it's like he can see me spiraling. His hand rubs calming circles on my back while pushing me forward towards the door.

"Sorry, not tonight." He calls back to the waiting paps.

We step inside the lobby and I relax just a little.

"Are you okay, Veronica?" Felix whispers in my ear.

"No…I…I'm sorry. I don't do pictures…" I mutter.

Felix stops and wraps his hands around the sides of my neck, using his thumbs to tilt my chin up. "It's okay. No biggie. I'm sorry that I didn't know."

"You couldn't have known…it's just that the only time we took photos as a family was the day my parents died. I don't do professional pictures because of that." I explain quickly, feeling silly. It seems so fucking stupid saying it out loud. A grown ass woman not being able to have her picture taken?

"I'm sorry, baby. Now that I know we can avoid it in the future, okay?" Felix assures me, pressing a sweet kiss to my lips.

I nod, feeling reassured because he didn't judge me. Even though I felt embarrassed by it, Felix didn't make a big deal. He understood and didn't push. Another piece of my heart tethers itself to him, growing more attached to this man by the second. If he breaks my heart, I might die.

We walk into the ballroom of the Drakos Hotel in downtown Westmound. The room is opulent, with vaulted ceilings, marble floors, and glittering chandeliers. Round tables are placed around the room, with a small area for dancing left open. Beautiful white floral centerpieces are on each table, and candelabras decorate the walls. It looks like it's straight from a fairytale. This hotel is the most upscale of the ones Felix's family owns, and it's always the home of the Winter Ball.

People dressed to the nines mingle throughout the open space, laughing and talking. A couple stands next to the doorway, and when they see Felix and I their faces light up. The man is tall and broad, with full dark hair and dark eyes. The woman is petite, with wavy red hair that falls down her back. Felix steps up to the woman and pulls her into a hug.

"Hi, ma." Felix kisses her on the cheek. He towers over her and has to lean down to do it. "Hey, dad."

The woman pats his cheeks and pulls away, peering around Felix to look at me.

"This is my girlfriend, Veronica Woods." Felix steps aside, gesturing to me with a smile.

"Mr. and Mrs. Drakos, I'm glad to finally meet you." Should I curtsey? Is that too much? I feel like standing here with a smile plastered to my face isn't the right thing to do. My body feels like it needs to be doing something.

"Please, sweetheart, call me Elsie." Mrs. Drakos' green eyes sparkle. Felix has the same eyes. Felix resembles his father in every aspect except his eyes. "I'm so happy to meet you." She pulls me into a hug, squeezing tightly before letting go and looking at me with pure joy on her face.

Mr. Drakos steps forward, reaching out his hand to shake mine. "Andreas. I'm glad Felix is finally letting us meet you." His accent is faint, but still has a tinge of Greek.

"It's my pleasure. This place is stunning, thank you for having me." My eyes keep getting drawn around the room to all the different people and sights. It's extravagant, and everyone at the event is the definition of elegance.

"This is my favorite building of ours. It's might be a little over the top, but I love it." Elsie says. "Perfect for a wedding." She winks at me and nudges Felix's side.

"Elsie, don't push them. You know how Felix is, he'll do the exact opposite of what we say." Andreas scolds her with a smirk.

A throat clears, revealing that Sav and Leah snuck in behind us at some point. Their timing is impeccable, breaking the sudden tension from Elsie's wedding comment.

"Oh! Sav, it's so nice to see you. And who's this beauty you brought with you?" Elsie pulls Sav into a hug too, patting his back.

"Hey, ma. This is Leah Crawford. She's my girlfriend, and Ronnie's best friend." Sav proudly introduces Leah. It's sweet, how excited he is to show her off.

"Look at you two, so cute together. Now Sav, you better not break this poor girl's heart." Elsie taps her foot, crosses her arms, and raises her brow.

"Don't worry, Elsie. If anything, she'll probably break mine." Sav replies, admitting how smitten he is with Leah.

Sav and Andreas shake hands, and then Sav drags Leah off towards the bar, leaving the four of us still standing near the entrance to the ballroom.

"Well, son, behave and make sure to show Veronica a good time." Andreas pats Felix's shoulder, shoots me a smile, and then pulls Elsie away from us to continue greeting the guests that are steadily entering the event.

"Come on, pretty girl. Let's get you a drink." Felix places a hand on the small of my back, leading us over to the bar where Leah and Sav wait for their drinks.

We sit at our table, waiting for the event to get started. Now that I've met the parents, I feel a lot more relaxed. I expected them to be intimidating and judgmental, but they both were actually very sweet. And they seem happy that Felix has a girlfriend that he's willing to introduce to his family.

The lights of the ballroom dim, and a hush falls over the crowd as Andreas takes the stage.

"Good evening, and welcome to the fourth annual Winter Ball!" Applause breaks out in response to Mr. Drakos' greeting.

"Thank you all for being here. As you all know, this charity event is near to the hearts of the Drakos family. With your help, we have been able to raise over five million dollars over the last four years, and the proceeds have gone to a different charity organization each year that supports survivors of abuse. This year's charity organization is RAINN, the Rape, Abuse & Incest National Network. We'd be honored if you would donate, anything you can, to support this cause. You'll find donation forms at each of your tables, as well as a box to deposit them in. With that being said, dinner is served!" Cheers echo throughout the ballroom, as well as thunderous clapping.

"It's amazing that your family does this each year." My head is on a swivel as I look around the crowded room. Every seat is full.

"It wasn't even a choice after what happened to Gwen." Felix replies darkly, seemingly lost in his thoughts.

I reach out, placing my hand on his thigh, which startles him out of his daze. "Gwen?"

"Fuck." He runs his hand down his face, shaking his head. "Forget I said that. Gwen would kill me if she knew I said anything. It's not my place."

"Hey, it's okay. I'll forget about it, and I won't mention it to her. Where is she, by the way?"

"She doesn't come to this event. Every year my parents try to convince her, but it's too painful for her." He replies quietly.

"Oh." Was Gwen abused by someone?

"That open bar is top fucking notch!" Leah chirps, falling into the seat next to me, not sensing the uneasy air around me and Felix.

"Well, the more boozed up the people are, the more they donate." Sav chuckles.

Wait staff begin bringing out the salads, setting one in front of each guest. The entire dinner Felix is withdrawn, his eyes dark and stormy. Leah and Sav are so wrapped up in each other they don't seem to notice the tense atmosphere.

I'm sad that Gwen didn't come, but from what I've gathered she suffered through something traumatic, and this event seems like a glaring reminder of that. I wonder if that's why she secludes herself so much. She mentioned that she didn't have any friends besides Leah and I, and she doesn't date either. It seems like a lonely lifestyle, but I can't imagine what she went through. It obviously still impacts her. I hope that Leah and I are able to bring her out of her shell as time goes on.

Chapter 24
Felix

Have you ever felt like you were drowning? And no matter how hard you kick your legs and try to swim, you're just sinking deeper into the water not making any progress? Sometimes you might even feel like someone or something is attached to you and dragging you down.

That is how I feel every year on this fucking day. Ever since that day five years ago when Gwen stumbled home in the middle of the night, beaten, broken, and abused. That December night was the worst night of my entire fucking life, and I wasn't even the one who was hurt. Seeing my baby sister battered broke my heart and spurred me on to become the vigilante killer I am today.

The event is for a good cause, and I know that the money we make doing it helps countless people, but it's still a brutal reminder every year of what Gwen endured. She can't stand coming to the event, wondering who knows the gory details of what happened to her, and searching the crowd for the faces of pity pointed at her. Not that there would be any, seeing as my parents were very good at keeping Gwen's identity under wraps during the investigation.

Gwen has confided in me that she's felt disgusting since that night, and that's part of the reason she doesn't have much of a social life. She's terrified that people will judge her or abandon her if they find out. She's been through therapy, and has worked really hard, but can't get past the idea that what happened was not her fault. One of the multiple problems with our society is that the victim is often shamed and blamed, when it should be the perpetrator that is shamed. But God forbid we ruin the 'bright future' of a young man who 'made a mistake'. It's fucking sick.

That's another reason I do what I do. When society and the law make the wrong call, it needs to be corrected. And we all know that no one likes to admit when they're wrong, and they often overcorrect and go in the exact opposite direction, digging themselves further into the pit that they created.

I thought that the event this year might be different. I hoped that having Ronnie by my side would make me feel less…hopeless. And I hate that I'm being so distant and cold to her right now, but I can't pull myself out of the ocean that's drowning me.

Dinner has come and gone, and I barely touched my food. I sit there, looking down at the chocolate torte, poking the tines of my fork into it over and over as it crumbles into a mess. I can tell that Ronnie is worried about me, feeling her eyes on me.

I feel so fucking weak and worthless. Sure, I killed the fucker who raped my sister, and I've killed countless other abusers, but no matter how many I wipe of the planet, more show up. It's a disease that will never be eradicated. And that thought consumes me. Not to mention I've been slacking, spending all of my free time with Ronnie instead of out there hunting and killing.

But it's not Ronnie's fault. I want to spend all my waking seconds with her. What makes me feel even shittier is that I don't regret for a second stepping back from my masked alter ego to spend my time with Ronnie. But part of my mind tells me that this thing rests on my shoulders, and because I'm choosing her over it, I'm letting everyone down.

But you know what? Why should it be me who rids the world of these pests? Why does it rest on my shoulders? The law should be doing its job. Society should be doing better. I've spent five fucking years chipping away at my soul with each monster I kill. Five fucking years of my life that I will never get back. And for what? I've saved people from torment, but there's always going to be more to go around. Why do I have to give up my soul to save everyone else? Don't I deserve to be saved too?

These last six weeks I've really been thinking about my future. I want Veronica to have all of me, well, whatever's left after the things I've done. I don't want to leave her to go hunting predators. While I've been lucky thus far, who's to say I'll continue with my fortune? What happens if I'm caught? Or if one of my prey gets the upper hand and takes me out? I can't leave Ronnie behind.

So, I'm choosing Veronica Woods, and I'm choosing me. I have one hunt left, and then I'm hanging up the mask. I've been digging, and what Ronnie said earlier today about hating photographs supports a theory I've been chewing on. I'm almost positive I've identified the murderer who took her parents away. In fact, I've even located the fucker. And he happens to still live in Westmound. I just need to find the perfect time to capture him.

The thought of ending his miserable life begins pulling me out of my ocean of hopelessness. But what really brings me back to the surface is Ronnie's small hand intertwining with mine on my thigh. Her thumb rubs circles on the back of my hand, and her fingers squeeze mine tightly, like she's afraid that I'll float away if she lets go. And she's right, without her, I'll cease to exist. I'll have nothing left of myself without her.

I squeeze her hand back, leaning over to press a kiss to her cheek. "I'm sorry." I whisper.

She looks at me with sadness, but also adoration. "It's okay, Felix. I'm here for you."

Veronica Woods is all I need.

Chapter 25
Ronnie

We're both exhausted by the time we reach Felix's penthouse. I don't have a very large social battery, and attending the charity ball drained it. Before Felix, I would crawl into bed alone and scroll mindlessly through my phone or watch one of my comfort movies to recharge. But something strange happened when Felix and I started dating. Instead of needing alone time and space to recharge my battery, I began craving spending my time with him. Being with Felix is better than any time I've ever spent alone. He makes me feel safe, happy, and cozy.

After I peel my gown off, I find one of Felix's t-shirts and pull it on. We both prefer it when I wear his shirts to sleep. He helps pull down my hair from the half up-do it's in, gently combing through the strands with his fingers. My heart flutters at the feel of his fingertips rubbing my scalp. Neither of us has voiced it yet, but this feels like love. It has to be. I've never felt anything remotely like it, until Felix.

Once my long waves are sufficiently combed through, I pull back the covers on Felix's king sized bed and crawl underneath. I basically live at his penthouse now, and anytime I have to sleep at my own apartment my heart aches with loneliness. I just sleep better with Felix's comforting presence near me, knowing that at any point I can roll over and snuggle into him. And I haven't had my recurring nightmare once while sleeping with him. He protects me, even from my own mind.

Felix slides in next to me, wearing only his black boxers. He turns on his side, pulling me so our chests touch. His arms wrap around my waist, and I dangle one of my legs over his. Being tangled in him is one of my favorite places. Felix's woody scent surrounds me.

His lips are pressed into the top of my head when he murmurs "I'm sorry about tonight, Veronica."

"You don't need to—"

"No, please let me finish, baby." His voice is hoarse, like he's holding back tears. "I hate this fucking day, Ronnie. I hate that my parents throw this huge ball, as if it's in honor of what Gwen went through. I know that's not their intention, they're trying to help others in the way that Gwen wasn't. But every year it fucking kills me. And the fact that Gwen can't face our family or the event just proves that we shouldn't be doing this. Why does it have to be a huge affair? My parents could easily raise the money without the ball, or even fucking donate to their goddamn charities themselves. The only thing that gives me solace is that the bastard who hurt my sister is dead. But even in death he tortures her and I can't do a fucking thing to help." Felix cracks on the last word, and I feel the wetness of his tears on the top of my head.

I breathe in shakily, desperately wanting to console Felix, but not knowing the right words to say. There probably aren't even any right words for this. All I can do is cuddle closer to him, pressing my face into his neck.

"My family won't even speak the fucker's name." Felix is vulnerable, on the verge of breaking as he whispers his truth. "It's as if saying it out loud might summon him back from the dead. He doesn't deserve to keep infiltrating our thoughts. He doesn't deserve my sister's mind, heart, or soul, and yet even in death he fucking has her vise grip. It's been five shitty years, and he's still wrapped around all of us, suffocating us."

"Felix…I'm sorry. I don't know what happened, but I'm so fucking sorry." My own eyes well with tears, reacting to the pain in his voice and the tension in his body.

"Gwen is a year younger than me." Felix sighs. "We were always close, she was one of my best friends. We had each other's backs, but I let her down. I moved away, wanting to go to college in New York. She stayed here, attending Westmound University. I should've fucking stayed here, been here to protect her. But I wanted to get away from my family and this life, just for a while, to experience the world on my own. I wanted to be somewhere where my last name didn't determine my worth. What a fucking mistake. Because I wasn't here for her, our entire lives were turned upside down. Gwen will never be the same, and it's all my fucking fault." He whispers into my hair, but it's almost like he's talking to himself and I'm just here as a witness.

"When Gwen was eighteen, she came out to our family and introduced us to her first girlfriend, Savannah." Felix is lost in memory. "It was a really big deal for her, and we were all so proud of her. Gwen hadn't dated before Savannah, and my parents were happy that she was with someone she liked enough to bring home. They dated for a year, and everything seemed to be going really well, until the night of the attack. Gwen and Savannah were at a frat party when they got into a fight. Gwen was a wild child, loved anything social, and definitely loved to party. Savannah was a quieter type, wanting to stay home and watch movies.

"Anyway…Gwen wanted to stay longer, but Savannah was done and wanted to go home. Gwen was mad that Savannah always wanted to dip out of things early, or skip altogether. Savannah was mad that Gwen always wanted to go out and party. Their social levels just were not in sync. So, Savannah ended up leaving the frat, and Gwen stayed. One of the frat boys, a star football player who thought he was hot shit, cornered Gwen once she was alone. He overheard the fight and told Gwen that he could make her feel better and forget all about Savannah. The guy told her that after she 'tasted his cock' she wouldn't be lesbian anymore." Felix sounds disgusted, and I don't fucking blame him.

Nausea roils in my stomach as he continues the story. I'm putting together the puzzle pieces and I don't like where this is going.

"Gwen pushed him away and decided to leave the party at that point. She was too drunk to drive, so she started walking home. What she didn't realize is that the fucking frat boy decided to follow her. He hit her over the head, knocking her down, before dragging her into an alleyway. That's where he…where he…" Felix lets out an anguished sob, choking on his words.

I pull back from him, wrapping my hands around his cheeks and forcing his eyes on mine. "It's okay. You don't need to finish."

This man who has been protecting me, saving me, loving me, has been carrying this burden. His whole family has, but he thinks it's his fault. I feel my heart cracking in my chest.

"Felix." When I start to speak, he shutters his eyes. "There is no way you could've known what would happen to Gwen. And even if you stayed here and went to Westmound U, it still would've happened. What, do you think you would've followed her to every party, every class, shadowing every single second of Gwen's life? No. There's nothing you could have done. What happened to Gwen was not on you. The fault lies solely with the motherfucker who hurt her."

"I know…but…" Tears slip down his black lashes.

"No buts, Felix. It. Was. Not. Your. Fault." I rub his tears away with my thumbs before leaning in to plant a soft kiss against his quivering lips. "And

I'm glad the shithead is dead. I hope he fucking suffered."

"He did." Felix responds quietly.

"Good." I push on his chest, rolling him onto his back. Straddling his hips, I lie down on his chest, listening to his heart beat. "Thank you for trusting me enough to tell me." I whisper into his skin.

His arms envelop me, cocooning me in his warm embrace. We lie like that, not saying anything, just listening to each other's breaths in the air. Slowly Felix's breathing deepens, and I know that he's drifted off to sleep, but I don't move. I fall asleep on his chest with his arms safely keeping me.

Chapter 26
Felix

The Photographer. That's what the media calls him, Arnold Burke. Of course, no one has put it together that it's Arnold Burke behind the nickname, not until I pieced the puzzle together. The thing about Arnold is that he wised up and stopped shitting where he slept. His last kills in Westmound were Erin and Dean Woods, Ronnie's parents. After that he changed murder locations every couple of years, making it nearly impossible to track his movements. Crossing jurisdictions complicates the case, although the FBI has been trailing him for years now. Obviously doing at shitty fucking job at it though.

What confirmed his identity for me was Ronnie mentioning that the same day her parents were murdered they had family portraits taken. I'd known about Arnold for a while, but he hasn't killed in Westmound in so long I dropped him off my radar. I only hunt in my immediate area, not wanting the fuss of traveling around the country preying on monsters. There are enough here to have kept me plenty occupied.

Like I said before, this will be my last hunt. My last hurrah as V, the masked vigilante. I'm fucking tired. All I want is to settle down peacefully with my girl and just live. Ronnie deserves the world, and I'm going to give it to her. I can't do that if I'm constantly distracted by the hunt. I'm even considering selling my cleanup and delivery business. Maybe it's time to move on from surrounding myself with death and finally fucking live.

I'd be lying if I said I wasn't nervous about today. I might have done something morally questionable. Okay, what I did is definitely fucked up. But you have to understand my point of view. I need to wipe the slate clean with Ronnie. I don't want our future to be built on deceit. So, I had to kidnap her, bring her to my barn, tie her up, and have her witness The Photographer's death, obviously. And then I'll do my grand reveal, admitting that I was her masked stalker all along. I need to show her the truth, and bring closure to her once and for all.

She will most likely be livid, on account of my gaslighting and all. But I'm positive with time and the application of my endless charm she'll forgive me. I love her, and I know she loves me. I can see it every time I look into her beautiful hazel eyes. I've got her, hook, line and sinker. That's the phrase, right? I've never been fishing in my fucking life, so don't yell at me if I got that wrong.

Annnnywayyyy. Back to the matter at hand. Arnold 'The Photographer' Burke is strapped down to my metal table, knocked out by a hefty dosage of ketamine. I do regret having to inject Ronnie too, but I had to get her here and I doubt she would've come willingly. Veronica is tied to a wooden chair next to the table Burke is on.

I want to give her the opportunity to join me in ending Burke. I'd love it if she participated, getting her revenge on Burke. We could share this experience, bathing in his blood and washing away the past, starting anew. And I know that gore doesn't bother her, she's an autopsy tech for fucks sake. The only thing that might hold her back is her conscience. That pesky part of the human brain that tells you what's right and what's wrong, as if everything is black and white, and convinces you not to do something because it's immoral.

Either way, I'm here for her. If she can't bring herself to help, she will watch. I'll bear the burden for her. I would do anything for my little fox. I'll slay her enemies and dance in their blood and entrails if she wants me to. I'd fucking kill myself for her, if that's what she wanted.

A feminine moan drifts through the barn, signaling that the sedative I injected Ronnie with is wearing off. Her head lolls to the side, as if it's too heavy for her neck, and she's unable to do more than flutter her eyelids.

I slip a straw into the cold bottle of water I have prepared for her, making my way to her side. I run my thumb down her cheek, and then across her plump lower lip.

"Fe...lix?" She rasps.

"I'm here, baby." I brush her loose strands behind her ears, and tip her head back. "Here, drink some water."

Her tongue darts out, wetting her dry lips. I place the straw in her mouth, and she gently sips the cool water, her throat working to swallow it down.

"Where?" Her voice is less crackled, but still rough due to the dryness of her mouth and throat.

"An abandoned barn in the hills outside of the city."

"What?" As Ronnie's eyes open, she winces against the bright light I have hanging above Burke.

"This is my kill room." I state, my voice even and calm.

Her head whips to the side, and her eyes snap to my face, well as much as they can while still coming off of the sedative. They widen as she sees the goat mask, concealing my features. Ronnie's chest begins heaving, her breaths becoming frantic as she tries to move her arms and legs against the restraints. Tears drip down her face, panic taking hold of her.

I crouch in front of her, gently cupping her face with my hands. "Shhhh, baby, it's okay. Shhhh." I stroke my fingers over her wet cheeks, wiping away the wetness of her tears.

Ronnie whimpers, thrashing her head to get away from my touch. My heart aches at the sight. She's terrified of me.

"Are y-you going t-to hurt m-me?" She cries, hiccupping.

"No, sweetheart, not at all. I'm here to help you."

"H-help me?" Her eyes collide with mine, although I know she can't see them through my mask.

"Do you see the man behind me?" I move aside slightly, angling my body to give her a better view of Burke, who is still passed out on the table.

Ronnie nods.

"His name is Arnold Burke. He's a serial killer, known as The Photographer."

Her gaze darts between me and Burke, confusion lining her features.

"He's the man who hurt you and destroyed your family." I explain.

Ronnie's face scrunches up. She narrows her eyes and tries to focus on Burke, examining his face.

"He killed my parents?" She whispers.

"Yes." I nod. "He's a serial killer. A photographer who targets families with an only child, taking pictures of the family and then murdering the parents. He leaves the child alive, but blindfolds them so they never see his face."

The color drains from Ronnie's face. "That's what he did to me. But why?"

"His parents were murdered in a similar manner when he was young, with the exception of the photography aspect. Only he can tell us for sure, but I think he was angry, lonely, and wanted to make others feel the way he felt." It's the only explanation that makes sense.

Some people, like Ronnie, rise above their situation and take their life in a positive direction. And others, like Arnold, use it to justify unleashing pain upon others. I guess Arnold and I are alike in that way, using the past as an excuse to exact revenge. And while I take it out on the filth of the world, he takes it out on innocent families.

"I don't understand, Felix." Ronnie's voice is tinged with pain, wrath, and fear all at once.

"What don't you understand, baby?"

"Why am I here? Why is he here? And why are *you* here, wearing *that* mask. Don't lie to me again, I can't fucking take it. Tell me the truth." She spits at me, rage winning over the other emotions coursing through her. Her anger is what brought her out of the drug haze she was in before.

"You were right the whole time, Veronica." I sigh, the moment of truth upon us. Will Ronnie accept this, or will she try to run? "I have always been the goat masked man. I used it as an excuse to follow you, get closer to you. From the moment I saw you at Terrance's office I knew you were it for me. You became my greatest obsession and my greatest weakness. But the night of your birthday, I took things too far. I'd never shown my mask to anyone, always hunting in the shadows. But that night when Micah…" I growl his name. "When he threatened Leah, I lost it. I love you, and by extension I love her. Obviously not in the same way, I see her as a friend and a sister…but you…you're everything. My entire universe."

Ronnie begins crying again, but this time they're tears of anger and anguish. I knew she would have a negative reaction to the truth, but I expected her to be hurt, not pissed. She didn't even react to me telling her I love her for the first time.

"You fucking stalked me? Broke into my house? Fucked me? And then you gaslighted me. Making me feel crazy and stupid for trusting a masked stranger, when you were the stranger all along?!" She's screaming at me now, her face contorted and red with fury.

"Yes, I did. I'm not sorry about it either. We both liked it, and you know it. You craved the danger and unknown. I only gave you what you wanted, no actually, what you fucking needed." I'm getting angry now, pacing in front of her. "Fuck! We don't have time for this, Veronica. Burke will be awake soon."

"I don't give a fuck, let him wake up! I deserve the truth, no matter how long it takes." Ronnie seethes.

I crash to my knees in front of Ronnie. "You're right, baby. I'm sorry." I reach my hand out to touch her chin, but she jerks her head away. "Five years ago, Gwen was beaten, brutalized, and raped. The fucker who did it left no traces of evidence, and it was her word against his. And unfortunately, the justice system believed him over Gwen. He was never arrested, nothing. They let him free, not even a fucking slap on the wrist. He broke her that night. And no matter how hard she works, she's still fucking broken, even though the guy is long dead. I took justice into my own hands, killing the piece of shit who killed my sister's spirit. The fucker who took her soul. I made him suffer, and then dumped him like the trash he was. But it wasn't enough."

Ronnie's anger has simmered slightly. She loves my sister, and hearing her story is hurting Ronnie.

"After that, I began hunting fuckers just like him." I exhale. It feels good to finally share this part of me with someone. I'm happy that it's Veronica. "When the law and society failed, I would take matters into my own hands. That is why I'm here, and that is why Burke is here. The law failed to catch him, and now it's my turn to right the wrongs."

"You're the vigilante killer." Her eyes are distant. She's piecing the puzzle together. "Mills, Giles, Clark..."

"Yes."

"And it was you who beat Micah in the parking lot." She doesn't say it as a question, but as a fact.

"Also, yes."

She nods absently, as if this is the most mundane thing she's ever heard. "And you want me here because..."

"Because you deserve peace and closure. You deserve to see the life drain from his eyes. And if you want, you deserve the chance to be the one to kill him." Ronnie's eyes focus once again, zeroing in on my face.

"Please, take off the mask. Let me see you." Her voice is small and pleading. "I need to see that it's really you."

I hesitate, but then nod. "Okay." I grip the chin of my mask, slipping it up and over my head. It falls to the ground beside us. Tilting my face up, I look at her, waiting for a response.

Chapter 27
Ronnie

The mask falls to the floor next to Felix. His black hair is tousled, falling across his forehead. His green eyes blaze like an inferno, ready to consume this entire barn in his heat. I want to reach out and touch his face, but my hands are bound to the sides of the chair. I need to feel him to know that this is real. This isn't a nightmare. He's so fucking beautiful, but he's also a monster. A monster that hunts other monsters. A monster who ends up saving the princess and making her fall in love with him, despite his flaws.

I should be afraid of him. But I'm not. I should be disgusted by his revelations. But instead, I'm falling deeper into his dark abyss. And that's what makes me so fucking angry, at myself, and at him. *This is so fucking wrong.* I shouldn't romanticize this killer before me. Yet, I can't help it. He's treated me better than anyone ever has. He's loved me, protected me, cared for me. Some of his choices are twisted and wrong, but doesn't the end justify the means? He's the vigilante. The one I praised countless times over the course of the last couple of months. Felix Drakos is doing what no one else dared. The first time he did it for the love of his sister. And this time, he's doing it for his love of me.

"Say something, Ronnie, please." Felix begs from his knees.

"I'm...I don't...I just..." I stutter, unable to get my thoughts to stop swirling in my brain long enough to form a coherent sentence.

"Burke is the last one, baby. I have to get rid of him, for you. But once he's dead, I'm done hunting. All I need is you. I want to give you every piece that's left of me. I want to love you, and give you the world." Felix reaches towards me, and this time I don't flinch away. "I love you, Veronica Woods."

I can see in his eyes that he means it. I nod. "Okay."

"Okay?" His face falls.

I didn't say it back. I can't. Not until he unties me and lets me go. "I need to make my own choice. I need to have the option to walk away."

Anger and hurt flash in his eyes briefly, before a mask of calm falls back over his face. "I will give you that choice. After we deal with Burke, I'll give you the option to walk away. Fuck, I'll give you the chance to kill me, if that's what you really want."

"No, Felix. The world wouldn't be the same without you in it. But I need you to give me the chance to make my own decision. It's the least you could do after lying to me for these past couple of months."

Movement behind Felix draws my attention. Burke must be waking up. The Photographer groans, his head moving slightly to the side.

Felix stands. "Do you want to do the honors?" He gestures behind him to Burke.

I shake my head. "No…I can't…Please, don't make me." It's not the idea of the gore that makes me hesitate. "I just can't bring myself to hurt someone, even if that someone destroyed my life."

"Okay. That's your choice. I will take this burden for you." Felix seems a little disappointed, but he shrugs it off and stalks over to the table.

Am I really going to let Felix kill a man for me? It's not like I'm forcing him to do this, he chose this. He wants to do this. But guilt still coils in my gut. If he does this, I'll owe him everything. Is that something I'm willing to do? What if he uses it against me? What if he uses it as an excuse to make me do things I don't want to? At the same time...he's not forcing me to participate. Although, he is forcing me to be present.

"Wait..." I call out to Felix as he rounds the table.

He pauses, standing by a rolling cart of miscellaneous tools and torture devices.

"Don't do this. I don't want to be in your debt."

Felix's eyes narrow. "There is no *debt*." He says the word with disgust, as if he can't believe that's what I'm thinking. "You won't owe me anything. I'm doing this for you because I want to, *need* to. I need you to be safe and feel peace. The trauma that this man caused has been clinging to your soul, and I want to cleanse it. After I do this, if you decide you don't want me...I'll let you go." His voice is pained on the last words. "But I want you to live the rest of your life knowing that the man who corrupted your innocence is dead. And he will never destroy another fucking family again. So, no, I won't wait. I'm doing this, whether you want me to or not. *I have to.*"

I nod, acquiescing. Felix has made up his mind. I have to trust that he won't hold this over my head. I have to believe that he will let me go if that's what I want after this. I don't know how I'll feel after watching him murder another human being. Will I be scared of him? Proud? Will my feelings for him grow even deeper? I don't fucking know. But we're both here, and he's doing this, and I'm watching it happen.

"Uhhhhhhhhh…" The Photographer groans, becoming more lucid.

I jolt in my seat, my heart racing. Suddenly, a thought pops into my head…how does Felix know this is actually the guy who killed my parents? Not only was I blindfolded, so I never saw him, but it was also so long ago that there's no way I'd be able to identify him by voice.

"Felix...how do you know it's him?" I hiss, as Burke keeps moaning and twitching on the table.

"Trust me." Is all Felix replies.

Felix stands at the head of the table, staring down at Arnold Burke as he slowly begins to wake. Any trace of kindness or love that was on Felix's face before is gone, replaced by malice and contempt. A scalpel glints in his hand. He gracefully flips it in the air once, making my heart stutter, before catching its handle.

Bending down, Felix's leather gloved hand pulls the skin of Burke's cheek taut. He raises the scalpel, and carefully, precisely, cuts one side of The Photographer's face from the corner of his mouth all the way to his ear, in a grim half smile. He pulls the other cheek, mirroring the cut. Nausea roils in my gut. I remember *everything* about that day. How could I ever fucking forget?

Images flash through my mind...

Chapter 28
Ronnie

The Day of the Murders...

It's a cool autumn day, a breeze swirling the fallen leaves into tiny tornadoes. Mom is so excited that we're doing family pictures today. She's always wanted to have 'a professional' take our pictures. Something to frame on the walls, besides my drawings and snapshots she's taken herself.

I'm wearing my Christmas dress. It's the nicest clothing I have, but this year it's a little tighter than last because I've been 'growing into a young woman', or so my mom says. It's dark red and velvety, with a poofy skirt and a white lacey collar. It makes me feel pretty, even though it's so tight across my chest that it's hard to breathe. My mom even shined my glossy black ballet flats, making them look almost new.

She curled my long black hair, and even fixed a big red bow in the back. Mom curled her hair too, but hers is a light brown and shoulder length. I got my thick black hair from my dad, and my green eyes from my mom. She looks pretty too, in her black dress and shiny shoes. My dad is wearing blue jeans and a black sweater.

We're at the park near my school, waiting for the photographer to come. Mom's smile is bright, her eyes shining with happiness. Dad isn't a fan of pictures, but for my mom and me he'd do anything. He's a really great dad. My parents are my favorite people on the planet. I might not have all the clothes and toys the other kids in my class have, but I think I still have the best life because of my family. Though, sometimes I wish I had a sister to play with. But my mom told me she can't have any more kids, and she calls me her little blessing. Mom and Dad had a son before me, but they said that he was in heaven and never came out of mom's belly.

"Mr. and Mrs. Woods?" A man calls out, striding towards us.

"Yes, that's us!" My mom replies cheerily.

"Are you the professional?" I ask. That's what my mom called him, the professional photographer.

The man laughs. "Yes, you could say that. Ready to get started?"

At first, it's exciting and fun to pose and take lots of pictures. But after a while my cheeks hurt from smiling, and my toes hurt from being bunched in my shoes. I don't complain out loud though, because my mom is so joyful and I don't want to hurt her feelings.

The camera whirrs once more. Click. "Okay, that was the last one." The photographer says. "I'll have your photos to you in a couple of weeks. It was a pleasure working with you all." He shakes dad's hand.

When we get home mom has me change out of my fancy dress right away, so I don't get it dirty. Dad makes my favorite dinner, buttered noodles with buttered toast. Mom and dad laugh over dinner. Someday I hope I have love like theirs.

After dinner we cuddle on the couch and watch TV together. One of our favorite shows to watch is 'America's Funniest Home Videos'. We watch together for a while, me sandwiched between mom and dad on the couch, before it's time for me to go to bed. Mom tucks me in and kisses me goodnight. I'm scared of the dark, so I have a nightlight that makes my ceiling look like it's covered in twinkling stars.

It feels like I just fell asleep when I'm startled awake by someone grabbing me and lifting me into their arms. I open my eyes but everything's dark and I can't see.

"Dad?" I ask.

"Shhhh…" The person says. It doesn't sound like my dad. He doesn't smell like my dad either.

"I can't see…" I whimper. I touch my eyes, and feel something covering them, a cloth. I try to pull it off my head, but the man holding me grips my wrists tightly in one of his large hands and holds them firm. "It hurts." I cry, sniffling and wincing at the pain of his tight grip.

The person doesn't respond. I hear his feet hitting our stairs as he takes me down into the main room of our house. The strange man tosses me onto the couch, and then ties my wrists and feet together.

The rope he uses is rough and scratchy, and it digs into my skin.

I hear my mom crying, and my dad trying to soothe her.

"Mom, dad?" I whisper.

"Shhhh, baby girl…it's okay…I promise it's okay…" My dad replies, trying to comfort me.

What's happening? I'm scared.

"Please, don't hurt us. Don't hurt my baby. Take anything you want." My mom pleads with the strange man.

"Please don't hurt us." The man mocks in a high pitched tone. "As if you could stop me, you little bitch." He growls.

His voice sounds familiar, but I don't know from where. I hear a loud thwack, followed by my mom sobbing. My dad shouts, yelling at the man for hitting her.

"Shut. The. Fuck. Up." The man spits. "Which of you wants to die first? Should I flip a coin?" He chuckles darkly.

"Why are you doing this!" My dad screams.

"Looks like it's going to be the father. Hope you're not queasy, mommy." He taunts.

I can't see anything, but I hear my parents weeping. This is a bad dream. This is the worst nightmare I've ever had. I'll wake up and mom will make me toast for breakfast, and then she'll take me to school. This is a dream. This is a dream. This is a dream.

The cries drag on for what feels like hours. I hear my dad grunting in pain, and my mom sobbing and begging the man to stop. A sickening squelch permeates the air, along with a gasp and a scream. My dad stops groaning, and my mom shrieks endlessly.

"Dean…no, no, no, no. Dean!" My mom's bawls are guttural and pained. She screams until her throat gives out and her breath leaves her lungs.

"Daddy?" I ask quietly, but he doesn't respond.

"Daddy's gone, little one." The strange man taunts in his dark and scary voice. "Mommy's turn."

My body shakes. I'm so scared, and my bladder releases all over the couch below me. The room smells like pee and something metallic. I can't see through the cloth, and I desperately want to know where my dad went.

Mom whines and howls now. The cloth covering my eyes is wet and heavy, sticking to my face as my tears soak it through. Mom sounds hurt and scared, and that makes this experience even worse. Mom and dad are the bravest people I know, and every time I'm afraid they make me feel better. But this time they aren't calming me, and I'm not waking up. Why haven't they woken me up from my dream yet? Why aren't they saving me?

I hear the strange man giggling, and the sound is so strange that it startles me. He laughs as I hear the sounds of gushing and tearing. My tummy hurts, and the smell of the room is making me feel sick. It smells even worse than it did a few minutes ago. It smells like one of the adults had an accident.

My mom wheezes, and then her sounds become silent. All I can hear is the sound of something dripping nearby, and the man's ragged breathing. Then I hear the whirr of a camera, and the clicking of a button. Over and over, echoing through the near silent house.

His heavy footsteps thud towards me. Is he going to hurt me too? The camera whirrs closer to me. And then I feel the brush of his breath against my cheek, and the warmth of his body as he leans down towards me. I feel something wet and warm touch my face, and I shrink back into the couch. The camera clicks again.

"Goodnight and farewell, little one." He doesn't say it in a menacing tone. His voice has calmed.

I hear his footsteps retreating, followed by the opening and closing of the front door. The silence is deafening. Will the man come back?

I sit, bound on the couch for hours, trembling and sitting in my own pee. I've tried calling out to mom and dad, but they didn't respond.

Sirens approach, and I've been on the couch long enough that I've realized this isn't a dream. The police sirens growing closer make it all the more real. I hear thumps and pounding on the front door.

"Police, open up!"

"Help me!" I shriek.

The thuds get louder as the house shakes. The wooden door splinters, and then bangs against the wall.

"Check the house!" One of the police commands.

"Hi, sweetheart." A woman must be standing in front of me, her voice close to my face.

The drenched blindfold slips off my face, and my eyes blink at the sudden light filtering through. It's morning now, sunlight streaming through the living room windows. The police woman stands in front of me, her kind blue eyes filled with sorrow and worry as she looks me over.

"Come on, sweetheart. Let's get you out of here." She croons.

Police swarm the house now, carefully walking through the house with odd white suits covering their uniforms. The woman reaches forward, untying the tight knots around my wrists and ankles. Her body moves to the side, and I see my parents across from me, sitting on two dining room chairs.

The buttered noodles I had last night come back up, vomit splashing the floor and the police woman's shoes. My uncontrollable sobs wrack through my body. Mom and dad are…hurt? No…it's worse than hurt. They aren't moving, and they're covered in blood. Their mouths are split into scary wide and bloody grins, and their eyes don't blink as they stare up at the ceiling.

"Oh, honey. I'm so sorry!" The police woman gasps, realizing I've seen my parent's dead bodies.

She lifts me in her arms and carries me outside.

Chapter 29
Ronnie

Bile claws its way up my throat, and I begin to heave. I thought that my parent's deaths desensitized me to gore, hell I work as an autopsy tech for fuck's sake, but seeing Burke carved up in the same manner they were is all too much. I squeeze my eyes shut, trying my hardest not to vomit. It's not even that I feel bad for him, he fucking deserves every slice Felix deals to his flesh. It's that when I look at him, I see my mom's vacant eyes, her slashed smile. My dad's slackened body strapped to a chair next to mom.

There's a part of me that truly believes the reason I'm interested in morbidity and gore is because my brain is trying to protective itself from the trauma of that night. It's trying to numb me to the horrors I've seen, making it something I see and live every day, *normalizing it*. It's not fucking normal. My entire life revolves around death. I've made it my goal to overcome the fear associated with dying by immersing myself in the idea of it. And honestly, I don't think I know how to truly *live* because of it.

I'm still stuck in the mindset of a child who witnessed the death of their parents. A scared child who never learned how to feel safe again. So instead of continuing to try, she gave up and embraced the uncertainty, the darkness, the fear. Made it her entire being.

I force my eyes open, and breathe in through my nose, out through my mouth. The metallic scent of blood lingers in the air. But I'm used to that scent. I'm used to seeing brutalized and carved up bodies. The only difference between Burke and my cadavers is that he's not dead yet. He will be though, Felix keeps pushing him closer to the veil between living and dead. It's a fine line that separates the two. At any moment, you could become one of them, one of the dead. Arnold Burke deserves death.

And even though my mind clings to the fear of that night, I push it aside. The Photographer can't hurt me anymore. Felix has him strapped down tightly, and there is no escape. I don't need to be afraid of him, the boogeyman from my nightmares. And my monster, Felix, is the reason that I'll finally be able to let this piece of me rest. He's here, slaughtering Arnold Burke, for me. He's ensuring that I'll never have to worry about the thief who took my family again. I have to watch the light fade from his eyes. I need to know that he's gone and that my parents have been avenged.

Arnold is quietly crying, still in a daze from being sedated. Blood drips down the gashes in his cheeks, pooling underneath his head. His eyes flutter, but he's not sober enough to open them all the way. He moans in pain between his sobs. I watch as Felix pulls out a stack of glossy papers from his pants pocket. Photos?

"Wake up, motherfucker." Felix shouts in Burke's ear, causing Arnold to startle, but he still doesn't have the lucidity to open his eyes fully.

Felix palms the scalpel again, slicing through the fabric of Arnold Burke's shirt until it opens and falls away, bearing his chest.

"Don't want to wake up yet, huh? That's okay…this'll help." Felix's voice takes on a calm, soothing tone, but underneath it is hidden malice.

Like he's holding a pencil, Felix begins tracing lines across The Photographer's chest. Starting just below his neck, he engraves letters into the skin, blood seeping from the newly opened wounds. The chair I'm tied to is on a pedestal, high enough for me to view everything that Felix does to Burke.

The first word, etched just below the hollow of Arnold's neck, reads 'Woods.'

'Jackson.'

'Gonzalez.'

'Castillo.'

'Rice.'

'Dunn.'

'Barton.'

The list goes on, each last name leaking blood over Burke's torso. As Felix cuts the last one into the skin above Burke's belt line, Arnold's eyes finally snap fully open, a scream of pain erupting from him.

Fifteen family names in total. Fifteen orphaned children, thirty adults murdered. When news breaks about Arnold 'The Photographer' Burke, will those children know peace? When Burke's body is found with the names carved into it, hopefully the authorities will connect the dots. Those children deserve vengeance as much as I do. And maybe some already know his connection to their tragedies, but I'm sure there are others like me who have been left in the dark.

"Good to see you finally joined us, Arnold." Felix sneers. "Let me introduce myself, I'm V, your executioner for this evening. And that beautiful specimen over there is my future wife. You might recognize her surname, 'Woods.'"

No comment on the 'future wife' thing. We can discuss that later, when Felix isn't in the process of murdering someone for me.

"What?" Arnold balks, confused. His eyes meet mine for the first time, widening as they do.

"Don't fucking look at her! You look at me." Felix growls, gripping the man's jaw harshly. "Was it so long ago that you need a refresher? Not to fear! That's why I brought these." Felix holds up the stack of photos, showing one at a time to Burke.

Whatever Arnold sees has him blanching.

"Ringing any bells? How about, Jackson? Dunn? Gonzalez?" Felix taunts.

"I don't know what you're talking about." Arnold spits.

"You know, you've been a very sneaky and naughty boy, Arnold Burke." Felix clicks his tongue, circling his prey. "Evading authorities for over a decade. Unfortunately for you, you picked my girl's family to fuck with. That was where you really fucked up, because no one gets away with hurting Veronica."

Arnold's eyes dart around, trying to track Felix as he stalks around the table.

"Help me." He pleads, glancing at me sideways again, trying to call on my sense of humanity. He doesn't realize that he's the one who took it from me.

Felix jumps on top of the table, straddling Arthur's body, and punches him in the jaw.

"Don't fucking look at her!" Felix roars, spittle flying as his fists land on Burke's face again.

Crunch. The sound of Burke's jaw cracking echoes in the air, followed by his shrieks of pain. His jaw hangs to the side, clearly displaced and broken. Felix beats down on Burke, losing control.

I should be scared and disgusted by Felix's outburst, but I can't convince myself to be. He's possessive and protective of me. And...I like it...no, it's more than like. I love it. I love him. Felix will do anything to protect me, and as he beats down on Burke, he proves it.

He's a beautiful monster.

Chapter 30
Felix

My chest rises and falls rapidly as I stare down at the mess I made of Burke's face. When I saw him looking at Ronnie for the second time, my vision went red and I flew into a rage. He doesn't get to look on her beauty, not after what he did to her. Fury floods my veins, and my red tinted vision homes in on the bastard's watery eyes.

"You don't get to fucking see her. She's MINE!" I bellow, picking up the scalpel that I dropped next to his head and driving it into his left eye.

Burke's eyeball squelches as the sharp blade plunges into it. I wrench the scalpel out, pulling his eyeball out will it. I push it off the end of the blade, and with a plop it lands on The Photographer's cheek. I make quick work of his other eye, ramming the blade in. This time when I pull out the scalpel, Burke's eye stays in its socket.

I can barely hear Arnold's howls over the rushing of blood in my ears. The room fades away as I look at his battered and bloody face. I'm taken back to the night that I took the life of Gwen's abuser. I destroyed his face much like I am doing to Burke. Each time I've killed over the last five years, I've felt a sense of justice and peace. But never anything as euphoric as when I destroyed Gwen's rapist. That same euphoria washes over me as I stare down at Burke. The ecstasy of knowing that I'm doing this for love. That I'm doing this for retribution, and doing so will protect the one thing that matters above all else, Ronnie.

I climb down from the table, ready to end this. Arnold Burke has lived too long, and it's time to put him behind us. All I want to do after tonight is spend the rest of my life protecting, caring for, and loving Veronica Woods. Soon to be Veronica Drakos, if things go my way.

"Puh-puh-puh…" Burke tries to beg, but his broken jaw is a serious hinderance.

"If you're trying to say please, know that it's too late. The moment you tortured and killed Erin and Dean Woods, it was too late for you. If you believe in God, pray now." My voice is a steel blade, cold and cutting.

Burke whimpers and cries, snot and saliva mixing with the blood on his face.

I glance up at Ronnie, checking to make sure she's okay and still with me. Even though she sees death every day, this situation is different. Seeing her parent's murderer taking his final breath is going to be an emotional roller coaster for her, and I need to be here to make sure she's alright. I need her to know that I'm here for her.

Ronnie's face is pale and covered in a sheen of sweat. Her breaths are heavy, but her eyes are filled with cool fury and determination as she looks at Burke.

"Veronica." I implore for her to look at me.

Her eyes lift to meet my gaze, and they soften slightly as she looks at me.

"Are you ready, baby?" I use a gentle voice with her, hoping to convey my love through my expression and tone.

She nods almost imperceptibly. "Do it." Ronnie rasps, her eyes trailing back down to stare at Burke.

"No…please, no." Burke wails, the words muddled.

I pick up the scalpel one last time, jamming it into one of his carotid arteries. Blood spurts out of the neck wound, slickening the tool and the table. Burke gurgles and chokes as his vital fluid steams out of his ruptured artery. Within minutes his body stops jerking, and the blood flow turns into a trickle. He's lax against the table, his eyes vacant and unseeing.

Ronnie and I wait in silence for a few minutes longer. We watch Burke, unblinkingly, to make sure that he's really dead. The blood has stopped flowing, and Arnold's body is pale. Gore leaks over the table, dripping onto the floor beneath. There's none left in him now.

"He's gone." I whisper, finally breaking the spell Ronnie and I were both under.

"I know." She murmurs, still unable to lift her eyes off his lifeless form.

I wipe my hands off on my jeans, stepping around the table to approach Veronica. She's shellshocked, unable to blink and remove her gaze from Burke. The ropes are still binding her arms and legs to the chair. Crouching in front of her, I reach around, untying each knot until she's free.

I'm directly in front of her, but her eyes are distant.

"Ronnie?" I say softly, placing my palm against her cheek. Her skin is cold and clammy. "Baby, look at me."

I stroke her face, sweeping my thumb over her cheek. Tears pool on her lashes, before spilling down her cheeks.

"He's dead?" Her voice is so quiet I nearly don't hear her. Ronnie slowly blinks.

"Arnold Burke is dead. You're safe." I pull her into me, pressing my lips to hers and then cradling her head to my chest. "I've got you, baby."

A sob wracks her body. She tremors against me as I hold her tight. I stand, wrapping her legs around my waist and her arms around my neck, hoisting her up. Ronnie tucks her head into my neck, her tears leaving a wet trail on my neck.

"Let's go home, little fox." I breathe into her hair.

***

When we get up into the penthouse, I strip both of us, putting our clothes into a pile to burn later. Veronica was quiet the whole ride here, staring out the window as the forest and then the city flew by. I never leave a corpse at the barn, always disposing of it right away, but taking care of Ronnie was more important. I'll go back later tonight when she's asleep and ditch Arnold somewhere in the city. That is, once I'm sure Ronnie isn't going to run away from me.

There's a giant soaker tub in my ensuite bathroom that I never use, but I feel like if there's ever a night where Ronnie needs it, it's tonight. I don't have any bubbles, salts or bath bombs like some girls like to use, but hopefully the warm water will be enough to soothe her. I turn on the tap and plug the drain, letting the tub fill over halfway before turning it off. Before going to get her, I scrub the blood that still lingers on my arms, hands, and face.

Ronnie is hugging her knees on the floor in front of the bed, her bare back pressed to the mattress. The wooden floor is cold, she's covered in goosebumps and shivering, but her eyes are still far off. I crouch in front of her, lacing my fingers through hers.

"Come on, sweetheart. Let's get you in the bath." I tug on her hands, and she doesn't fight me as I pull her to her feet.

I step into the tub first, then help her get in after me. We settle into the hot water, Ronnie resting between my thighs with her back pressed to my chest. We sit for a while, letting the heat soak into our bones and wash away the night we had. I purchased bottles of her favorite shampoo, conditioner, and body wash for when she stays over.

Once the washcloth is wet and sudsy with her heady vanilla and patchouli scented body wash, I slowly run it over her naked form. Taking care to clean every centimeter of her skin before rinsing the bubbles away.

"I love the scent of your body wash." I breathe in her fragrance, resting my face in the crook of her neck.

"The scent makes me feel calm." Ronnie's voice is raspy from her earlier tears.

It's the first thing she's said since we were at the barn. I try not to let her see my surprised expression, although inside I'm giddy to finally hear her voice.

"I can see why. It makes me feel the same way." I pull her hair back over her shoulders. "Dip your head for me, I'm going to wash your hair."

Ronnie obeys, slouching down and sinking under the water. Her black and green tresses fan out and float in the water, making her ethereal and mermaid-like. I expect her to pop back up once her hair is submerged, but she doesn't. Her hands grip the sides of the tub as she holds herself under. After a minute I begin to panic. Wrapping my hands under her biceps, I pull her out of the water, yanking her up until she's sitting straight.

She gasps and coughs, sputtering and heaving.

"Baby?!" I shift her body until she's facing me. My fingers are digging into her skin, as if I'm afraid that she might go under again.

Ronnie falls forward, her head colliding with my chest as a heart-wrenching sob breaks free from her mouth.

I wrap my arms around her protectively, clinging to her wet and wheezing body. "Shhhhh…it's okay, Veronica. It's okay."

"I'm sorry. I'm sorry. I'm sorry." She chants over and over, shaking against me.

"You have nothing to be sorry for." I reassure, even though I'm confused as to why she's apologizing to me.

"You k-killed h-him for m-me." Ronnie stutters.

"Yes." It's a fact.

She shudders. Ronnie doesn't say anything for several minutes, and eventually her sobbing stops.

"When I went under the water…everything was quiet. I wanted to stay there. The water muffled the voice in my head screaming that I'm guilty." She whispers into my skin.

"Baby, you aren't guilty of anything. You didn't do anything wrong. Burke hurt you and fourteen other children. He killed thirty people. He deserved to die."

"But his blood is on your hands because of me. You killed a man because of me." She cries.

"Arnold Burke wasn't the first person I killed, but he will be the last. You deserve rest, quiet, and peace, much more than he deserved to keep breathing. And if it makes you feel better, I would've killed him eventually anyway." That last part is a lie, he wasn't even on my radar until Ronnie came into my life, but she doesn't need to know that. Ronnie doesn't need to carry the burden of his death. "I killed him, Veronica. His death is my burden, not yours. And it's one that I'll gladly carry if it means that you got justice. Please, don't feel guilty or sad. I'll do anything to make you happy again. I love you so fucking much."

Ronnie blinks, the last trickles of her tears dripping down her cheeks. She looks up at me with her hypnotizing hazel eyes, and I can see the relief and hope in them.

"You're done with the vigilante thing now?" She asks, her palms pressed to my chest.

"Yes." My forehead rests against hers. "I'm done. I want to give you everything, every piece of me that's left. I want to spend every second of the rest of my life loving you, caring for you. There's no room for my hunts anymore, only you."

"Do you promise?" Her pleading, vulnerable eyes are locked on mine.

"Yes, forever. Always."

Ronnie's hands cup my neck. Our foreheads are still pressed together, our breaths mingling. She pushes her lips into mine, softly, tentatively. I thread my fingers through the wet hair at her scalp, pulling her closer into me until our bodies are crushed together. The kiss turns from meek and unsure to passionate and unforgiving. My tongue flicks the seam of her lips, causing a little moan to bubble in Veronica's throat. Her tongue meets mine, licking feverishly as we tangle. I swallow every gasp, whimper, and moan that escapes her lips. She tastes so fucking sweet, I want to spend every minute savoring her.

We're both breathless when our lips eventually part. Her hands claw at my shoulders and neck as she pulls back to look into my eyes.

"Thank you for saving me." She murmurs. Her eyes gleam. "I love you, Felix."

Fuck. She loves me. Veronica fucking Woods *loves me*. I slam my mouth back into hers, pouring every feeling I have for her into our kiss.

"I love you, I love you, I love you." I chant against her lips. "I'm going to spend every day telling you that and showing you. I'll give you the entire fucking world, anything to make you happy." Our kiss has broken, and we sit there panting against each other's mouths. "I need to be closer to you. Need to be inside you." My voice is pleading, my words cracking like I'll burst into tears if I don't have her right now.

Ronnie straddles my lap in the lukewarm bath water, my hardened cock jutting up between us. She pulls back, and looks down at me, ready and waiting for her warmth. Ronnie braces her hands on my shoulders, lifting up on her knees to position her entrance over me. I grip the base of my cock, steadying it for her to slide down and settle on me fully. Her eyes are still shiny with tears as they lock onto mine. I rub my thumb against her thigh soothingly as she takes the first inch of me into her. She slowly eases down, enveloping me in her tight, wet heat.

"Fuck, baby. You feel so fucking good." I gasp. "I'll never get over this. Over the feel of you."

I never want to stop holding her to me, consuming every gasp and moan she lets slip as we tangle endlessly. This time we're not fucking, we're making love. It's unhurried but passionate. Our bodies communicate with one another, giving our souls over to the other person.

Ronnie leans in to kiss me again. "Keep me safe. Forever." She whispers against my lips.

My heart leaps. "Baby, I will. You're mine, always."

Epilogue
Ronnie

Two months later...

"What if Sav and I move into the penthouse with you and Felix? That way we can keep being roomies." Leah whines.

"Babe. You know I love you right?" I grip Leah's shoulders. "We've had a good run as roomies, but I don't want to hear you and Sav going at it like rabbits anymore. The things I've heard coming from your room when he's been here have traumatized me. Like, you get yours, but I don't need to be third party to it."

Leah waggles her eyebrows. "You sure? You don't want to be in a throuple? Or maybe a foursome if we invite Felix too."

I laugh sarcastically. "Not a chance, babe. Not a fucking chance."

"Ughhh." Leah sighs. "I know, I'll just miss you. I know we didn't see each other often, but it was comforting to know that you lived here with me."

"It's not like we're moving across the country from each other, Leah. Not to mention, Sav and Felix are best friends. We'll still see each other all the time. Besides, aren't you excited? You're moving in with a *boy* for the first time. Think of all the sexy shenanigans you can get into together."

"I can't wait to christen every single surface in his cute little craftsman. Where should we start? I'm thinking the kitchen counter. Or maybe the deck…" Leah taps her chin, grinning wildly.

"You two are freaks of the highest order." I shake my head.

"And you love us anyway." She teases.

"I love you. Still not sure about Sav." I joke. Sav is actually a great guy. He and Leah are perfect together. I'm happy that she's found someone just as wild as she is.

"Veronica, I'm hurt." Sav's voice echoes down the hall from our front door.

"I'm kidding! Geesh." I raise a brow. "So sensitive." I mouth at Leah, giggling.

"His ego isn't the only thing that's sensitive, if you catch my drift…and if you don't, I'm talking about his cock." Leah raises her hands, spreading them until they're about a foot apart. "It's this big." She whispers conspiratorially.

I smack her arm. "It is not!"

"Oh, it is. Wanna see?" Sav says from behind me.

I shriek, startled by his sudden closeness. "Ewwww. No thanks!"

"Your loss." He chuckles.

"Are you hitting on my girlfriend, Sav?" Felix's arms are crossed and his brow is raised as he stands in the doorway.

"Nah, man. Just playing around." Sav raises his hands in placation. "You know I wouldn't do that do you. Unless you were into it, that is. In which case I'd totally cuckhold you."

"You motherfucker!" Felix lunges, tackling Sav to the ground. They wrestle, rolling around on the bare carpet. This isn't the first time I've seen these two wrestle like this. They still act like little boys sometimes. It's endearing, in a way. Felix laughs as Sav struggles in his hold.

"Boys! You're going to get rug burn doing that!" I walk over, trying to break them apart. I manage to grab ahold of Felix's ear. "Why do I feel like I'm the only adult here?!"

Sav starts laughing as I tug Felix's ear, forcing him to stand.

"Ouuucchh." Felix mewls. "Baby, I was just defending your honor."

I release his ear, patting him on the cheek. "You people are going to be the death of me."

Sav and Felix are truly brothers, in everything but blood. They bicker, tease each other, and fight, but the love they have for each other is unbreakable. Sav is naturally a flirty person, and he knows that it riles Felix up, so he takes any opportunity to flirt with me. Felix knows that it's a joke, but he still likes to rough Sav up for it.

"Well friends, I think it's time to go." I clap my hands together. "All the boxes are gone, apartment is clean. As clean as it can get anyway."

Leah sniffles. "Goodbye, Bessie." She pats the kitchen counter affectionately.

Felix, Sav and I all look at each other with bewildered expressions.

"Sunshine...who's Bessie?" Sav whispers.

"The apartment, duh." Leah cries dramatically.

"You named your apartment Bessie?" Felix guffaws.

"You should hear what she named my—" Sav spouts before Felix punches him in the stomach.

"Not...cool..." Sav wheezes.

Once Sav recovers, we take one last walk through of the apartment that Leah and I have shared for the past few years. It's bittersweet. I'm not attached to the apartment per se, but I am attached to the memories we've made here. We weren't even twenty when we moved in together, and it feels like we've grown so much over these years. We've seen each other's heartbreaks and triumphs, been each other's rocks. And it's not like that won't be the case anymore, but things will be different.

Leah is moving into Sav's cute little craftsman on the edge of the city. I'm moving into Felix's penthouse. Instead of being one hallway apart, we'll be twenty minutes apart. And we haven't been that far away from each other since before I moved in with the Crawfords in eighth grade. Although I'm sad to end this chapter with her, I'm also so excited to begin our new ones. We both have found our other halves. The missing piece of our puzzles. Our soulmates.

We lock the door for the last time as we leave our dingy apartment behind. It wasn't anything special, but it was ours.

***

Felix pulls his Jaguar into the spot next to my Kawasaki. It's nice to have it in an indoor parking garage, and not to mention in a nice area of town. At my old apartment I was always worried about it getting stolen or busted up, but here my ride is safe. And with Felix here, I'm safe too. He's a crazy obsessed stalker, but he's my crazy obsessed stalker. He'll beat up anyone who tries to hurt me. Is it normal to have your boyfriend be so absolutely consumed and infatuated with you? Probably not...but I love it. It makes me feel like I'm his entire universe. He's beyond dedicated to me.

We take the elevator up to the penthouse. Felix stands next to me with a blissful expression and his hand caressing the small of my back. The first few weeks after the ordeal with Burke were rough for us. I dealt with a lot of guilt and remorse. Not on behalf of Burke, but on behalf of Felix killing him for me. Felix was so patient and gentle with me while I worked through my emotions. I've finally gotten to a place of acceptance. Felix proved he would do anything for me, and I love him more than I thought possible. Sometimes it actually fucking hurts how in love with him I am.

Felix unlocks the door to our penthouse, following me as I trail through the hallway. I can't believe I live in this gothic fairytale apartment. It's the nicest place I've ever been, and it's mine now. Ahead I can see the glow of the fireplace, the light from it flickering across the walls. As I round the corner I stop in my tracks. The entire living area is covered in black candles. Scattered around are hundreds of sprigs of snapdragons in varying shades.

I spin around on my heel. "Felix...what—"

He pushes me back against the wall, his body holding me captive. "I love you, Veronica Woods." He kisses the tip of my nose. "I want to spend the rest of my life by your side." He kisses my forehead. "I can't live without you. I truly believe that if I ever lost you, I would die."

"You're not going to lose me, Felix. I love you." I respond in a breathy whisper.

"Let me finish, baby." Felix entwines our fingers. "From the second I saw you at the medical examiner's office, I had to have you. You're it for me. My everything." He presses a soft kiss to my lips before pulling away and dropping to one knee in front of me. His hands leave mine, one dipping into his pocket to retrieve a small velvet box.

My heart skitters.

"Marry me, Veronica Woods." His gaze is filled with adoration and longing. He flips open the top of the box to reveal a ring with an iridescent, shimmering gem of labradorite in a dewdrop cut. The band is gold, and five small diamonds ring around the rounded part of the labradorite gem.

"It's stunning…unlike any ring I've seen before…" I'm breathless.

"That's why I picked it. It reminds me of you." Felix says fondly. "Please tell me you're going to say yes, Veronica." His voice takes on a shy and pleading tone.

"Of course I'm saying yes, Felix." I stroke his cheek and hold out my left hand for him to put the ring on.

He pulls it from the velvety pillow, sliding it on my left ring finger. It's a perfect fit.

"How'd you know my size?" I ask.

"I measured your finger the first night you slept here." He admits slyly.

I scoff. "You're fucking insane. But I love it, and I love you."

He stands up from the floor, pulling me into him and kissing me with fervor. I melt into his arms, unbelievably happy. This man is my world.

Epilogue II
Ronnie

One year later...

"Are you ready, honey?" Darcy Crawford asks, handing me my bouquet of purple snapdragons.

Darcy and Elsie both helped me get ready this morning, slipping me into my black lace gown and lacing up the corset back. My hair cascades down my back in waves, with a glittering gold and labradorite barrette holding half of it back. Elsie lifts the short train of my dress, while Darcy helps me slip into my black heels.

"I'm ready." My heart pitter patters in my chest, and my tummy is full of butterflies.

Felix and I brought our parents here to Santorini, Greece, to be the witnesses for our elopement. We wanted Sav and Leah to come along, but Leah is six months along with her twins and her belly is so round and uncomfortable that the long flight to Greece wasn't in the cards. I wish Gwen could be here, but she has finals this week and I wasn't about to ask her to drop everything to fly halfway around the world. Jake Crawford, my adoptive dad, will video call Sav, Leah and Gwen to have them watch the ceremony, so in a way they'll still be with us.

We're getting married at a boutique hotel just off of Perissa Beach. Felix is enamored with Greece, and after we visited Santorini six months ago, we decided this was where we wanted to get married. My heels click along the stone floors, Darcy trailing behind me to hold the train of my dress, and Elsie at my side. We make our way down the hall towards the open-air atrium.

Felix stands in his black tux, waiting for me with Jake and Andreas by his side. Felix's hair is tousled, as always, but the messiness of it adds to his charm. When he sees me in the doorway, his face splits into a grin. I can see the gleam of his shining green eyes from here as he looks me up and down, devouring me with his gaze.

I return the gesture, letting my eyes linger on the way the tux hugs the thick muscles of his thighs and biceps. The sun glitters behind him, illuminating his form, making him appear before me like a fallen angel. My heart leaps. Felix Drakos is mine. He's marrying me. He's committing his life to mine. There's something profoundly beautiful about two souls coming together like this. Swearing ourselves to one another for the rest of eternity, in this life and the next.

Elsie gives me a reassuring squeeze before stepping to stand by my side next to Darcy. I face Felix, blown away by his enigmatic allure.

"You're so handsome." My voice is filled with awe as I observe the man who is about to become my husband.

Felix smirks. "You're a goddess, baby."

The officiant clears his throat, and I join hands with Felix as the woman begins.

The ceremony is over in the blink of an eye, and before I can catch my breath, we're slipping our wedding bands on and kissing for the first time as a married couple.

Our parents give us each hugs as Leah, Sav and Gwen cheer from the laptop that we're video chatting over. Happy tears are shed from all parties as we laugh together. Two families and two hearts becoming one.

The Crawfords and the Drakos are flying out tomorrow morning, but Felix and I start our honeymoon right away. We booked a suite to share at this hotel, and that's where we head as soon as the parents finish congratulating us.

We'll be spending a week here in Santorini, and then moving on to Athens for another few days. I couldn't have imagined a more beautiful place to start my life as Mrs. Felix Drakos.

Epilogue III
Felix

One week later...

The sun sets in the Mogostou Korinthias Oakforest near Athens. My little fox and I are staying in a secluded cabin here, perfect for the activities that I have planned.

My blood thrums in my ears as I follow the sound of her footsteps pounding away from me, sticks cracking as she sprints over the forest floor. My hot breath fills my mask as I chase after her through the dense woods. I let Ronnie think she's escaping me, let her think that I've lost her trail. But the truth is, I'm tracking her phone. When I replaced it after the Winter Ball last year, I modified it just a bit. I'm honestly surprised she hasn't caught on by now. This isn't the first time I've tracked her using the phone, and it won't be the last. She'd probably think it's cheating for me to use the GPS to follow her through the forest, but I call it using all the tools at my disposal.

The little dot on my screen stops, about nine hundred yards away. Neither of us are used to this amount of running and exertion, so Ronnie must be getting worn out.

My steps are silent as I continue my trek towards where her dot stopped. I no longer hear the sound of her thumping steps or panting breaths. Where is she? I'm standing on the spot where the GPS says she should be. I look around, trying to spot Ronnie, but her black outfit blends into the night and I don't see a sign of her.

"Veronicaaaaa…" I call out, my voice low and menacing.

I step forward and notice something metallic glinting in the moonlight. Her phone, discarded on the ground. Fuck.

"Ronnie?!" Fear creeps into my voice. Why the fuck is her phone laying on the ground like this? Did something happen to her? "VERONICA!" I scream. I thought we were secluded enough to not run into anyone else, but what if I was mistaken? What if someone has her?

I'm about to take off running when I hear a snapping sound behind me and then feel the cool press of a sharp blade against my throat.

"The hunter becomes the prey." Ronnie purrs from behind me. "Nice try with the tracker on my phone. I figured that one out months ago though."

"Jesus fuck, Veronica. You scared me." My heart feels like it's going to explode from my chest.

"Isn't that the point of this game?" She coos, pressing the blade harder into my skin.

I hiss at the sting as the knife presses enough to draw a thin line of blood. "Fair point." I grit out. Before she can fight me, I grip her wrist and twist it just enough for her hand to open and drop the knife. As it falls, I reach out and grip the handle with my other hand.

With her wrist in my grasp, I spin her around and press her front into the oak tree in front of us. I drag the knife down her cheek, not forceful enough to cut her skin, sending a shiver through her body. I push my goat mask up my face until it rests atop my forehead.

"Oh, little fox...you had me for a moment there. But I will always be your hunter and you will always be my prey." I run my tongue over the shell of her ear before biting down on her lobe.

Ronnie cries out and wriggles beneath me. Her ass grinds against my already throbbing cock. This is one of the games we play. She pretends to run away and fight me, all the while loving the chase. Ronnie admitted that she missed our times together when I was her stalker. I was stoked when she told me that, because I missed it too. After that we began playing these games, me donning my masked man persona for her, and her giving in to him.

I reach between Veronica and the tree she's pressed against, fingering the waistband of her leggings. Goosebumps trail behind my fingers as I caress her skin. I stab the knife into the tree above her head, making her jump.

"Do I scare you, little fox?" I croon.

"Yes." She whimpers.

"Good. You should be scared." I bite down on the crook of her neck. Ronnie will have bruises from my teeth in the morning. I plan on leaving my marks all over her body.

My hand slips underneath her leggings and panties, stopping to cup her warm pussy. I growl, her wetness coating my fingers as I spread her lips and stroke my middle finger down her slit. "Already wet for me? You bad fucking girl."

"Always for you." Ronnie pants.

I strum my thumb over her clit, dipping down to her entrance and then swirling the wetness back up. Her peachy ass presses harder into my groin as she arches her back and moans for me. My cock twitches in response to the feel of her rubbing against me. It strains against my zipper, but I need to make her cum for me before I get my own fix.

My fingers leave the warmth of her cunt, causing Ronnie to whine at the absence. I quickly grip her waistband, tugging her leggings and panties down her ass and legs. She steps out of them, letting me remove them completely. Once she's bare from the waist down, I flip her around until she faces me. The pack I'm carrying slips off my shoulders. I bend down to pull out one of the lengths of rope I brought on our excursion.

I grip her wrists in one hand, wrapping the rope around them until they're tightly bound. When I meet her eyes, I see them gleaming with feral lust.

"My wife is such a bad little slut for me, isn't she?" I groan.

"Mmhmm. I am." Ronnie moans, rubbing her thighs together in search of friction.

Raising her arms, I hook the rope tied around her wrists over the knife I stabbed above her head. Her body stretches taut and she stands on her tiptoes to ease the pressure pulling on her shoulders. The knife in the tree is Ronnie's, but I brought my own as well. I pull it out of my pocket and click it open, moonlight shining on the blade. The shirt that Ronnie is wearing tonight is one she knows I will destroy. She knows better than to wear nice clothes when playing our games. I grip the fabric in my hand, slicing the knife down through the collar until it hits the hem. The cotton rips apart, fluttering off to the sides to reveal her heaving, bare breasts.

"Fuck. No bra, little fox?" I lean down, taking one of her pierced and peaked nipples into my mouth. Sucking, licking, biting.

Ronnie squirms underneath me while I run the tip of my blade around her other nipple.

Her nipple pops out of my mouth as I back away. The second length of rope I have tonight is longer. Rummaging through my bag, I slowly pull it out and hold it up to her. It's long enough to wrap around the tree several times. I wind it around the trunk once, tying it off and securing it around Ronnie's hourglass waist. She looks at me in confusion, but underneath her bemused expression I see absolute trust.

I wrap the rope around the tree trunk again, and then once more. But on the third time I lift both of her legs and secure the rope underneath her knees, opening her pussy and ass to me. Ronnie's naked body is suspended against the tree now. I can see her cunt glistening, waiting to be teased, fucked, and filled with my cum.

I put the knife away before dropping to my knees before her. My mask has long since slipped off my head, falling to the ground near my pack. My tongue flicks out, the flat of it stroking from her opening to her clit. I groan at the taste of her sweet pussy. I could bury my face and cock into it several times daily and it'd never be enough.

My tongue circles the nub of her clit, flicking against it before I suck it into my mouth. Ronnie's hips grind and buck against my face, pushing her pussy further into my mouth. Her wetness drips down my lower lip and chin while she mewls above me.

"I fucking love the sounds you make, pretty girl." I groan into her cunt. "You make me so fucking hard."

"Please, Felix, fuck me." Ronnie cries.

"Not yet, baby. You need to cum for me first." As much as I want to shove my cock deep into her tight cunt right now, I love how sensitive her pussy gets after cumming first.

Taking my index and middle fingers, I thrust them into her entrance. I curl them, pumping against her g-spot, her cunt making sloppy wet sounds as I move in and out of it. My mouth is on her clit again, nipping and tugging at it with my teeth. Ronnie shrieks as I suck on her bundle of nerves hard, curling my tongue around it and brushing against it. I feel her cunt pulse around my fingers before liquid gushes out of her, drenching my face. My eyes find her face, seeing that her neck is arched back, her head pressing into the tree trunk and her eyes are rolling back in her head from the force of her orgasm. Her cries and screams become silent as her body trembles and jerks against the ropes holding her up.

After I drag the last wave of her orgasm out of her, Ronnie's body goes lax in her bindings. I drink up every drop of her cum from her pussy like it's the tastiest nectar I've ever had.

"Fuccckkk, Veronica. You taste so fucking sweet." I groan, dragging my tongue up her slit one last time before standing. "Are you ready for my cock, little fox?"

Ronnie moans and nods, her eyelids fluttering. "Please." She begs. She's tired from her intense orgasm, but I'm not through with her yet.

I grip my cock in a fist, dragging it up and down her wet folds, hitting her clit on every upstroke. Every time my head hits her sensitive nub, she moans. When my dick slides past her entrance, she pushes her hips forward, trying to push it inside.

"Tell me you want it." I command.

"I want your cock, Felix. Please. I *need* it." Ronnie whines, her eyes open and pleading.

"Anything you want, pretty girl." I slam inside her to the hilt, forcing a gasp out of Ronnie. My hand grips her ass cheek so hard that it'll leave finger shaped bruises. I slide all the way out to the tip and snap my hips back in until my pelvis and balls slap her cheeks. Again and again. All the way out, all the way in. Hitting her cervix with each punishing thrust.

Each time I ram into Ronnie's tight cunt, her body jolts with the force, and she screams in pleasure.

"My wife likes to be fucked hard, doesn't she?" I growl, leaning in to take her lip between my teeth and bite.

She whimpers. "Yes, I do. Yes…please…more."

My thumb finds her clit, pressing down and adding friction with each stroke of my cock inside of her. "Cum for me, Veronica."

I pinch the nub of her clit between my thumb and forefinger, and that's all it takes for her to shatter around me. Her cunt squeezes tightly around me, making it hard to keep thrusting. I feel her clit and pussy pulsing as I milk out her orgasm. She screams and cries, the sounds echoing in the dark forest around us. It's secluded out here, and there's no one around to hear her pleasure.

Her tightly wound body relaxes once again, and I follow close behind her with my own release. I roar as jets of my cum fill her warm, wet cunt. I could live inside of her. I need her more than I need oxygen.

"Fuck, baby." I pant, resting my forehead against hers. "You're so fucking perfect. I love you."

"I love you too, Felix." She sighs contentedly.

I untie the rope around her knees and waist, gently setting her feet on the ground below. Then I unhook the wrist rope that's still slung over the knife that I stabbed into the tree. Once her wrists are untied, I rub them gingerly. There are red marks from where the ropes rubbed her skin, but I plan on taking care of the injuries when we get back to our cabin.

My lips caress hers, before I lift her into my arms and carry her back to the cabin. Her head rests against my chest, jostling as I carry her.

Ronnie looks up at me with love and trust. "I'm so happy you're my husband."

Author Note

Thank you for reading "It's Always You". I appreciate your support. Follow me on TikTok, Instagram and Amazon for new releases and updates!

Tiktok: @author_autumn.l.belle
Instagram: authorautumn.l.belle
Amazon: www.amazon.com/author/autumnlbelle

Other Works:

Romantasy:
Series: Souls Trilogy
Soul of Fire & Starlight (coming soon)

Dark Romance:
Series: It's Always…
It's Always You
It's Always Savage (coming soon)

About The Author

Autumn L. Belle lives in Minnesota, near Minneapolis/Saint Paul with her husband, Nick, and her corgi, Rory. During the day she works as I.T. support, and during the night she spends her time reading and writing all things smut.

When she's not writing and reading, she's jamming out to Ghost and Sleep Token, listening to spooky podcasts, watching horror movies, or playing video games with her friends.

Made in the USA
Monee, IL
13 June 2025